CACKNACKER'S FURY

Cacknacker's Fury

Paul Wright

BLACK ACE BOOKS

First published in 2009 by Black Ace Books
PO Box 7547, Perth, PH2 1AU, Scotland

www.blackacebooks.com

© Paul Wright 2009

Typeset in Scotland by Black Ace Editorial

Printed in England by CPI Antony Rowe
Bumper's Farm, Chippenham, SN14 6LH

A CIP catalogue record for this book
is available from the British Library

ISBN 978–1872988–87–0

The publisher acknowledges support
from the Scottish Arts Council
towards the production of this volume.

Scottish
Arts Council

For Bev and Corin

1

Sol Singleton lived to work and hated it when his annual summer holiday came around. This might seem surprising to the outsider, for his job, judged by most criteria, was not a rewarding or fulfilling one. It was not capable of meeting deep and complex human needs, it involved no profession of oaths and there was no sense in which it could be seen as somehow furthering Life's great work. It involved no difficult skills that had to be developed over the years under the tutelage of a master. It was simply what it was, a lowly position within a company that existed to service the everyday needs of everyman.

It would be wrong to say that Sol's work stimulated him. There was no challenge in it, and no sense of achievement at the end of it, merely the satisfaction of a job well done. It was routine, with little happening in the course of the day that had not happened the day before, and a thousand times before that. The best that could be said was that his work engaged him from time to time. It can be counted a plus that his working environment was pleasant and harmonious and that his colleagues were agreeable, and occasionally kind and amusing. Sol's work, in short, went a long way to fill the time given to him on this earth and was the rock upon which his existence was built. In this he was not so different from the majority of the population.

Being removed from his routine workaday world created

an underlying sense of unease, which Sol countered by inventing new routines, so that the day did not lie before him as a blank sheet, or as something unknown that could throw surprises at him. Every two-week summer holiday was a challenge to occupy himself, and a test of patience. So he would return to work buoyed by the fact that the holiday was over for another year and things were back to normal. He would have been happy to forgo his holiday, but this was against company policy. It believed staff returned refreshed, both physically and mentally, from a long break, which was to the benefit of both employer and employee. Sol did not share this view, but there was nothing he could do to overturn the rule.

Sol received his name from his mother, who had studied astrology. The day after his birth she was well enough to draw up his horoscope and observe that the Sun was (as she put it) 'happily aspected and well positioned within the diurnal circle'. This led her to conclude that her son would be of a sunny disposition. As it turned out, he was not. On the contrary, he was rather cool and unemotional. He was drawn to sunny people, however, much preferring them to lunar types, whom he found to be touchy, moody and a tad cantankerous. As a teenager he thought about changing his name, but decided in the end not to. He might not be sunny, but he decided his given name could be taken as short for Solus, which was more appropriate to his character. For, although he liked other people, and generally got on well with others, he was just as happy to be alone; indeed, he was probably happier.

That Sol, come the summer holiday, did not seek, as millions do, the rejuvenating waters of a warm sea can be put down to an unfortunate incident in his childhood. When he was a boy his family passed a fortnight each year at a seaside cottage. His father taught him to swim and also to row and paddle. Sol took particularly to a fibreglass kayak that even with the limited strength of a young boy he could control and propel with some ease. Each year, as he grew more confident, he would venture further out in his little craft – until one year, as he attempted to return to the shore, he found he was making no headway.

It was a calm, sunny day, with barely a swell, but no matter how hard he paddled he found himself being pushed out to sea, as if by a hidden hand, which was both perplexing and alarming. He was wondering what he could do when a passing motor boat slowed, steered towards him, and eventually stopped. Sol, who was close to tears, explained the difficulty and asked for help. He and his little craft were taken in tow and returned to the shore. His rescuer explained that the tide had turned. It was a strong tide – four-and-a-half knots. He would have exhausted himself attempting to combat it and eventually would have been carried a long way from the shore. Sol had heard of tides. He knew they went in and out, but hadn't appreciated they represented a danger.

Sol seemed none the worse for his scare, but the next night he had run screaming from a different sea – a subconscious sea, the *mare tenebrarum*, a nightmare – and sat bolt upright in his bed, sweating and short of breath. And the following night he dreamed he was being pulled helplessly into the appalling expanse of the Atlantic and toward the maw of a furiously spinning maelstrom.

Nor did it end there. The following spring he was with a school party on a day trip to the continent. At the ferry port, as he stepped on to the gangplank, he experienced once more the same irrational terror of his nightmare. He was impervious to all persuasion and reassurance and had to be taken back to the school. Within him had developed a loathing for the sea, and for Thor the thundering god of tides and hidden, treacherous ocean currents. There were tides, Sol learned, that even fish couldn't swim against and which could drag large boats on to the rocks. There were tides that could draw a man down to icy depths where even an aqualung was of no use. There were tides that surged inland in towering waves, up rivers, seeking unsuspecting prey. There were tides that retreated far from the shore tempting individuals to examine the exposed sea-bed and, when they had been lured far enough, turned on them and made them run for their lives.

It reassured Sol that their menace could be countered with science. But if they were predictable, it was only up to a point, for there were occasions when the elements made a mockery of the mathematics.

2

On the first day of his holiday Sol awoke at the same hour he always did, showered, breakfasted and then set off to the newsagent's to collect a paper. On his return he spent about three minutes reading it before turning to the crossword. Sol had the sort of mind that could make short work of crossword puzzles. Generally he completed them on the bus to work before the journey was half over. He would then throw his newspaper dismissively on to the nearest empty seat and make a show of shaking his head in frustrated annoyance at how undemanding it had been. The other travellers would pretend not to notice, but once Sol had alighted at his workplace, they would circulate the discarded paper amongst themselves to learn Sol's solution to the clues that had left them stumped.

'Right!' said Sol, aloud, as people often do who live on their own. 'What have we got today. Let's see: "Sharp merchant is merchandise." Oh dear, is that the best they can do?'

And he wrote 'tart' in the appropriate place. He completed three other clues with equal facility but then – unprecedentedly – came to a halt. He lingered a minute on the clue, then passed on to the next, which was equally baffling. He knew well it was futile to linger more than a few seconds; you saw it right away or not at all. Clues did not (or should not) yield to time or patience. He looked for the name of the compiler, but there wasn't one. That this was not the usual compiler was plain. And though he complained often enough that the puzzles were too easy, it still irritated him to have to get used to the ways of a new compiler.

He put down the newspaper and picked up a book, which he read for about half an hour. Then he tidied the flat and prepared an early lunch. After lunch, while in the bathroom, he caught his own reflection in the mirror. He moved his head from side to side, and said aloud:

'Yes, definitely getting a little shaggy. I'll go for a haircut. That'll occupy about two hours. Walk in the park afterwards, shopping, home, cook meal, television. Bed. Another day gone.' He felt satisfied and smiled at his reflection.

At the hairdressing salon he usually patronized the reception-ist turned the pages of a leather-bound book, and with each turning leaf an appointment receded into the future.

'Sometime in the next half-hour would suit me well,' said Sol assertively.

The woman smiled, not certain if he was joking.

'You'll appreciate, I am a regular customer,' Sol added.

'We might be able to squeeze you in – in October?'

'I've something on in October, and I'm not sure I want to be squeezed at all, as you put it. As if I was a blackhead, or some irritating afterthought. But if I have to be squeezed in, I'd prefer tomorrow.'

She made a pretence of checking the book. 'Can't do tomorrow. Booked solid. *Sorry.*'

'I can usually get an appointment no bother.'

'Alas, we can't go on repeating the past endlessly,' replied the woman, sounding, Sol thought, like a New Age therapist. 'I don't like to turn customers away, but . . . you could always try somewhere else.'

While Sol was sure there must be other hairdressing shops

within the town he had no knowledge of their precise location, so he simply walked the streets looking about him. As he turned into the high street he could see men working at the roadside. A number of stones from the pavement had been removed from their customary position and lay around haphazardly. There was a dreadful screeching noise as one of the thick square slabs was cut with a high-speed rotating saw. A cloud of fine dust filled the air and settled on nearby cars and windows. Sol stood a moment, waiting for the cutting to be complete. But it was not and the workmen seemed unwilling to make concessions to passing pedestrians. So he turned left, into a side street, and walked along it a little way to the beginning of a service road that ran parallel to the High Street and between two rows of shops. He would use this, he thought, to bypass the bothersome roadworks, rejoining the High Street at a point beyond them.

There was some activity in this service road. At the back entrance of one of the shops boxes were being unloaded from a van and carried inside, while from another a figure emerged and deposited some empty cardboard boxes into an already overflowing skip. As Sol continued he was surprised to see – on what was after all a back alley – a shopfront, with a plate glass window, a sign and a door. He stopped to survey it. The sign read:

Hairdresser

To the point, unadorned, and mercifully devoid of silly puns.

Sol was puzzled. He was sure he had passed this way before but had never noticed any such shop. He attempted to squint between the gaps in the slatted blind but could not make out any of the features within. He hesitated, then pushed open the door. A bell jangled somewhere inside.

He stood in a small reception area. There was a doorway, opposite the one he had entered, filled with hanging strands of beads, alternately round and ovoid and set in a larger, repeating pattern of dark and light woods.

'A nice touch,' Sol thought. 'So much better than plastic strips.'

He was about to examine it more closely when there was a dry rustling sound, as of a Latin percussive instrument, as the wooden curtain was swept aside to reveal a man of much the same age, height and build as Sol.

'Hello,' he said, with a hint of suspicion.

Sol stared. He then smiled and appeared embarrassed. 'I, um . . .'

The man rested his arm against the door jamb waiting for Sol to finish.

'Forgive me,' said Sol. 'I couldn't help noticing—'

'Yes?'

'That we're a little similar in appearance. Remarkably similar, actually, if we look past the hair and the clothes.'

The man studied Sol for a few seconds, then answered:

'Don't know. I have trouble remembering what I look like.'

'Well, believe me, there's definitely a resemblance. A marked resemblance.'

The man shrugged. 'So what? How many ways can you arrange two ears, two eyes, a nose and a mouth.'

'I think there's more to it than that,' began Sol. 'For instance—'

'What can we do for you anyway – don't tell me! You want a haircut!'

'Er, yes. I do, actually.'

The man smiled. 'Of course. Now, let's see . . . ' He opened the salon's appointments book at the first page, glanced at it, and then at his watch. 'Well! Talk about luck! The only free slot we have today, and it's right now.'

'Fine. I'll take it.'

'No time like the present, eh?'

'Do you find that as well?' asked Sol.

'Name?'

Sol informed him.

'Hi. I'm Parlando.'

'Par-lando!?'

'Yes. Par*lando*. Why?'

'Oh, nothing. It's not a common name in these parts, that's all.'

'Okay, it's not my real name, if that's what you're driving at.'

'I wasn't—'

'Krebs. Krebs is my real name.'

'Ah! Yes. I can see why you changed it. Parlando seems much more appropriate for a man of your profession. I mean, if you'd elected to drive a steamroller for a living – say – then Krebs would be perfectly appropriate.'

'I toyed with Splendido.'

'Possibly a bit immodest,' offered Sol after some reflection. 'And people would expect a conjurer, or some tawdry showman. They'd phone the salon asking if you "do" children's parties. No, I think your decision was, again, the right one.'

'Names are so important. I can't understand why some people just accept the one they were given at birth, if it has nothing to do with what they are. It's just a random name. Mind you, Sol's not so bad.'

'Thank you.'

'Now would you like me to cut your hair?' asked Parlando, a touch impatiently, as if it had been Sol that introduced the digression.

'If you would be so kind, yes.'

Parlando held out his arm, ready to sweep aside the curtain, but then hesitated. He looked at Sol.

'Don't assume,' he said, 'just because you were able to get an appointment right away, that business is bad.'

'No, I won't.'

'It's actually very good. If you'd come here this time yesterday, I would have turned you away. But we had an unfortunate cancellation, and – you've not been here before, have you? I mean, you didn't get that haircut here.'

'No. I usually go . . . down the road.' Sol gestured vaguely.

'Yes. The less said about them the better.'

'Is it so bad? My hair?'

Parlando laughed sardonically. 'I think we can probably salvage something.' He reached out and ran his fingers through it. 'First thing is a good wash. And some conditioning. I've just the thing that'll put life back into it. After you.' And he indicated the curtained entrance.

'This is amazing,' exclaimed Sol, astonished at the space that opened up before him. 'It's much bigger than I imagined.' He looked back through the curtains to confirm just how narrow and modest was the frontage. He laughed. 'I mean—'

'How big did you think it would be?' asked the hairdresser. He appeared quite anxious to hear Sol's answer.

'What? Oh. Let me see. Say, 35 by 25 by 12,' replied Sol, who had a good head for figures.

'Feet?'

'Yes.'

Parlando surveyed the room. 'It's funny, most people think it should be about that big. And I can see what you're saying. There is a certain seemliness about the dimensions you suggested, a pleasing proportion. But I'll say to you what

16

I say to the others: if that was all the space I had to work in, I wouldn't last a week in this business.'

'Economies of scale,' said Sol, remembering a phrase from his secondary education.

As well as spacious, the salon was luxurious. There were thick carpets of burgundy and cream, soft music and sweet scents. There was lustrous chrome that caught the light and portrayed a distorted world in miniature. Floral displays were in abundance. At each of the many work bays there were soft, flexible chairs that could bend and rotate to match the dimensions of the quirkiest body. Sol complimented Parlando on the décor, and told him he was surprised that something so opulent should be found here in the town. Would it not all be more at home in the most exclusive area of a wealthy and cosmopolitan city?

Parlando chuckled. 'You're very kind. That's where we started out. But I don't know. Put it down to egalitarian principles. Dreary little provincial towns like this need a leaven for the lump. Of course, I still get customers from the city. They've followed us here. I can't turn them away. They're like old friends.' He stopped walking and looked at Sol. 'Perhaps in time you'll become an old friend too. It's really one big happy family here.' And he invited Sol to savour the harmony that pervaded the salon.

'I don't see why not. I'm so far very impressed. However, and excuse me for being so proletarian, but luxury has a price – and, well, how much will this haircut cost me?'

'I don't know, Sol. I don't impose a price structure on my customers. I ask them to put their own value on the service they receive. Wait until you've seen the end result and then pay us what you think it's worth. Here!' He pointed to a hatchway. 'We'll get fixed up with shampoo and conditioner.'

Once more Sol was amazed by what he saw. It was like

an old-fashioned pharmacy, with shelves lined with bottles of coloured liquid. There were benches where white-coated technicians sat blending liquids with beakers and measuring cylinders. There were even Bunsen burners, and bulbous flasks linked by lengths of glass and rubber.

'All our customers have their own individual blends. If you continue to patronize us, we'll get one for you too. Once we get to know your hair. We'll start with something basic, though.' He called over one of his staff. 'Some Formula 23 for Sol, with a touch of 11; about eight parts to one.'

'Very good,' answered the technician.

'Of course,' continued Parlando, 'we produce everything on the premises. That's the only way you can be sure what you're getting is good. Would you like to see? We've a few minutes. Your washing bay's not quite ready.'

They went through a door next to the 'pharmacy' into a short corridor that led to a production plant where soap was produced in stainless-steel apparatus, along with all the other toiletries and lotions that were used in the salon. There were carboys of caustic potash and drums of coconut oil.

'Alas, we can't grow the coconuts locally. We import them from Sri Lanka. We find they're the best. This is where we crush them.' Parlando pointed to a press, which was in the process of being loaded. 'We couldn't get permission for an alkali plant, so we buy that in. Somewhere up north. But to be frank, alkali is alkali, however and wherever it's made. It's the organic stuff that's so unpredictable. The perfumery's next door, but we could perhaps leave that for another time. I think Rachel is now waiting to wash you.'

Sol lay in Washing Bay 7, on his back, almost horizontal, his neck resting in a groove on the rim of a heart-shape sink. It was an odd position, he thought, and perhaps not altogether intended. The young woman named by Parlando as Rachel appeared to struggle with the controls of the sophisticated chair so that he was pivoted and jolted this way and that, up and down, till finally he was flipped so vigorously that his whole body lost contact with his seat. Rachel had giggled and apologized. Sol suggested the sensitivity mechanism might be at fault. Sensing a risk of being catapulted across the room if the adjustments continued, he assured her that his present horizontal position was tolerably comfortable.

Rachel soaked his hair with warm water and then worked in a palmful of Formula. He enjoyed the feel of her fingertips moving back and forth over his scalp in a slow rotational motion. The shower was adjusted so that once more warm water flowed over his hair, and as it did so she coaxed out the suds with her hand.

'Not too hot, is it?' she asked.

'No.'

'You know the good thing about this Formula? It really cleans without making a lot of suds.'

'Really?'

'Yeah, really,' she replied, a defensive edge to her voice, as if he had doubted her statement. He was about to reassure her on this point when she continued:

'You don't need a lot of suds to get things clean. People think you do, but you don't. It's not the suds that do the cleaning. They're just like, you know, air . . . mostly.'

'Really!' exclaimed Sol, modulating his inflexion to sound as if he had been ignorant of this fact and so now was grateful to have had his wonderment at the world increased.

She turned off the tap. 'There, that's you. Listen, I've got to leave you for a minute. I'll be back. Don't go away.'

Sol was not sure how long he lay there, but his neck grew increasingly uncomfortable where it rested in the ceramic groove, until it felt as if gripped by an irate schoolmaster. His face felt hot and there was a ringing in his inner ears. He shifted his body a little this way, a little that, but the relief was only temporary. When still the woman did not return, he decided enough was enough. Awkwardly he sat up. He reached for a towel, rubbed his hair, then patted it into some sort of order with the palm of his hand.

He noticed a curved sheet of shoulder rubber on the table next to his chair and tried to reach it as little streams of water were already finding a way past the plastic cape and dampening his shirt collar. It was, he recalled, similar to the rubber shield he had been given to guard his genitals when last he was X-rayed.

'I'm not intending to breed in the foreseeable future,' he had joked to the woman who had conducted the procedure.

'It's just a precaution,' she had replied.

'Isn't it funny how rubber and precautions seem to go together?' Sol had said, attempting to push the conversation to a more intimate level. He liked women in clinical white coats.

Impatience now drew Sol back to the present situation. He reached out and touched a red-knobbed lever attached to the chair. There was a hydraulic 'shoosh' and he instantly withdrew his hand. Tentatively he gripped the lever once more and, with relatively few movements, adjusted the chair to the vertical position.

'It's really not so difficult,' said Sol to himself.

He removed the cape, then wiped away the water that was still running off his hair.

He drummed his fingers on the arm of the seat. More time passed, but Rachel the hair-washer did not return.

Sol's attention was then caught by the sound of flowing water from the next washing bay. He stood up, put his ear against the wall and listened for a few seconds. Then he noticed a forked stream slowly advancing underneath the partition. He shook his head and began to wonder

20

about the quality of a salon that had at first impressed him.

'It's no good having flash beaded curtains, and a perfumery,' he said to himself, 'if you don't get the damn basics right. Like plumbing, and staff that stay in one place.'

He looked up and down the corridor outside his bay, but there was no-one in sight. He knocked gently on the door to the next bay, then entered. There was a man lying back in the chair with his head resting on an overflowing sink. He lay quite still, seemingly oblivious to Sol's presence.

'Um, excuse me,' said Sol. 'I think I should tell you. Bit of a problem, I'd say.' He stepped forward and turned off the tap, although water continued to cascade from the basin. Sol stepped out into the corridor and called out:

'Hello?'

But once more no-one answered.

He re-entered the washing bay.

'What a mess! What's she thinking of?' continued Sol, directing his remark at the supine form. 'Wandering off. My washer disappeared too. It's really not – hello?'

There was no response.

Sol moved closer, peered at the face in the bowl and realized he was looking at a dead man.

He should have been horrified, but he was not. Yes, there was a little frisson of shock at the moment of realization, but mostly his reaction was one of puzzlement. Things like this shouldn't happen in a hairdressing salon. Plenty of people die under surgery and occasionally at the dentist, under anaesthesia. But at the hairdresser's? Surely not a venue generally associated with mortal hazards. People didn't send you cards saying 'Good luck with your haircut!', did they? Yet this unfortunate fellow had come to this salon for a routine haircut and one of the employees, so it seemed, had managed to drown him.

21

Sol heard hurrying footsteps. He turned to face the door just as Parlando burst in. He looked, aghast, at the corpse, then at Sol.

'What the hell's going on here?' he shouted.

'I think he's—'

'What have you done?'

'Me? I've not . . . What have *I* done?' replied Sol, his finger pointing at his own chest, an expression of pained innocence on his face.

Parlando looked more closely at the corpse. He picked up a limp wrist and felt for a pulse. 'My God. He *is* dead!' He looked accusingly at Sol.

'Well, you don't think I had anything to do with it – do you?'

'I don't see anyone else. What are you doing in here anyway? I told you Bay 7.'

'I know. But I was left. I saw the water on the floor and came through.'

'You came through. You didn't come when you heard a man drowning, though!'

'I didn't hear anything.'

'Don't be ridiculous! Have you never seen a person drown?'

'No.'

'They don't just lie there and suck in water, you know. They thrash and struggle like mad. Fight for breath.'

'I didn't hear anything, I tell you,' replied Sol, growing angry.

'Oh my God, I don't need this. It'll ruin us.'

'What about the girls? Maybe they saw something?'

'Who was attending to you?'

Sol reflected. 'You said her name was Rachel.'

'Rachel?'

'Yes.'

'*Rachel?*'

'*Rachel!*'

'I see,' said Parlando wearily. 'It might interest you to know we've got three Rachels here.' He paused. 'One's on maternity leave, one left last week, and one phoned in sick this morning.'

Sol was about to point out that there were actually, then, only two Rachels working at the salon, when Parlando continued:

'She told you her name was Rachel?'

'No. You did.'

'And you believed her?'

Sol seemed bemused. 'Look here—'

But Parlando was looking over the body. He seemed calm once more. There was even compassion in his expression. Sol also fell silent and looked down at the body, and a certain solemnity crept into the moment.

'The thing is,' observed Parlando, 'whoever may have killed him – and I'm not saying who. It's not for me to go accusing customers. It may even have been an accident. Let's not rule that out.'

Sol nodded.

'But the thing is,' continued the hairdresser, 'it's too late for the most important individual in this drama. Him.' And he indicated the corpse with a movement of his head.

Sol could only agree. 'We'll need to call the police,' he suggested.

'I don't think so,' answered Parlando firmly, and almost before the words were out of Sol's mouth.

Sol looked at him quizzically. 'What do you mean? Of course we have—'

'I can deal with it, thank you.'

'But it's the law!'

'I said, *I* can deal with it.'

23

'Well, I'll call them, then.'

'No! No police. Definitely not,' said Parlando hotly. 'Do you want to ruin me? I don't want to spend the next twenty years in a stinking prison cell. Do you?'

'*I*'ve not done anything! *I* didn't kill him!'

'You tell that to the police. I'm not sure they'll believe you. It all looks a bit suspicious, doesn't it?'

'Bloody hell, this is ridiculous. I was reclining in my chair, all the time.'

'Okay, I believe you.'

'The girl will tell you—'

'Rachel? Ah yes, Rachel. The girl who left last week, phoned in sick, and is having a baby.'

'No, the girl who washed my hair.'

'See how easy it is to get confused?'

'I'm not confused.'

'Aren't you?' Parlando put his arm around Sol's shoulder. 'Just trust me, okay? I know what I'm doing. Leave it to me. This thing will never have happened. All traces of the incident will be erased. It will be as if the clock were turned back.' He pushed open the door of the bay and looked up and down the corridor outside. 'Now let's get this body shifted.'

The corpse was heavy and as they transported it down a narrow winding staircase the head banged on every step.

'Christ sake!' said Parlando. 'Have some respect for the dead!' He was at the front with one of the corpse's legs under each arm. Sol, at the rear, had the harder task of trying to lift a dead weight upwards by the wrists. He was uneasy about handling dead flesh. He wasn't particularly squeamish, but had read somewhere that – though living skin is a very effective bactericide – once death supervenes, microorganisms multiply rapidly. He had tried to support the weight with his hands under the torso, where at least there was clothing between his hand and dead skin, but he could not keep a grip.

'Rest a minute,' said Sol. They had reached the bottom of the stairs, and that was a blessing. Strange chemical smells hung in the air. Sol could see into a room where flasks and other experimental apparatus bubbled away.

'What's all this, then?' he asked.

'Don't trouble yourself,' snapped Parlando. 'Just things to do with the operation of a hairdressing salon. It's not as simple as people imagine to run a place like this. Look!' He threw open a door. 'This is the laundry. Okay? No great mystery. There's a lot of washing to do in a place this size.'

Sol looked into a room filled with noise, steam and stainless steel. It did indeed seem to be exactly what Parlando said.

'Come on, let's get the job done.'

'I may decide not to make you my regular hairdresser,' said Sol.

'Suit yourself.'

'Where's it going?'

'We can just drag it now. Here!' He handed Sol a leg.

A man emerged from a room to Sol's left, stepped over the corpse, and continued down the corridor.

'Here! This room *here*,' said Parlando, after they had dragged their load along several more corridors.

Inside, the room was tiled white and it was cool enough for the water vapour in their breath to condense.

Sol dropped the leg he was holding and stood transfixed. On a slab in front of him was a cadaver. A female, about thirty years old. Her head had been shaved.

'Yes, yes, I know,' said Parlando before Sol had a chance to say anything. 'These things happen, all right?'

Sol looked at Parlando. 'What the bloody hell's going on here?'

25

'Look, this one's nothing to do with you. This time tomorrow it won't even be here.'

Sol looked over the body on the slab. To his shame, it crossed his mind that she had a nice figure. 'And did this one drown too?' he asked.

'I don't know, I'm not a pathologist. Now let's go, or do you want to stand here gawping at her all day?'

'No.'

'Good. Then help me lift this fellow on to the slab. Thank you.'

'What happens now?' asked Sol.

'Don't worry, we have people who'll take care of him. And her. It's quite complicated, preparing a body for burial. Or cremation, or whatever. You can't just sling it out the back and let the dogs eat it, you know.'

Minutes later the two men stood in the foyer.

'And remember,' warned Parlando. 'Not a word.' Looking at Sol's still-damp hair, he added

'You didn't get your cut, did you?'

'Just a wash.'

'Well, we'll skip the charge for that, in the circumstances.'

'Thank you.'

'Pleasure.' Parlando opened the door to the street and a bell rang somewhere close by.

They exchanged solemn nods, and Sol left for home.

3

Sol paced restlessly around his flat. More than once he picked up the telephone with the intention of phoning the police. But he never made the call. He went to bed in an agitated frame of mind and slept fitfully. Images of the dead appeared in his dreams. In one, he was in a kayak on a calm sparkling sea, paddling towards a white Lilo which was floating slowly out to sea. On it lay a naked young woman. As he approached she seemed to drift away. The sky darkened and the sea grew turbulent. When finally he reached the white Lilo he discovered only a rotting, maggoty corpse, with skin the colour of a peeled potato. Horrified, he turned his kayak and paddled furiously. But he could not escape. He and the stinking corpse were pulled towards a great vortex, were sucked in and spun furiously. Each dizzying revolution took him further from the lip and closer to the densely black opening at the centre of the whirlpool. Sol was terrified and at the same time burningly curious as to what he would find there. He awoke with a cry, sweating and breathless.

He lay on the bed reflecting on the images that were still vivid in his mind. The kayak was the one he once owned, that was plain. The woman had looked familiar, a cross between the Rachel who had washed his hair and the body on the white slab. He felt tired and drifted easily into sleep once more, which this time was deep and untroubled, so that he awoke refreshed in mid morning. Moreover, the events of the previous day now seemed remote and unreal.

He showered, breakfasted, then walked to the newsagent for his daily paper. He returned home, settled himself in a chair, and turned directly to the crossword.

'Let's get the old mind into gear,' he said. But it was much the same as the day before. He raced through half a dozen clues and then was unable to progress.

Sol thought he might eat out that night, on his own, as he usually did, with a book, so that his fellow diners would think he was an eccentric writer, or a scholar who chose to use the time productively, rather than someone who had no partner or close friends.

He turned to the features pages, where a review of a recently opened seafood restaurant caught his eye. The critic – one Breen Maricaibo – began by saying she and her partner had had a 'little fallout' on the way to the restaurant and they were still 'snapping at each other like demented piranhas' as they studied the menu. However, the excellence of the food by stages dissipated the animosity so that by the last spoonful of salmon mousse they were smiling at each other, they were playing footsie during the main course, and by the time the sweet arrived she was squatting on the table-top filling the otherwise hushed restaurant with lusty atavistic howling. Sol, like the huge majority of readers, was not the least bit interested in the tedious day-to-day details of a journalist's life and so moved on.

He turned to another page and a blaster headline caught his attention.

ASBESTOS HORROR
by Ganny McIlwham
Environment Correspondent

A wave of pathological terror swept the town today after a single fibre of asbestos was discovered in a sealed container in an underground bank vault.

According to one unconfirmed source, grown men wept and tore off their own limbs rather than risk coming into contact with the horrifying substance – whose lung-rotting deadliness comes in a variety of bewildering colours.

Local councillor Krige Nimgimmer said: 'It's a tragedy and a catastrophe. The end of civilization as we know it. But it doesn't mean the town isn't a nice place to live and raise a family. It is, and there are excellent amenities and good shopping, and generous rates and rent holidays for new businesses.'

Jarry Gowser, chairman of the Ratepayers' Association, said something should be done about it. 'Something should be done about it,' he said.

A police spokesman said the force was being coy about the whole thing: 'There has been a complaint and we're monitoring the situation. It's too early to say at this stage of the investigation if it's an asbestos-related incident or not. But we're keeping an open mind and not ruling anything in or out.'

Continued on Page 17

'Hmm,' mused Sol. 'A slow news day, I would say.'

He looked at his watch, threw the newspaper aside, put his jacket on and left the flat. He had a dental appointment.

The dental receptionist explained that Sol's regular dentist was not at work. There had been a telephone call three days previously, from Patagonia, where his parents had retired to raise beef cattle. They had been doing rather well, but there had been an accident and his mother was not expected to recover.

Sol expressed his sympathies then turned his attention once more to the woman's lissom white-coated form.

'There is a locum to take his place,' said the receptionist. 'Would you like to see him?'

Sol replied that he would, adding that one dentist was much like another in his experience.

'I wouldn't be too sure,' she replied with a little smile, and asked him to go on in to the surgery.

The nurse, older than any Sol had encountered before, greeted him and repeated what the receptionist had said about the absence of the regular dentist, Dr Corrigan.

'Yes, I've been told. Most unfortunate circumstances,' said Sol. He looked at the dentist and then, with puzzlement at the nurse.

'Yes, I know,' she said, wearily. 'He's blind.'

As if her statement was a cue, the dentist stumbled into a table and scattered some instruments on the floor.

'Pick them up, would you, Hetty?' he said. 'And put them through the sterilizer. Don't just put them back on the table. They'll need to be cleaned. People come in here with dog merde on the soles of their shoes, you know. I can smell it before they've left the waiting room. This is what happens when you're blind. Your other senses grow sharper. Everyone has a smell. I can smell Hetty. I can smell you. You probably don't realize how much you smell.'

'Dear, really,' Hetty said, and looked apologetically at Sol.

'Oh, it's not a bad smell. Not unpleasant. Smells don't have to be bad. But I would recognize you if you came again.'

30

'I should perhaps explain', said Hetty, 'that though my husband may have no sight, his other senses are unimpaired – he works by touch much of the time. I act as his eyes to a limited extent. I can guide his hands.'

'How was Dr Corrigan on the blindness issue?' asked Sol.

'We sort of skirted around it,' admitted Hetty. 'When we spoke on the phone he didn't ask, so we didn't bring it up. My husband is a fully qualified dental surgeon, after all.'

'Oh, I don't doubt,' said Sol.

'I wasn't always blind, you know,' said the dentist.

'It happened about ten years ago,' explained Hetty.

'Just woke up one morning and everything was black,' continued the dentist. 'Doctors were stumped. Said it was some sort of virus and it would probably go away in its own time. But it didn't. Never seen a thing since. Completely black. Most blind people see shapes, you know. Outlines and things. I see nothing.'

'Well,' said Sol, touched by the man's plight. 'It was very courageous of you to continue as a dentist. Many might have given up.'

'What was I supposed to do?' the blind dentist asked sharply. 'Stand on a street corner and sell matches?'

'They don't do that any more, Bernard,' said Hetty, gently.

'Or sit making bloody paper poppies all day?'

'We're of that generation,' said Hetty. 'We were taught just to soldier on.'

Sol studied the dentist. He was a tall man. Very tall, with a thin, striated neck the colour of old parchment. He seemed to be for ever craning, as if his blindness were the consequence of being stuck in a hole, such that if he could only peer over its edge he might see something. When he moved his head it appeared to rotate in a quantum

31

fashion rather than as a continuum, seemingly able to get from one position to another without passing through any points in between. Sol could think of no great evolutionary advantage this would give a creature – not even an eagle, which was the beast the dentist most resembled in profile. And not just an eagle, but a Semitic eagle. And not just a Semitic eagle, but a Semitic eagle whose father was a rabbi who could trace a direct lineage back to the prophet Ezekiel.

Indeed the nose was prominent.

'Is the patient in the chair, Hetty?'

'Not yet, dear. No.'

She smiled at Sol and invited him to sit down. After a moment's hesitation Sol took his position.

'Now,' said the dentist. 'I should tell you. Because I rely so much on touch, I don't use gloves. That's a modern thing anyway. They're not essential. But you can be assured, my hands are clean.' And he held them up for Sol to see, front and back.

Hetty guided the dentist closer to the patient.

'Just close your mouth to start with,' said Hetty.

'Relax,' instructed the dentist. 'I like to get a general feel of the shape of the face. The jaw line.'

When he had run his fingers over Sol's jaw, he asked him to open wide. He slid a couple of fingers inside and ran the tips, very lightly, along the gums, and over all the surfaces of the teeth. Sol could taste the brackish residue of antiseptic soap.

'Don't need mirrors. Mirrors distort anyway,' said the dentist. 'Don't have to go prodding gums with those minia-ture gaff things – can't even remember what they're called, been so long since I used one. Barbaric. Ahh! Some tartar there. Did you get that, Hetty?'

'Yes, dear. I've written it down.'

'There's some gum recession too. At the front. Not a lot I can do about that, I'm afraid. Write that down, Hetty!'

'Yes, I know, Bernard. I know what to do. You don't have to keep telling me.'

'Fingers are sensitive, full of nerve ends,' said the dentist as he continued to feel the inside of Sol's mouth. 'Do you know which part of the body has the greatest concentration of nerve ends? Hmm?'

'Earlobe,' replied Sol, although it came out as 'eghrurbb'.

'No, it's not the tip of the penis.' The dentist smiled, the only time he did in the whole session. 'Most people think that. Most men, anyway. No, it's the earlobe. I ask you, what's the point of that? Nature got that one wrong. A few token nerves to let you know when it's cold, or when the wife's nibbling it. That's all the nerve ends you need in an earlobe.'

The dentist withdrew his fingers, which seemed very thick to Sol. Too thick for a dentist, more befitting a grave-digger or a farmer.

'Oh, do excuse me,' said Sol. 'I appear to have dribbled.'

Hetty handed him a tissue, and also a tumbler of liquid the colour of dilute blackcurrant cordial. It was antiseptic wash.

'Just rinse and spit,' said Hetty.

'In the bowl, if you please,' added the dentist, severely.

'Dear, you don't need to say that.'

'You do, though, Hetty. You do! You have to spell it out. Some of the riffraff you get coming for treatment these days.'

'Not this gentleman, dear. I must apologize—'

'No need,' said Sol, who had adapted to the dentist's manner. 'I can see your husband has a very subtle sense of humour. Very dry. Pawky, as the Scots say. Said without a smile.'

'But that's the way it should be,' said Hetty. 'It's always struck me as conceited to laugh at one's own witticisms.'

33

'What are you talking about now?' asked the dentist in a voice of weary irritation.

'Nothing, dear. Nothing at all,' replied Hetty, her tone peevish. 'I was just trying to be friendly to the patient, but I suppose *that*'s not important.'

The dentist walked into the table again and a number of implements fell on the hard floor with a bright ringing sound.

'Don't worry, dear,' said Hetty. 'The other ones will be clean now. They've had their ten minutes in the sterilizer.'

'Yes, well. Let's get on with it then,' said the dentist. 'You need two fillings. One quite urgently, the other we can nip in the bud.'

'We could do them now, if you like,' suggested Hetty.

'The thing is . . . ' began Sol. So far he had been impressed with the dentist's steady hand and diagnostic sensitivity. But a filling? A screaming drill? What use a steady hand if the diamond tip missed the mark and burrowed ferociously into soft tissue?

'If you're busy just now, then we could leave it until tomorrow,' offered Hetty.

'The thing is . . . ' replied Sol who did not generally struggle to find the right words.

'Bloody thing's not working again!' exclaimed the dentist plaintively.

'It's not switched on, dear. You have to switch it on.'

She flicked the power switch and the drill burst into life, almost leaping from his hand, like an angry serpent.

'Thing is . . . ' said Sol once more.

'It's okay,' said the pained but dignified Hetty. 'You don't have to say anything. We understand.'

'Thing is that Dr Corrigan and I go back a long way. I do feel it should be he who carries out the work.'

'Of course.'

'I feel it would be underhand and disloyal if I—'

'Please don't worry about us. We'll get by,' said Hetty. She looked away and seemed to be struggling to hold back tears.

'I mean, perhaps a clean?' offered Sol. 'As I'm here I might as well—'

'Don't patronize us!' barked the dentist. 'You don't need me to clean your teeth.'

'I just thought—'

'Clean your own bloody teeth! What's the world coming to?'

'I'm just trying to be—'

Hetty intervened. 'He was just being kind, dear.'

'Don't need his charity.'

'He gets like this,' said Hetty. 'He's a proud man. It's been very difficult.'

'Yes, I can appreciate,' said Sol getting up out of the chair. 'Well, thank you both very much.'

'Just get out, would you?' said the dentist. This time Hetty said nothing in Sol's defence.

'Yes. I was just going, actually. I, er . . . thank you. Goodbye, and good luck.'

Parlando drew back the curtain at the same time as Sol walked through the door of the salon.

'I knew you'd be back,' he chimed. He seemed happy, pleased with himself.

Sol closed the door. 'That's more than I did. How did you know?'

'Because you've unfinished business here.'

'A haircut, you mean?'

'I suppose there's that, yes. No, the other thing.'

'What other thing?'

'I found a way to get you out of the hole you were in.'

'What hole? I'm not in any hole.'

'Not any more you're not. Thanks to me.'

Sol stared at the hairdresser and was once more struck by the uncanny likeness to himself. And yet no-one else had commented on this. He thought some of the staff might have turned their heads when he walked through the salon yesterday; a double-take. Or it would have been an obvious handle for the hair-washer – Rachel, or not-Rachel – to have begun a conversation with.

Sol sighed. 'I'm not sure why I came back, actually. I, er—'

'Guilt. Guilt draws us back, like a dog to its vomit.'

'But "guilt" suggests I've done something wrong.'

'Don't you believe it, Sol. Guilt needs no object to attach itself to. Listen.' Parlando seemed to consider something for a moment. 'Why don't you come through for a coffee?'

'Well, I—'

'In the office. We can have a cosy little chat. I'll let you in on what's happening.'

'That would be something,' answered Sol. 'I'd certainly like to know.'

As they walked through the salon, Parlando called to someone a little way off. 'Oh, Rachel!' He mimed holding a cup and tipping it to his mouth. 'If you wouldn't mind, love. In the office.'

Sol looked to where the request had been directed, but it could have been aimed at any one of a number of young women.

'Rachel's back at work, then?' he remarked.

'What?'

'Didn't she phone in sick yesterday morning?'

'Did she?'

'That's what you said.'

'Oh yes. Rachel. Of course. Gippy tum. She's better now.'

'And the other Rachel?'

'Shhh!' Parlando held his finger to his lips and said, sotto voce:

'We'll talk about her in the office . . . 'Ah good,' said Parlando as they stepped through the doorway. 'Coffee's ready.'

Sol looked to a desk where indeed there was steaming coffee in a silver pot, and two small cups of fine china. There was also a plate full of fancy French cakes.

'How did . . . ? That was quick!'

He looked to Parlando for an explanation, but none was forthcoming.

'You do worry about inconsequential things, Sol. Just help yourself, okay?'

As Sol sipped his coffee the events of earlier in the day came back to him. 'Tell me,' he asked. 'Would you employ a blind hairdresser?'

'I shouldn't really say it, especially in front of a customer,' Parlando replied, 'but sometimes I think I have. Some of them haven't a clue when they come here.'

'Why do you take them on?'

'Because it's my job to teach them. To pass on what I know. If they leave here better than when they arrive, then my work has been done.'

There was on one side of the spacious office a bank of CCTV screens. Sol squinted into one and saw fuzzy images which appeared to represent two boiler-suited figures standing over a steaming cauldron, which now and then one of them stirred with a large paddle.

'What's happening here?' Sol asked.

Parlando walked over and stood by his side, as Sol pointed to the screen.

'Is that hair they're pouring in?'

'I believe so.'

37

'Why?'

'Because . . . ' Parlando giggled uneasily. 'I suppose I should know, shouldn't I?' He pressed a button and the image vanished. He pointed to another screen. 'I wanted you to see this, anyway. That was where you were yesterday.'

Sol leaned forward. 'Where I was washed? Bay 7?'

'No. Next door.'

'You mean where—'

'Exactly.'

'The unfortunate—'

'Quite. Do you notice anything unusual?'

Sol studied the grey image. 'No.'

'Good.' Parlando smiled. 'Good. There is nothing unusual. Everything's back to normal.'

They both watched as the attendant massaged Formula into a customer's hair.

'Business as usual, I would say,' said Sol.

Parlando smiled again. 'I tell you, things couldn't have worked out better.'

'Really?'

'Fortune has smiled on us. Come and sit down. I'll tell you about it.'

They sat at Parlando's desk.

'What's the perfect way to get rid of bodies? What do you think?'

Sol felt uneasy at the question. 'I really don't know.'

'Oh, come on! You read books, you're a man of wide knowledge. What do you think?'

'Well . . . ' Sol thought. 'I did see a film where they put a body – they were on a ship, this couple. They wrapped it in a blanket and just shoved it through the porthole.'

'Brilliant! We'll just charter a bloody steamer, shall we?' Parlando picked up the phone and, not taking his eyes off Sol, stabbed randomly at the keypad. As soon as a voice answered, he smiled and returned the receiver. 'Just as well I didn't let *you* take care of things.' He laughed. 'No, we don't have to go to sea. In fact, we don't have to do anything. It's all taken care of.'

'What? What's taken care of?'

Parlando laughed again. He patted Sol's thigh. 'Good. I like it. You've got the idea. Funnily enough, you were part of the way there when you said "film". That's the key. I don't know if you know, but they're shooting a big scene for a new film in the town.'

'I didn't know, no.'

'Down at the churchyard, at the edge of the common?'

'Ah! I passed by there. I wondered what that was all about.'

'It just so happens that this big scene is a funeral. Indeed, the funeral of the tragic couple around whom the entire plot revolves.'

'So?'

'So, two bodies, two coffins. Perfect.'

Sol thought about what Parlando had said. 'Okay, just to get it perfectly straight. There's a film involving a funeral. And the two bodies I witnessed – at least I think I did, it all seems very unreal – two real-life dead bodies are going to be, as it were, props in this film, and buried in a pretend funeral?'

'Very good summary. Just so.'

'Hmm. Okay,' said Sol. 'Let me play Devil's Advocate here for a moment. If it's a film, it's not real. It's pretend. Ergo, not a real funeral. Yes? No-one really dies in films, do they? Not really.'

'Exactly. But that's the whole point. For this "funeral"' (Parlando's index fingers etched the quotation marks in thin air) 'we don't need all the paraphernalia. We don't need post-mortems, we don't need death certificates, we don't need undertakers, and nor do we need officials who ask awkward questions.'

'Yes, but let's take it step by step. Supposing . . . well, how are you going to get the bodies on to the set, for a start? Without arousing suspicion?'

'It's done. Taken care of.'

'How?'

'Doesn't matter. As we speak there are two coffins containing bodies waiting to be lowered into the ground. The hole's already been dug. Ashes to ashes. They've been embalmed. All the bits that go off really quickly have been removed. They've had all the make-up on. You know? Full-facials from the undertaker.'

'It's possible, as it's only a film,' continued Sol, 'they might not follow the whole procedure. They might not bury anything. They might cut and take their lunch break just as the coffins are being lowered. Then what?'

'I've seen the script. They *do* get buried. It's a wonderful scene. Immensely moving. It's all there. The Latin chants, the altar boy swinging the censer. A choir. The jilted lover throws in a handful of dirt, then the embittered parent. The crowd melts away and the gravediggers – four of them, honest working-class types – start shovelling in the earth. Dust to dust, amen. I know this director. I do a lot of work for him – hairstyles for the cast – and he's big on authenticity. There's no way he would compromise with some half-arsed funeral scene where the coffins are not even buried. He has his reputation to think of, and he thinks about it constantly.'

Sol nodded, as if to commend Parlando on his argument. 'Okay, but just suppose they look *inside* the coffins, and discover there really *are* bodies in it?'

'Suppose they do,' replied Parlando, calmly. 'Suppose they do. Are they going to think, "Hello! someone's trying to dispose of some real dead bodies," or are they going to think, "Pretty realistic, these corpses. Props have done a great job here."? What do you think, Sol?'

Sol reflected awhile. 'I'm thinking, how did a man like me, who has never had so much as a parking ticket in his life, get sucked into this? I'm thinking, it's not right somehow: everyone deserves a proper send-off.'

'And they've got one! They've got a fantastic funeral!'

'No, it's not the same—'

'There'll be hundreds of people. There'll be . . . it's all in the script. It's magnificent in concept. And big. It's a big scene. It's so big they can only afford to do it once. Must be right first time.'

'But it's not *real*, is it? The *priest* isn't real, for example, is he?'

'He's a great character actor. Good as any ordained priest, and probably better. His words are taken verbatim from the sanctified . . . liturgy, or whatever they call it.'

'You're ignoring my point,' said Sol.

'Honestly, you're such a nit-picker.'

'I think it pays to be sceptical in this life. And cautious.'

'Scepticism is one thing but . . . ' Parlando tried to think of the second thing, but couldn't. 'You know, you can stretch scepticism just as much as belief. That's what I'm trying to say.'

'I just get the feeling – how shall I put it? You're not the one in control. There's someone else, someone I don't know about, who's pulling the strings.'

'You're saying I'm not in charge?'

'That did occur to me, yes.'

'I – work – for – no-one!'

'Fine.'

'I'm my own boss. That's all a hairdresser has to aim for. To open a shop, be his own boss, and cherish the illusion he's master of his own destiny.'

'Okay, okay.'

'Because otherwise . . . do you seriously think anybody wants to spend the whole of their working life, fifty years, just cutting hair? Just listening to the tedious chatter of asinine customers when you could be paying someone else a pittance to do it for you?'

'Well, you know, it's a job. Jobs need to be done.'

'Platitudes. Clichés.'

'It's not my cup of tea, certainly,' admitted Sol defensively. 'And it's not like that at my work. We only talk to communicate information germane to our work.'

'It's not my "cup of tea" either. That's why I built up all this.' Parlando gestured towards the cathode-ray representation of his empire.

'You've done very well, Parlando. I applaud you.'

'Don't be so surprised! When it comes to business, hairdressing has a lot going for it. It's up there with the essentials. People will die, people will be born and people have to eat. Hair will grow, and needs to be cut. We can't stop it. Even when it stops growing on our head, it grows in other places. Even when we're dead it keeps on growing. It doesn't know when to bloody stop!'

'Yes,' said Sol. 'There will always be a demand.'

'And of course, we haven't even talked about vanity. There's no shortage of vanity in the world, and it isn't going to go away.'

'And yet for all that—'

'I know what you're going to say. People do fail at hairdressing, despite the great potential for success. Some of my staff leave to "set up on their own", as they put it. And who can blame them? I give them my blessing, when what I should really say is: "Write No Hope Business Ltd on the sign above the shop. At least then when you do fail miserably no-one can accuse you of being unrealistic." I don't mind if

42

people want to reach for the stars, Sol, but, for goodness sake, how long's the human arm?'

'Two, three feet?'

'And how far's the nearest star?'

'Alpha Centauri? Oh, about four light years.'

'Exactly. You do the arithmetic, Sol.'

'I think I see your point. But we digress. To return to the matter in hand. You seem to have thought things through carefully, and in all your arguments there's a peculiar logic. I'm not saying this funeral plan won't work. It's just, I'm not exactly sure what's been going on and—'

'You don't have to know. It's not important that you do. I've not asked you to help in any of it. All I'm asking is that you draw a line under it all. Just get on with your life and forget about all this.'

'Yes. It's been a bit unsettling. I'd like to put it behind me.'

'Good. Fine.'

'One thing, though.'

'Yes?'

'I wouldn't mind that haircut at some point.'

Parlando smiled. 'Of course.'

'If you can fit me in?'

'As it happens, we've had some cancellations. Quite a few, actually.'

'Oh?'

'I think there must be a virus going around, or something. We'll book you in on the way out. Would you excuse me a minute? Coffee goes straight through me.' And Parlando left the room with alacrity.

Sol drifted over to the CCTV screens and scanned them. The day-to-day work of a busy salon continued. He pressed some buttons and watched the images change.

'Hello! What have we here?' It was a room with a small

43

bed, and nothing much else. A naked form glided into view, then out again. Sol wondered if there was any way of remotely adjusting the camera in that room, but then the young woman appeared again, this time full-frontal to the camera. Now with another body behind her.

'What are you looking at?'

It was Parlando, returned, still adjusting his zip.

'Nothing really.' Sol stabbed some buttons in an attempt to get rid of the image, but all he got was a different aspect of the same scene.

Parlando stood next to him. 'I see. Little bit of a voyeur, are we?'

'Not really. What is this anyway?'

Parlando looked at the screen. 'I think it's pretty obvious what it is.'

'No, I mean, why is it taking place in a hairdressing establishment?'

'No-one's forcing you to watch, if you find it all so bloody disgusting.'

'I don't think it's disgusting.' In fact, Sol was rather taken by the naked young form and found it hard to take his eyes off the screen.

It was as if Parlando could penetrate his thoughts. 'Look, we're both grown-ups. You don't have to be prissy. If you're interested you just have to ask for "Bay 17" when you book in. Okay? They'll know what you mean. Bay 17.'

'Yes, thank you, but I don't usually—'

'Yes, I know. You don't have to pay for it. Scores of big-busted wantons beat a pathway to your door every Saturday night. Is that it?'

'I don't do too badly,' replied Sol, although in reality he knew he didn't do wondrous well when it came to women.

The door of the office opened and a secretary hurried in.

She appeared agitated. She was about to speak, then noticed Sol, who had turned to look at her.

'Don't worry, Ruth,' said Parlando. 'Sol's okay. But what is it?'

'The police are here!' she gasped.

'Police! What do you . . . ?' Parlando hurried to the screens, pushed Sol aside, and scanned them.

'Where, for God's sake?'

'In reception.'

He zoomed in on the two men, who appeared to be admiring the wooden curtain.

'Shit!' Parlando looked severely at Sol. 'What have you been saying?'

'Nothing. Don't keep accusing me.'

'Okay, okay. Just keep calm. Let's all of us keep calm. *Calm.* Let me think. Right, I've got it. You pretend you're me.'

'What?'

'Yes, we could maybe swap clothes.'

'Whatever for?'

'It'll – no. No, you're right. It'll just make things more difficult.' Parlando seemed to be turning things over in his mind. 'I want you to come down with me,' he said.

'I don't see what all this has to do with me.'

'Just come with me. Whatever I say, back me up. That's all I'm asking. I'm not telling, I'm asking.'

Sol sighed. He gestured helplessly. He was truly confused. He began to protest.

'It's not a lot to ask, is it?' pleaded Parlando. 'After what I've just done for you?'

'I'm not sure I can help you. I—'

'Good! Excellent! Don't say anything, though, unless it's to back me up. Right? Have you got that?'

Sol nodded warily.

4

The camera did not lie. In the reception area of the salon stood a police inspector and his sergeant.

'I'll not beat about the bush,' said the senior man. 'I'll leave that to others. No, I'll get straight to the point: there's been a disappearance.'

'I see,' said Parlando, uneasily.

'Yes. A lady phoned HQ this morning, somewhat distraught. She said her husband did not return home last night.'

'So what?' answered Parlando.

'You might say. Yes, I'm broad-minded too. I'm aware this isn't the first time this has happened with a husband and wife, and usually it's nothing more than adultery, which is a civil matter.'

'What's it got to do with me, Inspector?' asked Parlando.

'We did a check on his movements, if you'll excuse the infelicity of the expression. As far as we can see, his last known whereabouts was here: in this establishment, where he had an appointment. For a haircut, I imagine. Possibly a shave, or a wash and brush-up, as they used to call it.'

'I think we can clear this up quickly, Inspector. If this man had an appointment here, his name will be in the book.'

'The book?'

'The appointments book. What was his name?'

The inspector addressed his sergeant:

'Ginge, what was that name again?'

The sergeant, who was writing everything down, flipped back a few pages of his notepad. 'Dowt,' he answered.

'Doubt?' asked Parlando.

'No, Dowt,' corrected the inspector.

'Do you suspect foul play?' asked Sol.

Parlando, one eye on the inspector, frowned at Sol.

'Yes, I do actually, now that you ask. After twenty-five years in the Force one gets a nose for these things.' He paused for effect. 'I think we're looking at murder.'

'Oh, come on, Inspector,' said Parlando, laughing unconvincingly. 'People bumped off at the barber's! You've been reading too many Victorian melodramas. You'll be asking to see the meat pies next!'

Ginge scribbled away busily.

'Perhaps you could take down some of this man's particulars,' said the inspector, pointing at Sol.

Ginge obediently turned his attention. 'Name? . . . How do you spell that?'

'With combinations of three letters there is rarely anything to trap the unwary,' replied Sol, a little superciliously, keen to establish his intellectual superiority in the situation.

'He's only being thorough, according to the rules laid down. Just oblige us, if you wouldn't mind.'

'And you work in this establishment, here, do you?' asked Ginge.

'I ask you!' said Parlando, again laughing rather uneasily. 'Does he look like a hairdresser?'

When Sol informed Ginge where he did work, the inspector interrupted once more. 'An office you say? That's funny, that. I've a niece who wants to work in an office. I'll tell her I met you, she'll be most interested.'

'Would you like to see the appointments book?' asked Parlando. 'I'm sure nobody called Dowt has been here.'

'Might have used a false name,' suggested Ginge.

'All in good time. I'd like to look around the premises, if you don't mind.'

'I do, actually,' replied Parlando.

'Ah!'

'Shall I send for some back-up, chief?' asked Ginge.

'I'm sure that won't be necessary,' said Sol. 'I mean, why should he object to your looking around? There's nothing to hide here. It's a hairdressing salon, for goodness sake! Not a charnel house! He's merely thinking of you and your time, which he has no wish to waste. I understand this can constitute a criminal offence.'

'Yes, indeed,' said the inspector. 'But I would still like to eliminate the salon from my enquiries, as it were. So . . . if you would be so kind?'

'In that case,' answered Parlando. 'But as my friend says, there's nothing to hide.'

'This way,' said Sol brushing aside the curtain, which, despite the uneasy situation, continued to emit a soft, swishing, calming sound when thus disturbed.

No-one paid much attention to the quartet as they entered the main chamber. The two officers wandered about the floor looking up and down, left and right. Sol and Parlando walked two paces behind.

'It's much bigger than you imagine, isn't it?' said Sol at one point.

The inspector turned to look at him. 'It's not the size that surprises me,' he remarked. He addressed his sergeant. 'Notice anything odd, Ginge?'

'Have actually, chief, yeh,' said Ginge, without looking up from his notepad.

'Have you?' replied the inspector, surprised. 'What?'

'Well, it struck me as a bit odd that here we are in some fancy poncing hairdresser's and there ain't a bleeding mirror in sight.'

'What?' said the inspector. He looked around the room. 'He's right. Not one. Well spotted, son!'

Parlando was dismissive. 'As if people wanted to sit and stare at themselves for an hour! I've no wish at all to encourage narcissism. If people want to look at themselves, they can do it at home. I believe most people can afford a mirror these days.'

The inspector seemed shocked. 'But how can they see what's happening? You might be making a right pig's ear of it, and they wouldn't know till too late.'

'Inspector, we don't make pigs' ears here. People come here sometimes with hair like a pig's ear and we turn it into a silk purse. When people come to this salon for work on their hair, they put themselves entirely in our hands. If they are not a hundred per cent confident about the service then I don't even want them here in the first place.'

'Don't know if I could be doing with that.'

'If people really want a mirror,' said Parlando, impatiently, 'we'll bring them one at the end. But you really have to ask why. It's not as if they're seeing themselves. It's just a mirror image. A reflection. It's sobering to think: you can never see your actual head. I can see yours! You can see mine, and we can describe them to each other. But in the whole history of mankind no-one has ever directly seen their own head.'

'Not even Janus,' confirmed Sol. 'He could stare down at his own arse, but not his own head.'

'Yes, well. I know which I'd rather look at,' said the inspector.

'What's through there, then?' asked Ginge, pointing with his biro to a door.

'Oh, nothing really,' answered Parlando casually.

'Nothing!' exclaimed the inspector.

'You mean,' said the sergeant, with a good helping of sarcasm, 'like a vacuum? Interstellar space.'

Parlando and Sol exchanged anxious glances as the two detectives opened the door and looked at what lay beyond.

'Nothing, you say?' said the inspector.

'In a manner of speaking,' answered Sol. 'Nothing germane to your inquiry.'

'I'll be the judge of that, if you don't mind.' The inspector looked from Parlando to Sol, then back again. 'Lead on, if you would be so kind.'

'It's really only staff rooms, storage rooms, washing rooms. All the stuff necessary for the running of a successful business.'

The inspector stopped walking. 'What about in here? Here, Ginge. Give the door the old heave-ho, would you? The lumbago's playing up a bit these days.'

'I think you'll find the door's open,' said Parlando.

The group entered. There were two men in boiler suits and leather aprons slowly stirring a bubbling vat.

'Phwoar!' exclaimed the inspector. 'Pongs a bit in here.'

'What they up to then?' asked Ginge, ready to write down the answer.

'Oh, just waste disposal,' replied Parlando. 'We use some noxious chemicals for dyeing, and—'

'Dying?' exclaimed the inspector.

'Keeps the grey at bay,' said Sol.

'Ah! That sort, yes.'

The search continued in a desultory fashion, with the inspector now and then pointing to a door, asking to be admitted to the room behind it and then for an explanation as to its purpose. Parlando answered and Ginge noted down the replies.

51

'And what goes on in here?' asked the inspector as he looked into the white-tiled room with the marble slabs. 'The last time I was in a room like this there were bodies laid out.'

'Stiffs,' said the sergeant.

'We hardly have need of a mortuary in a hairdressing salon,' said Parlando.

'I can understand you mistaking it for a mortuary, inspector,' said Sol. 'It has that feel about it.'

'What's it used for, then?'

'Well, we, um . . . ' said Parlando, and looked towards Sol, who prompted him.

'Surgery.'

'Surgery?' exclaimed the inspector, looking around.

'Yeees,' said Parlando uncomfortably.

'In a hairdressing salon? What sort of surgery?'

'Oh, very basic stuff.'

'They do a very good line in leeches,' said Sol.

'I suppose that makes you a barber-surgeon?' said the sergeant.

'Barber-surgeon!' exclaimed Sol. 'That's it. One of the clues in my crossword. Nine across, six and seven. Funny how it comes to you, isn't it?'

'What's that, then? Barber-surgeon?' asked the inspector.

'In the old days it was like the two trades were the same, wasn't they?' said Ginge.

The group returned to the main salon, where the inspector's attention was caught by the vibrant colours of the 'pharmacy' with its rows of bottled toiletries.

'This is where we make the shampoos, conditioners, and various other preparations that we use in the salon,' said Parlando, anticipating the policeman's question.

'Ah, yes. Very interesting. Bit like down at forensics – eh, Ginge? Blooming marvellous what they can do down there.'

Parlando handed the inspector a bottle of viscous orange liquid. 'This is our best stuff. I'd like you to have it, inspector. I'm sure your good lady could use it.'

The inspector took the drift. 'Ah yes, thank you very much, yes.'

'I'd appreciate it if you didn't mention any of this,' and Parlando gestured about the salon, 'to the authorities. A man's only trying to make a living and there's so much red tape these days. Health and Safety, Taxman, Planning Department. You name it—'

'VAT?'

'What?' said Parlando, alarmed.

'Are you registered for VAT?'

'I, er—'

Sol stepped forward and handed the inspector another bottle of coloured liquid. 'I think you'll find everything is in order in that department.'

'Yes, of course,' said the inspector, pocketing the bottle. 'I'm sure that's the case. I've no reason to suspect otherwise.'

There was an awkward silence.

'Um, let me think now. I'm sure there was something else,' said the inspector.

Parlando looked at his watch, with an exaggerated sweep of his arm. 'Lord! Is that the time?'

'Yes, I suppose I should be getting back to the station.'

'Let me show you out,' offered Parlando.

'Before you do – you mentioned an appointments book.'

'Did I?'

'Is it handy? I'd like to see it.'

'It's in reception,' said Parlando. 'Why are you so interested in my appointments book?'

'I'd like to take it down to the station and run a check on some of the names—'

'Take away the appointments book? Don't be ridiculous! How am I supposed to know who's coming to the salon, and for what?'

'It would be chaos without that book,' added Sol.

'Very well. As you wish. We'll just need to copy the names. Sergeant! Over here with your notebook, my lad.' The inspector looked over his shoulder. 'Where's he got to then? Ginge!'

'Who's that?' asked Parlando.

Sol looked at him, puzzled. Parlando indicated he should play along. Sol shrugged, and wondered what advantage Parlando had seen in the situation.

The inspector was looking around him, bemused. 'I'm sure I had an assistant when I came here.'

'I don't think so,' said Parlando, and once more gestured surreptitiously to Sol.

'I don't remember seeing anyone else,' agreed Sol.

'That's funny. We usually go around in twos, you know. Here, that's a good one! Why do policemen go around in twos?

'What?' answered Parlando, defensively.

'No, it's a joke.'

'Ah! Very good!' Parlando forced a laugh. 'Yes, very funny.'

One of the salon girls brushed through the curtain.

'Ah! Ann, my lovely! How are you?' said Parlando, and kissed her on the cheek. 'Have you seen the inspector's colleague?'

'His colleague?'

'So you didn't see anyone either! Just as I thought.' He indicated that she should leave. 'There you are, Inspector. A considerable body of evidence appears to be building up. Evidence that you came here alone.'

The inspector shrugged. 'Perhaps you're right.'

'Could be cutbacks?' suggested Sol. 'Joking aside, some-one high up has ruled it an extravagance to go around in twos all the time.'

'That wouldn't surprise me. Oh well. Thank you for your co-operation. I'll be off. But I would like to see that book sometime, at your convenience.'

'Before you go, Inspector,' said Parlando.

'Yes?'

'Just one more thing.' He put his arm around the detective in a chummy, man-to-man sort of way. 'If there's any problem of any kind I'm sure we can sort it out in a manner that's satisfactory to us both – but particularly to you.'

'Oh yes?'

Parlando nodded. 'Yes. When it comes to giving satis-faction there are one or two of my girls . . . If you get the picture?'

'I think so. Yes. I did happen to notice when I was passing through the salon there were several right little corkers. I even fancied one or two were giving me the eye.'

'That doesn't surprise me, Inspector. A mature, disting-uished-looking man like yourself.'

'Shall we say tomorrow,' said the inspector, addressing Parlando once more. 'I can—'

'Ah, tomorrow! Tomorrow we're closed.'

'Oh, and why's that? If you don't mind my asking.'

'Don't be so diffident, Inspector. It's your job to ask questions.'

'There's been a family bereavement,' chipped in Sol.

'That's right,' said Parlando. 'A funeral to attend.'

'A funeral? Someone's died, then?'

Parlando's tone changed once more to one of uneasiness. 'That's right. My, um, Uncle Delgardo. He's ninety-one. My great-uncle. In Tibet. He was . . . gored by a yak.'

'Oh, that is sad. It's like they say, isn't it? You never know

where you are with yaks. A bit like Alsatians. Oh well, my
condolences. If not tomorrow, then the next day. Oh! Blow
me down, no! Can't make it. Bit of a do on, down at the
Recreation Ground. The Vice Squad are taking on Forensics
at cricket. Why don't you come along? Should be a laugh.'

'I don't think so,' said Parlando. 'I hate cricket. I'd be
bored stupid.'

'As you wish. Till next time then.' The inspector walked
out through the red door and a bell rang somewhere not far
off.

Parlando let out a sigh of relief. 'Thank God! How do you
think it went?'

'So-so,' answered Sol.

'Listen, um. This funeral tomorrow—'

'The film, you mean?'

'Of course. The film. You didn't believe all that stuff about
my Uncle Delgardo. Did you?'

'No.'

'I do have an uncle Delgardo, but he wasn't gored by a
yak. It was a bull. I'll tell you about it some day.'

'The funeral?'

'Ah yes. Well, I was thinking. I'd feel happier if one of
us was there. Just to see, you know, that everything went
off okay.'

'When you say "one of us" – you mean you'd like me to
go?'

'I say, would you?'

'Why me?'

'You are on bloody holiday after all!' snapped Parlando.
'And it's for your benefit!'

'Mine?'

'Christ, you ungrateful little . . . I'm only trying to help
you! Sorry, sorry. I'm getting a little tense. We both are.'
Parlando poked his head through the curtain and looked

around the salon. 'Let's keep our voices down, eh? That sergeant might still be snooping around the shop. I don't know what's happened to him.'

'I'd be a lot happier, and it would make life so much easier,' said Sol, 'if you told me exactly what you have and haven't done. It's all a mystery to me.'

'Sure, sure. But not now, okay? I'm way behind – thanks to these idiot policemen. There are people waiting to get their hair cut. They've been waiting for ages. I'm not sure what I'm going to say to them. Later. Okay? We'll have a drink – no I'll treat you to a meal at the Riverside. Best restaurant in town. Langoustines the size of armadillos, and every bit as tasty!'

'Very nice. Thank you. We'll do that.'

'Not tonight, I'm afraid.'

'No?'

'No. After tomorrow, when everything will be sorted.'

'Fine. Just give me a call. Now, what am I supposed to be doing on this film set?'

'Just . . . keep an eye on things. Make sure everything goes according to plan.'

'But I don't know the plan.'

'Make sure the coffins are buried. In the ground. That's the only part of the plan you need to know.'

'Okay. I'll do that.'

'Thing is, Sol, I *trust* you. You're very good at thinking on your feet. You see, I hate people asking me questions. I just panic. I was like that at school. I don't know why. I just tense up. But you – you just bat them away.'

'Yes, I've always been quite good with questions,' acknowledged Sol.

'You ran rings around those stupid policemen.'

'Wasn't difficult.'

And they both laughed.

'So do I just turn up on the set, or what?'

'At eight o'clock. They're expecting you.'

'Are they?'

'Yes. I arranged it earlier. I know the director.'

'Ah, yes. You said.'

'He owes me a favour. But even if he didn't, he would still have done it. He's that kind of guy. Just turn up at eight, and keep an eye on things. Use your common sense if, you know, anything . . . '

5

Sol awoke a little later than usual next morning. After breakfast he looked at his watch and realized there was no time to go out for a paper. So he picked up the one from the day before, turned to the crossword page, and entered 'Barber-surgeon' in the appropriate place. He read the clue again. "Royal roe a cut above at t-time."

'Hmm,' he said. 'No wonder I couldn't get it. That's not right. "Royal roe" is caviar, which is not the same as sturgeon. Not sure about this compiler. It needs to be more . . . "Cut above double-act slices sturgeon to a T." I don't know what it's coming to when you have to find the bloody clues yourself, as well as the solution.'

He read Ten Down:

'Does Hannibal up the ante in a poker game with Dalai Lama? (2 Letters.)'

'No', he concluded, and entered an 'o' in the space after the 'n' in surgeon. Moments later he laid down the paper and set off to take the bus to the common where the filming was taking place.

At the site entrance he was questioned by a security man, who seemed satisfied that he was indeed expected and let him pass. He asked one or two people where he might find the director and eventually found himself in the presence of a man sitting on a folding chair studying a script. He looked up as Sol approached.

'You must be Parlando's friend.'

'Yes, I am. How do you do.' He half expected the man to remark on the resemblance between himself and Parlando, but he didn't.

'This is Rossan,' said the director, indicating a man standing a little way off, dressed in clerical garb. 'He's third assistant director.'

'Just don't call me gopher, okay?' said Rossan, laughing.

'I can't imagine why I would,' answered Sol.

The men shook hands.

'Well, of course it would be out of order for you to do so,' said Rossan. 'I mean, a film set is so medieval with its hierarchies. I'm incredibly important compared to you and yet—' he indicated the director, 'hardly fit to kiss this man's shoes.'

'Really, Rossan!' laughed the director. 'Let's write that out of the script, shall we? You're my highly valued assistant. The film wouldn't get made without you.'

Rossan, obviously flattered by the compliment, said:

'Oh, I'm sure it would!'

'You're probably wondering why he's dressed like that,' said the director to Sol.

'He's not truly a man of the cloth then?'

'The last time Rossan was in a church was when he was christened.'

Rossan laughed loudly once more, pleased to be enjoying a joke with the most important man on the set.

'Anyhow,' said the director. 'Let's get this bloody show on the road, shall we? Enough frivolity. Making a film's a serious business.'

'Of course, yes, right,' answered Rossan. He looked at his watch and turned to Sol. 'We've not got a lot of time, so we'd better get you sorted out.'

As they hurried over the muddy common Rossan explained what the film was about, and outlined the day's schedule.

'It's the funeral scene. Tragic lovers. It's actually the penultimate scene but we're filming it first. Sometimes logistics dictate. Of course, you'll know that. Scenes are often not filmed in the order they appear in the script.'

'I didn't know that, actually.'

Rossan stopped walking and looked at Sol, a little concerned. 'You have done this sort of thing before? I mean, been an extra?'

'Oh yes,' lied Sol. 'Now and then. Here and there, you know.'

'Good. You see, we get all sorts of people who really haven't a clue and say, "Oh, we just wanted to be in a movie. No-one told us we'd have to act, or anything."'

'Timewasters.'

'Exactly! That's a good word for them. They really do waste everyone's time, which is so precious when you're making a film. Speaking of which . . . '

They passed by a plot, about fifty yards square, that had been transformed into a graveyard. A group of men were struggling to erect a cumbersome model, made from polymer, of an ancient yew tree.

Sol looked around. 'Shouldn't there be a church?'

'Well, that's the thing, see. There is a church, but not here. About a hundred miles away. In Shropshire, I think it is. Wonderful, late Gothic and all that. But we couldn't film there, in the churchyard. They were all right about filming inside, but not out amongst the graves. And they wouldn't let us dig. No. They were very definite about that. I don't know why. Respect for the dead, I suppose. I mean, people are so bloody touchy about the dead. It wasn't as if we were going to exhume bodies and sell them to medical students or anything. So we've had to go to all the trouble with this damned replica. This', and he indicated round about, 'is identical in every detail to a part of the churchyard in Shropshire. Hence the yew tree. A thousand years old, it's supposed to be. So, once we've finished here, we'll pack everything up, and head for the actual church. There are some lovely shots planned. Sun streaming through the stained-glass . . . everything. Then, of course, we just splice things together. In the cutting room. That's where films are really made, you know. It's all in the editing. That's what I'd like to do. That's my ambition. I certainly don't want to be a third assistant director all my days.'

'I'm sure you won't be, Rossan. Everybody in the film business knows third assistant director is just a stepping stone, don't they?'

'Exactly, yes.'

The two men came to a large rectangular hole about six feet deep. Next to it were two coffins, one in rosewood, one in beech.

'Ah,' remarked Sol. 'These will be the—'

'Tragic lovers, yes,' answered Rossan. 'Two hearts, one love, one grave.'

'And the rose grew round the briar . . . '

They stood silently a while, as if they were real mourners. Then Sol leaned forward. He noted that the lids had been screwed down. He ran his hand over the polished wood of one of the boxes, then grasped a brass handle and attempted to lift. The coffin barely moved.

'Oh!' exclaimed Rossan. 'I didn't realize there was something in there.'

'It doesn't surprise me, knowing this director and his passion for verisimilitude. In my experience you can tell if people are manhandling an empty coffin.'

'Yes, of course,' agreed Rossan. 'There'll be, er, something in there. To give it weight.'

'Sandbags, perhaps?'

'That's what I would use.' He giggled. 'Mind you, knowing this director, it wouldn't surprise me if he was using real bodies.'

'It wouldn't surprise me either,' said Sol, smiling. 'But you still haven't told me about . . . You know, about the . . . ?' And he indicated Rossan's outfit.

'Glad you reminded me! Yes, you'll need to know. Well, the funeral scene is a big scene. Biggest in the film. It's so big, in fact, that we can't retake it. Has to be right first time.'

Sol nodded. He could appreciate that.

'It's a period piece, so what we absolutely can't have is someone like a tea-boy in jeans coming accidentally into shot. That's why everyone on the set must be in costume that's appropriate to the period.'

'I see. Yes. A precaution.'

'Exactly. Which reminds me.' Rossan patted his hair. 'This won't do, will it? Fine for a trendy sixties vicar, maybe. Not a fifties country parson, though. I need a trim. But let's get you kitted out first.'

'What part am I playing?'

Rossan consulted his clipboard. 'Let me see, let me see . . . a mourner, one of six hundred and thirty-two. A distant relative, or perhaps just a well-wisher moved by the couple's tragic plight. You'll stand nearer the back.'

Inside the capacious wardrobe trailer there were racks of exotic and elaborate costumes, as well as some plainer ones. Sol pulled out something colourful and read the label:

'Grandee from the court of Ashoka the Great. Circa 200 B.C.'

He pulled out another, described by its label as:

'Bengal Lancer (other ranks) c. 1850.'

'They can't be using these in this film, can they?'

Rossan looked at them. 'Bengal Lancer? Wouldn't have thought so.'

The door opened and a young woman carrying a little suitcase came in.

'Ah, Sally! My haircut,' Rossan informed Sol.

Sol recognized the woman from Parlando's salon. He said hello, but she barely responded – as if she could tell from a single brief glance that he was no-one of importance within the context of the film.

Rossan pulled up a chair. The girl snipped away at his hair. Sol watched. He looked at her buttocks, which he judged too pronounced. Like a Hottentot's. 'They'd be a real turn-off in bed,' he told himself, though not with great conviction. And he glanced at them again.

As she worked she recounted enthusiastically how she had just washed the hair of Butters Nicobar.

Butters Nicobar! Sol was distinctly unimpressed. Yes, she had been in a number of films, but was very over-rated in his view. She always played the same part in exactly the same wooden way. The dignified, upper-middle-class English matron who, whatever the calamity, always kept a lid on her emotions and put on a brave face. An obvious choice, though, for the grieving parent.

'We could probably give yours a trim too, old boy,' said Rossan, as he stood up, brushing hair from his cassock.

'No time for that!' said Sally, packing her case. 'I've got other people waiting. Important people.'

'Your boss owes *me* a haircut, actually,' said Sol severely.

'Hold on, hold on,' said Rossan, eager to head off any unpleasantness. 'Fair's fair. She's got work to do, Sol—'

'Bloody right. Important work.'

'Sally, love, I – you carry on. I've just had an idea for a part for Sol.' He consulted his clipboard. 'Yah. A photographer. The press are very interested in the funeral, naturally. So we've got someone at the graveyard snapping away. There's a costume, I saw it earlier. Fifties style, with a mac and hat. Thing is, if you wear a hat, we won't need to see your hair.'

'Fine. Let's do that,' said Sol.

'As I recall,' said Rossan, 'there's a little bit of action involved. You stand at the front of the mourners and take a flash photograph as the coffins are being lowered.'

'I think I can manage that.'

'All a bit disrespectful, if you ask me. Taking pictures at the grave-side. But that's what the script says.'

Sol looked in the mirror and frowned. The hat was fine, particularly set at a raffish angle. The mackintosh too was quite presentable. But the trousers were baggy and the bottoms lay corrugated on his shoes, touching the ground behind his heels; a reminder that he lacked the ideal proportion. His legs were shorter than average for people of his waist size. If he thought he was going to be scrutinized, Sol generally wore striped trousers in an attempt to deceive the eye of the beholder. He had once, at a dance, been rebuffed by a woman who told him his legs weren't long enough.

'They reach the ground,' he had riposted. 'That's perfectly long enough.' Well, not exactly riposted. Rather he had thought, some time after the event, that that was what he should have said.

'You don't have any safety pins, do you, Rossan?' Sol asked now.

But Rossan was already about his business.

* * *

Sol strolled about the set, waiting to be called for the filming. In the mock churchyard the giant yew tree was in place and, from a distance, looked quite authentic. The team which had erected it stood in a little knot eating sandwiches and drinking from hip flasks. Sol wandered among the maze of headstones, in granite, red sandstone and dark, polished composite. There were simple square slabs, ornate Celtic crosses, even a family vault surrounded by black railings. At the head of one 'grave' there was a statue of an angel, with palms pressed together and eyes turned heavenward. On others there were brass urns and floral tributes. And there was a good mix of old and new, with stones polished and pristine and inscribed with ornate gold lettering, while in other places stood dull grey slabs, mottled with lichens and pitted by time and storm, to mark the resting places of persons who had supposedly lain dead for two or three centuries.

He read some of the inscriptions and they were as you would expect in a real-life cemetery. But then he noticed one or two unlikely names:

'Dipper Macaroony', 'Dash Squib-Diddly', 'Fribbler Sucknimble'; 'Pup Mordecai'; 'Borad and Findo Umbelisha, Beloved Brothers, *In their death they were not divided.*'

'Conjoined, perhaps?' mused Sol. Then another inscription caught his eye:

'Here lies Old Cacknacker. Died aged 176. Who gives a f***ing s**t?'

'I can't think that's part of the script,' muttered Sol.

The stone next to it marked the supposed resting place of someone called Margaret, who had apparently lived to be two hundred and eleven.

There was an epitaph:

Bye Bye Maggie
   Scraggy; shaggy and slaggy;
   Then saggy and baggy.
   How much better
   If you had been called Susan.

'Puerile doggerel? Or a simple but poignant comment on the starkness of life and the inevitability of death?' wondered Sol.

As an afterthought someone had scrawled in chalk:

'I dun her round the back!'

'This might', reflected Sol, 'refer to a moment in a budding romance when a couple slipped away from a roistering party to the privacy of the back garden and consummated their love under the moon and stars. Equally, it might allude to an act still proscribed in certain God-fearing nations as—

Sol broke from his musings on the epitaph as he saw two members of the props team were walking towards him. They were dressed as grave-diggers, for the Big Scene, with flat caps, moleskin trousers, waistcoats and white collarless shirts. Moreover, their costumes fitted them perfectly.

One of them called out:

'Oi, snot! What you up to here? Sniffing round like a dog looking for somewhere to point its piss.'

Sol observed the two men. They were both big. The one who had spoken was long, lean and pale. Almost albino. With bold, confident strokes Life's Sculptor had carved his features into sharp, well defined interlocking planes, but seemed to have grown bored, or weary, with the second man (who was called Clowsie) and not bothered to differentiate his head from his neck, or his neck from his shoulders. Malevolence burned in Clowsie's eyes, but in his friend's cold, pale eyes there was nothing. Nothing at all.

Sol thought the better of a clever or abrasive response.

67

Seeing no advantage in establishing his mental superiority, he replied honestly:

'I don't believe I'm up to anything. Just looking around.'

'You found some problem with the set?' asked Choy, the lean man.

'I wouldn't say that, I—'

'Then just what would you bloody say?'

'The yew tree is excellent. I saw you putting that up. Um, and many of the gravestones are very good. I did have a tiny problem with some of the names.'

'The names?' said Choy.

'Yes, some of them struck me as—'

'Screaming ponce!' snarled Clowsie.

'What's wrong with the bloody names?' asked Choy, who maintained a menacing calm.

'Bang him one, Choy! Make his head rattle, boy. Only way to teach these damn spunk-monkeys.'

'That's one way of doing it. Yes, Clowsie. You see, you've upset my friend. He doesn't like to be told. Too many damn people have upset him before, trying to tell him this and that.'

'Well, I er, didn't mean to upset him, but in this business you have to expect a little criticism from—'

'Damn grunting pisser! Let's sting him, Choy. He's asked for it.'

Choy put his hand on Sol's shoulder and looked him up and down.

'What the bloody hell you supposed to be, dressed like that?'

Sol felt humiliated, but replied calmly:

'Why, a press photographer, of course.' He looked down at his trousers. 'They, um, preferred a looser fit in those days.'

'If you're a photographer, where's your fucking camera?'

Clowsie thought this hilarious and hooted with laughter.

68

'Good point, actually,' said Sol who realized that he indeed had not been issued with that vital prop. 'I'd better go and get one. Thank you for, er, pointing out the deficiency.'

The two men watched as Sol walked away.

'Don't worry, we'll get him round the back afterwards,' said Choy. 'Give him a real doing then. No mucking about.'

'I'll land him a few stingers, then you can have him, Choy,' said Clowsie, the prospect plainly enthusing him. 'We'll put him through it, eh?'

'We'll lay it on thick all right,' said Choy. 'Just like Old Cacknacker used to.'

The filming passed without incident. Sol felt increasingly embarrassed about his costume, not only because it wasn't a good fit, but because he realized, looking around at the other costumes, that it was almost a parody of itself. He noticed some of the film crew looking askance at him. He wished he could just have been the anonymous extra at the back after all – which he could have been, had it not been for that snotty hairdressing girl. He cursed her, and wondered how he might get his own back.

When the time came he was asked to step forward, take a flash photo, then step back to his original position. They only did one take, and it seemed plain from the director's reaction that the shot would be unlikely to make the final version. On the other hand a lot of time was lavished on the 'gravediggers'. Sol hated to admit it, but Choy, Clowsie and the two others cast in those parts did look good in their costumes, an impression enhanced by the stark contrast in their appearances. There was spontaneous applause following the cut from the scene when the quartet, solemnly and in unison, took off their flat caps and laid them across their chests. It was true what they said: the camera seems to like some people and not others.

At the end of the day Sol returned to the costume trailer, where he was surprised to discover the inspector, who was dressed in a bizarre policeman's uniform, with an A-shaped tunic, secured with a large brass-buckled belt, and a top hat.

'Ah, nice to see you again,' he remarked. 'I didn't know this was your line.'

'What on earth are you dressed like that for?' asked Sol.

'They said we had to be in costume. You see, it's in case—'

'I know all about that, but why this anachronistic thing?'

'I beg your pardon?'

'It's out of date.'

'A policeman seemed appropriate, for a man of my profession. This is Scottish, by the way.'

'Yes, but it's 1850s, not 1950s.'

'Do you think so?'

'I think things have come on a little bit up there, you know.'

'Oh dear! I hope I haven't gone and spoiled the film.'

'What brings you here anyway?'

The inspector tapped the side of his nose. 'Suspicion!'

'Suspicion?'

'Indeed.'

'Well, I just wonder if you're wasting your time coming here, inspector. I mean, it's only a pretend funeral. No-one has really died.'

'That remains to be seen,' he replied, enigmatically.

As they stepped down from the caravan, two men were waiting, a little way off. One of them carried a pole of polished wood, about four feet long and as thick as a big man's thumb. When they saw Sol with the inspector they appeared disturbed and spoke furtively.

'He's in with the fucking rozzers, Choy,' said Clowsie, as if this represented some betrayal.

'Pissing bumsucker! What's he gone and told the rozzers for?' asked Choy, in the tone of an innocent wronged.

'I can tell that stink a mile off. Fucking rozzer, he is.'

'Plenty of stink, Clowsie, and did you see his get-up? Shitting rozzer alright. Better act normal, man. Can't afford to mix it with the law right now.'

They stood aside as the inspector and Sol walked by. Sol smiled and wished them both good day.

'We'll get him another time,' murmured Clowsie as Sol passed out of earshot.

'You bet. We'll sell him a ticket to the last night of a dodo show. Final curtain and no encore. End of run. No-one treats us like that and gets away with it.'

6

The next day, the third of his annual holiday, Sol awoke with a runny bottom. He immediately blamed the mobile canteen on the film location, whose beefburgers, he recalled, were of a particularly sinister mien. He wouldn't have eaten one, but had been hungry; there was nothing else, and they were free. Of course, the stars of the film were not fed beefburgers. They sat with the director and his assistants at a cloth-covered table under a red canopy. Nor did they stand in a queue at the hatch of a stinking mobile kitchen. Their food was served at the table and arrived on silver dishes, hot and aromatic. Moreover, he was sure, it hadn't given them runny bottoms.

He had stood watching from a little way off. At one point, as a platter was uncovered, Butters Nicobar had remarked:

'My, what cute little lobsters!'

'Langoustines, actually,' corrected Rossan, who simply oozed obsequiousness in the elevated company. 'From Loch Fyne.'

The company chortled and another of the stars remarked:

'Oh Butters, you are an arse sometimes!'

That provoked more laughter; but with her, rather than at her. Butters didn't seem to be offended, although the strait-laced, aloof character she always played would not have tolerated being called an arse under any circumstances.

When lunch was called, Sol had hailed Rossan, presuming

he would be dining with him and the director. But Rossan had been very stand-offish. Sol had walked alongside him in the direction of the top table, chatting away. But when he took a seat at the table, Rossan told him:

'All these are taken, actually. There's the burger van, if you're hungry.'

As if that wasn't bad enough, just as Sol vacated the seat, Sally the hairdresser had come flouncing across in her tight blue trousers and sat down at the table, where she was welcomed by the smiling Rossan. It was plain to Sol they had an arrangement. He secured her a seat at the top table, where she too could fawn over the stars. Later on she would drop her pants for Rossan in one of the trailers. There were perks, it seemed, even for third assistant directors.

Sol had felt embarrassed, even humiliated, as he walked away in his mackintosh, hat and baggy trousers. Normally something like this wouldn't have worried him. On a normal day, the words would have been there and he would at least have retreated in good order. He might even have charmed his way into a place at the table. Actors are vain and he had enough experience of life, knew enough about the stars of this film, to engage them. But he had been knocked off balance, first by the gratuitous aggression of a pair of barbarians, and then by the fickleness of Rossan. The old one-two had so stunned him that he lacked the spirit to meet the situation head on. He had been defeated by circumstances. This always depressed him, and he wished he had stayed at home.

With his turbulent bowels, Sol didn't want to venture from the house. He estimated that once things started moving in his gut he could hold out for about a minute. Beyond that he could not be held responsible. It would take at least nine minutes to get to the shop, buy a paper and return home.

So he ruled out that idea. He picked up the paper of two days ago, turned to the crossword he had already begun and scanned the clues anew.

A couple of the names from the pretend graveyard danced before his eyes:

Squib-Diddly, and the Umbelisha brothers.

'Yes, of course. Seven across. Squib,' thought Sol. '"Insignificant brother loses long sea fish on line. (5 letters.)"'

'Sibling. Ling is an elongated sea fish. *On line* – Q, yes. *Squib* for *insignificant* is rare these days, but it suggests this new compiler is a mature individual. And very likely a woman, with her taste for associative logic.'

Sol thought that if he himself was having problems with the crossword, then what about the rest of the readership? The local paper was published in the city, but was regionalized to cater for readers in the town and surrounding countryside. The editor was a city man who treated the rural readers with such barely disguised contempt that, following a particularly vituperative leader, a group of prominent locals had written in:

> Don't call us bumpkins! Call us yokels or daft country folk if you want, but don't go calling us bumpkins! Just 'cos we eats turnips all the time and keeps goats in the kitchen, don't mean we're simple. Oh alright. Call us bumpkins then.

And the editor had continued to do so, confirmed in his opinions.

Sol picked up the phone. He wanted to speak to Parlando, to brief him about the pretend funeral and to point out a flaw in his 'perfect plan'. The gravediggers had shovelled in earth for the cameras, but had not filled the hole. A JCB had arrived later, on the back of a truck, to finish the job.

Sol watched as it was done, but it occurred to him that this was council land and if he recalled correctly, at least one developer had submitted a proposal to build houses there. If it was sold in the future – as it probably would be, in whole or part – then, when building began, digging would be unavoidable; to lay sewage, water and gas pipes. And when two coffins were uncovered, questions would be asked. Sol grew anxious at the possibility and had to tell himself once more that he had done nothing wrong. At worst, very worst, all he had done was not pass on to the authorities some information – no, not information; just a suspicion regarding a crime that might or might not have been committed.

A sing-song female voice answered from the salon.

'I'm sorry, Parlando's not available,' she said.

'Yes, he is,' insisted Sol. 'You haven't even asked him, have you?'

'I beg your pardon?'

'Does he just happen to be standing next to you?'

'He's with a customer actually.'

'Is that Sally, by any chance?'

'It's Rachel, if you really must know.'

'Ah! Rachel. A few things I'd like to ask you.'

'Sorry, I'm busy.' And the line went dead.

'Damn slattern,' muttered Sol.

He grabbed his jacket, then winced and rested the flat of his hand against his turbulent bowels. He returned his jacket to the peg. The visit to the salon would have to wait until tomorrow.

The telephone rang.

'That'll be Parlando,' thought Sol.

But he was wrong. It was his own elder brother, Charles.

Sol and Charles rarely met up these days. Generally they would only see each other at family funerals (and once at the funeral of a friend they hadn't realized they had in common).

76

Certainly it was unusual for Sol to receive a phone call from his brother.

'I'll get straight to the point,' said Charles. 'I've got this ticket for a Murder Mystery Weekend – you know the sort of thing. You turn up, and there are clues, and actors, walks in the grounds, drinks and nice meals in the evening . . . '

Sol said, yes, he had a vague idea.

'The thing is, something's come up and I can't go now. It'd be a shame to waste it, seeing as how it's paid for, and there are no refunds. And, well, I thought it might be your sort of thing. You like crosswords, and are quite good at solving things. So I thought perhaps you'd like to go along instead of me.'

Charles was a perfectly affable and agreeable soul, and yet was probably best known for his conventionality. Indeed, 'Orthodoxy was his middle name' might have been his epitaph, had he already died.

'Didn't realize you were into that sort of thing, Charles.'

'Well, you know. One has to occupy oneself somehow.'

'Can I ask what it was that "came up" – as you put it – that prevents you from attending?'

'Oh, something the wife had planned, forgot to tell me.'

'I bet!' thought Sol, who quite liked his brother. The reason he didn't see him more often was because of his shrewish wife, with her nagging voice of grating crow-dryness. Charles hadn't always been Mr Conventional. He'd had the life squeezed out of him. 'Old Chas? He's all right,' people used to say. 'Especially with a drink or two inside him. Quite witty sometimes. Good sense of humour. Pawky, as the Scots would say.'

'She was always one for springing little surprises, wasn't she?' said Sol. 'Oh, and that reminds me. Something I wanted to ask you. Something that happened the other day. Came across someone who looks like me. Yes, it was extraordinary, as you say. I mean, we're brothers and we don't even look alike. But it got me to thinking – you read about these things – did I ever have a twin at all? You know, one who was sent away, or mysteriously disappeared?'

There was a silence at the other end. Then Charles coughed. 'Um, I think you can go to – Somerset House, isn't it? – to check on these things. That's in London, by the way. Not Somerset. Ha! I mean, it's not for me to say, is it?'

Sol knew Charles well enough. He was a man of integrity to whom lying did not come naturally. He was also an uncomplicated man, very poor at dissembling, and the more he tried, the more he revealed of what it was he was trying to hide. *Yes*, he admitted after more prevaricating. There *was* a twin that Sol had never known about, who drowned aged two in the stream that ran along the bottom of the garden of the old house. It also emerged there was an older sister who had vanished one day, feared abducted by gypsies, and another sibling, Raymond, younger than Charles but older than Sol, who died in a 'regrettable' incident at prep school.

'That it's regrettable goes without saying,' remarked an astonished Sol. 'What happened, exactly?'

'Oh, I don't know. One of those things. It was different in those days, Sol. You didn't make a fuss. You didn't ask questions. The word of a headmaster was good enough.'

'And were there any others?' asked Sol, not entirely seriously.

'Just the two girls. They were fostered out when times were hard.'

'I didn't realize Mother was so fecund.'

'As you say. But you know, people were poorer then, the families bigger.'

'What about the girls? You know, the ones who were fostered? Surely they survived.'

'Er, no. Actually. Heard through the grapevine they'd succumbed to some mysterious virus.'

'Anything else I should know about, Charles?'

'No. I think that's it. Except for Gidney. You know about Gidney, of course.'

'Who the hell's Gidney? And what kind of name is that? For anyone?'

'Surely . . . You mean? Oh dear! Mother said she was going to tell you. Once you came of age.'

'It must have slipped her mind. Perhaps you could tell me now.'

'It's really not up to me, Sol. I mean, I don't know that I should be the one to – It's rather, you know, awkward . . . '

Sol could feel the discomfort in his brother's voice. Charles had grown rather portly with the advancing years, to the extent that the outer hole of his belt struggled to consummate its relationship with the brass spur of the buckle. And he sweated much more than he used to, particularly when he found himself embroiled in 'awkward' or 'embarrassing' situations. Sol could picture him at this very minute: dabbing his bulbous forehead with his handkerchief, and nervously running a finger between neck and collar (his wife insisted he wear a tie, even in the house, in case anyone called unexpectedly). Nevertheless, he did inform Sol about the last of the siblings he never knew. It happened when Sol was about three and his sister Gidney was just a babe. The two of them were together in the living room, the mother in the kitchen. She heard a noise, a dull thud, and went through to investigate. There was the baby lying limp on the floor with Sol standing next to her. It was assumed she had rolled off the settee and cracked her little head on the uncarpeted floor. Two or three times Sol was questioned by his parents, but each time he simply burst into tears and cried again and again that he hadn't done anything.

'It was put down to accidental death. I remember well the day,' said Charles, who had been twelve at the time. 'A very sad day. Poor little Gidney. I don't think your mother was really quite the same after that. She loved that child – more than any of us, I think.'

'Did people think I was responsible?'

'No, not really. Well, you know. The police have to ask questions. And the coroner.'

'What do you think, Charles? You were around.'

'Me? Um, I was quite young. It was a long time ago.'

'You think I might have—'

'Oh no! Nothing like that. My own brother? No, shouldn't think so. An accident, they said. You know, I was sure Mother told you all this. It really is remiss of her.'

Sol was silent and reflective.

'Anyway,' said Charles, eager to change the subject. 'What was the name of this chap who resembled you? The one you thought might be a twin?'

'Parlando.'

'Parlando! Italian, is he?'

'It's an Italian word, Charles. An operatic term. No, it's not his real name.'

'I see. Anyway . . . you're all right for this weekend, are you?'

'What?'

'The Murder Mystery Weekend.'

'It's very kind of you to think of me,' said Sol, searching for a way out. 'Is there no-one else who might like the ticket?'

'I've tried everyone else. You're my last resort. Go on, Sol! Why don't you give it a try? I was saying to someone only last week that you need to get out more.'

Sol was surprised to realize he was reluctant to turn down the opportunity. Nor was this anything to do with

80

not wanting to offend his brother. It was rather a strange feeling of excitement which he simply couldn't explain. And if nothing else, a weekend away would help fill the time on his holiday, which was still barely halfway through.

So he agreed to accept Charles's invitation for the Murder Mystery Weekend.

'Splendid. I'll tell the organizers it will be thee rather than me.' And Charles explained where the event was due to take place.

'That's a bit out of the way, isn't it?' replied Sol.

'Of course, I'm forgetting. You don't have a car. But you could always hire one for the weekend, couldn't you?'

'I suppose so.'

'Let me know how you get on.' Charles then spoke at length about how these things were run, and some of the people Sol might bump into.

Sol's mind wandered, as it was wont to do when his brother spoke at length. Eventually he interrupted:

'I'm sorry, Charles. I'll have to ring off. I need the toilet. Badly.'

Later that day Sol found himself somewhat melancholically reflecting on the several siblings he had never known, and more generally on his past.

His father's passion had been metals. Real metals, that were solid, strong, lustrous, malleable and ductile, but not those impostors – such as the alkaline earths – that gained their status from the chemical pathways they preferred rather than their physical properties. His work was winning metals from the ores that others had hewn from the earth. When Sol was quite young his father took up a position with a tin-mining company and the family moved to the Far East for three years. The company was prepared to pay the cost of a three-week sea voyage, but because of Sol's fear of the sea, they had to fly, a journey that took twenty-four hours in those days, with refuelling stops at Istanbul and Karachi.

His memories of the time were few but sharply focused. He recalled his father holding up a lump of sticky mud, pointing to a red vein within it, and declaring, 'Tin.' His father knew how to make that red vein into something shiny, solid and useful. He could recall their bungalow and its garden and its trees from which sprouted a strange but tempting red-skinned fruit. It was too high up for him to pluck, so he fetched a broom and swung at the laden branches with this. He dislodged some of the fruit, but also some of its guardians, the ginger fire ants. Perhaps a dozen fell on him, in his hair, on his bare arms and legs, and inside his shirt. It felt as if cigarettes were being stubbed out on his flesh.

Sol recalled fondly the old *amah*, a kindly, wrinkled Chinese lady who wore what he mistook for pyjamas. She took him to the market once or twice, where he was fascinated by the big open-mouthed fish lying on the slabs, and horrified when, at the *amah*'s instigation, a chicken had its throat cut and was thrown into a filthy dustbin to thrash away the last minutes of its life. He could still see in his mind's eye the spots of blood flying into the air, and conjure up the dull sound of wings beating against the metal, at first frenzied, then sporadic and feeble.

'Fresh. Must fresh,' explained the *amah*. It was only in later life that Sol understood what she was trying to communicate: that dead flesh rots quickly in the Tropics when there is no refrigeration.

The *amah* had her own room adjacent to the kitchen, and leading off that room, for her exclusive use, was a squat toilet. Sol remembered asking his mother why the indigenous people had nothing to sit on when they used the toilet. He could not recall the answer. But he could recall one day observing a large cockroach crawling out of the dark, ceramic opening. As it moved circumspectly across the stone floor, Sol crushed it with some hard object and watched with revulsion as pus the colour and consistency of mayonnaise oozed from the broken blood-red body. Still when he shopped, if he was in vacant mood (as generally he was in a supermarket), he could not look upon the slim bottles of salad cream, or the stubby jars of mayonnaise, without thinking of cockroaches.

Sol's father had hoped to impart his love of metals to his sons, and each night, before they went to bed, he would read to them from a textbook.

'Cobalt. A lustrous silvery-blue hard metal. Ferro-magnetic. Melting point 1495 degrees centigrade. Abundant in the earth's core, much less so in the crust. Mostly mined in the Congo, Morocco, Sweden and Canada. Stable in air, but slowly attacked by dilute acids to form a variety of salts . . .

'Platinum, a lustrous, silvery white, malleable, ductile metal whose density is surpassed only by osmium and iridium.'

And so on.

The father was disappointed that his sons asked no questions, and that they could not answer when he questioned them on what he had just read. And although he didn't say it, he was disappointed that neither of his boys pursued a career in metals.

About two years after returning from the Far East his father fell ill. Dangerously ill. He remained in his sickbed for nigh on a year. The company doctor ruled out the possibility that the illness was 'in any way whatsoever' connected with the mercury and cadmium ores he had been working with when he fell ill, and put it down to 'something picked up out East', which had mysteriously lain dormant until this time. He recommended Sol's father retire early. The company too thought this a very good idea and duly retired him on a pension generous enough to erode any intention of seeking legal redress.

Sol's parents currently lived abroad in comfortable circumstances. They sent him cards now and then, always suggesting he pay them a visit. He would reply, thanking them, but saying he was too busy at work.

Besides, to be honest, he did not really like flying either.

7

On his way to the salon the next afternoon Sol called into a car-hire firm and was told there was nothing available for the coming weekend. He walked to the only other service in the town, where the staff were most apologetic. Normally, they explained, they could have obliged him, but three of their vehicles were presently off the road. The head gasket had blown on one while the other two had been involved in a collision with each other. There was a five-ton lorry available, if that would suit, and if he had an HGV licence.

Sol didn't.

So he made his way to the salon, where he found Parlando at the reception desk, looking through the appointments book with one of his senior staff.

'Thank you, Julia,' said Parlando. 'I'll catch up with you later.' He turned to Sol. 'I was expecting to hear from you yesterday. I was a little concerned.'

'You can blame your staff for that. I phoned, but was given the brush-off. I won't name names, but—'

'Don't be so swift to chide, Sol. They're only following instructions. Having said that, they should, in the circumstances, have fetched me. Well?'

'Well what?'

'Did everything go . . . well?'

Sol summarized the day's filming, omitting the episodes

with soapy Rossan and the two bullies, which he judged to be of no interest to anyone but himself.

'Why was the inspector there?' asked Parlando. 'Do you think he'd had a tip-off?'

'I did ask him that question, and formed the impression he was there on a hunch. To poke around a bit. But he didn't find anything. The two coffins are now under six feet of soil and I don't think he can order an exhumation in respect of a fictional burial.'

Parlando smiled. 'I knew I could trust you. I think we should draw a line under the whole thing now, don't you?'

'I've said that all along.'

'I'm sorry, Sol. I'm forgetting my manners. How are you anyway? Are you enjoying your holiday?'

'Actually,' replied Sol, 'I was hoping to get away at the weekend, but I'm having difficulty hiring a car. You don't know of anywhere, do you?'

Parlando thought briefly before naming the town's two car-hire establishments.

'I've already tried both.'

'Well, I suppose there's always the city. You're bound to get one there. But wait a minute – what am I thinking about! Why don't you borrow one of mine?'

'Really?'

'Why not? I've got three cars. Can't use them all at once.'

'Three? Business must be good!'

'It is, yes. I could have four cars if I wanted. But that would be ostentatious. No man needs four cars.'

'Well, that's very generous of you, Parlando. Thanks very much.'

'Not at all. Least I can do. You've been really helpful, Sol. I appreciate it.' Parlando went to the drawer of the reception desk and took out some keys. 'The white Ford. You probably saw it outside.'

'Thank you. Is it insured for me?'

'Insured, taxed, MOTd, tuned to perfection. Runs like a dream.'

'Excellent. And what about—'

A bell rang somewhere, the door opened, and in walked the inspector.

Sol and Parlando exchanged glances.

'You again!' exclaimed Parlando.

'Er, yes,' agreed the inspector, somewhat diffidently.

'I thought you were going to a cricket match, or something.'

'That was yesterday. It was all over rather quickly, actually. Forensics had acquired the services of a very handy pace bowler. Name of Jonny Walpurgo. You may have heard of him?'

'No,' replied Parlando, much quicker than he needed to.

'Had a trial with the County as a schoolboy, I'm led to understand. A tad nippy, as they say, and can swing it both ways – if you'll pardon the expression. Not that it's considered a slur these days, or illegal – more's the shame, if you ask me. Didn't work at Forensics, this bowler. Was just a friend of a friend of someone who did. Ringers, I think they're called. Was a bit of a barney about it in the bar afterwards. Rather spoils it all, if you ask me. What about your funeral? Did that – what's the expression now? – go off well?'

'Funeral?' repeated Parlando, somewhat bemused.

'That'll be poor old Delgardo,' prompted Sol.

When this didn't register with Parlando, Sol leaned towards the inspector and said, sotto voce:

'He's still rather upset about the whole thing. Try not to, you know, stir things up.'

'Ah yes, of course. Apologies. Sometimes better to draw a line under it all.'

'My sentiments exactly, Inspector. We were just saying that, in fact.'

'What brings you here anyway?' asked Parlando.

'Thought I'd like to poke around a bit more if you don't mind.'

'I do mind, as it happens,' replied Parlando, growing heated. 'This is a place of work. A policeman "poking around", as you like to put it, hardly adds to the ambience of the salon, does it? How many times does a man have to "poke around" somewhere, for goodness sake?'

'Something I learned early on in my career,' said the inspector, holding his ground. 'If you don't poke around, you don't find things. I'd like to start with that book there, if you don't mind.'

'The appointments book? I don't think you'll find anything of interest in there. Um, there are good reasons why it's not appropriate or convenient to . . . ' Parlando looked helplessly at Sol.

'When you said "poke around", Inspector, it reminded me,' said Sol. 'Didn't you want to, em, interview Barbara?'

'Ah! Barbara!'

'A right little corker, to use your own words.'

'I'm glad you reminded me.'

Sol addressed Parlando:

'You remember? I'm sure the inspector would rather be "interviewing" Barbara somewhere private.'

'Yes,' agreed Parlando, catching the drift at last. 'I'm sure I can arrange something. I believe Bay 17 is free right now.'

A bell rang, the door opened, and a burly man walked in. 'All right, Guv?'

'Who are you?' asked the inspector.

'I'm your DC.'

'Where's the usual man. Wotsisname? Jenkins.'

'Rang in sick. Got the shits, he said.'

'Charming!' said Parlando.

'Well that would explain why he disappeared the other day, I suppose,' said the inspector, glad something had been cleared up.

'He's alright inni? Old Jenkins. Carroty-top.'

'Yes. More familiarly known as "Ginge".'

'Bit of a smart-arse, though, if you ask me.'

'Don't think anyone was,' retorted the inspector.

'Yeh, well, you got me for today.'

'And what's your name?'

'Erskine.'

'Erskine?' The inspector appeared to think about this for a while. 'It's a bridge isn't it?'

'Dunno, Guv.'

'Somewhere in Scotland.'

'Couldn't tell you, mate.'

'Erskine!' thought Sol. 'That's another bloody crossword clue! "Bonnie lady frightened as cross partner finds more than one way with cats." Bonnie/Clyde, bridge over, Bonnie Scotland. Skinning cats. Frightened out of her skin. (H)er skin. Erskine. That's definitely suspect. That's just rambling, random associations. Might as well be on a psychiatrist's couch.' But more than indignation he felt the unease we all feel when the laws of coincidence are contravened. Why should the clues of a crossword puzzle seem to be resonating with the flow of events in his day-to-day life?

'Cor! Fuck me gently!' Erskine had parted the wooden-stranded curtain and was looking into the main salon. 'You seen in here?'

Parlando was quickly at his side, anxious to discover what had happened. 'What? What's wrong?'

Sol joined them, then the inspector. They all peered into the salon, where everything seemed to be in order.

'I'm putting in for a bleedin' transfer,' said Erskine and

laughed a fatuous, lewd laugh. 'All that minge! Eh?' And he laughed again. 'You lucky buggers!'

Parlando and Sol looked at one another and then at Erskine with puzzled expressions.

'Look at 'er,' Erskine pointed. 'I'd give 'er one!' His eyes alighted on another young female. 'Whooa! I'd slip her a crippler. Look at the tits on that! Blimey. Should be illegal, eh?' Erskine stuck out his tongue and panted like a dog. 'Oi, Guv! Want me to poke around in 'ere a bit?'

'You keep that thing in your trousers!' admonished the inspector. 'We've got work to do. You can help me check the names.' In an aside to Parlando he added, 'I'll come back to Barbara later, if you don't mind. Er, the book? If you please, sir.'

'Very well,' sighed Parlando wearily. 'But not here in reception. In my office, please, where you'll be out of the way.'

'As you wish. Erskine, grab the – Erskine? Where the bloody hell's he got to?'

Erskine was already in the salon. Beaming broadly, he nudged Sol with his elbow and indicated a pert blonde a little way off. 'Christ, would I give 'er one!'

'Perhaps', said Sol, 'it might be easier if you indicated those girls to whom you wouldn't "give one".'

'Yeh, right!' replied Erskine, laughing out loud again.

In the office the inspector opened the book at the first page. He turned to Parlando. 'Now, perhaps you'd be so kind as to tell me a bit about some of these people listed here. For example: Parlane McFarlane?'

'What about him?' asked Parlando.

'Scottish, is he?'

'Canadian, actually.'

'I see.'

'Are you looking for someone Scottish?' asked Sol.

'I don't know who I'm looking for until I find them,' replied the inspector, rather sharply.

Erskine laughed. 'Yeh, that's wot they say down the station.'

'Now, this person here: Chogleigh Undenthigh. Is that how you say it?

'Schhog-leyh,' corrected Parlando.

'Can you tell me anything about him?

'Not really.'

'Then what about Jimmy Bloot?' continued the inspector.

'Comes here regularly. Salt of the earth, Jimmy.'

The inspector looked up. 'Is he now. Well, I may return to him. Certain suspicions came into my head at the mention of his name.' The inspector moved his finger down the list of appointments. 'Juppy Candela. What about him?'

Parlando burst out laughing. 'I'm going to tell *her* you said that,' he remarked.

'Yes, point taken. Then what about Ron Bonsai?'

'Lovely man. Always a good word for everyone.'

'Pikey Soffit?'

'Ah!' exclaimed Erskine. 'That's our man, Guv.'

'Is it?'

'Yeh. Pikey, bleedin pikeys.'

'It's just a name,' said the inspector. 'Doesn't mean he is one.'

'Remind us,' said Sol. 'What's a pikey?'

'Gypo,' replied Erskine. 'Can't trust pikeys.'

'What, never?' asked Parlando.

'Nah. They're fuckin' – what's the word?'

'Untrustworthy?' offered Sol.

'Yeh. Any trouble, you can bet there's a pikey behind it.'

'I don't believe he's a gypsy,' said Parlando.

'Don't be so sure, squire. Old Johnny Gypo, he don't always go round selling clothes pegs. Or play the old violin in

some toff restaurant, with an 'anky wrapped round 'is 'ead.'
And Erskine mimed a man playing the violin.

'That's that then,' said the inspector, exhibiting an unexpected vein of sarcasm. 'We'll just go and arrest this Pikey
Soffit, shall we? "Being a gypsy in a built-up area"!'

He looked severely at Erskine, then at Sol and Parlando
with an expression which said: *See what I have to work
with?* He turned to the book once more. 'Now then. Dondano
Dandini? Who's he, when he's at home?'

Parlando shrugged. 'Just someone who chooses to come
here to get a decent haircut.'

'Yeh,' said Erskine. 'But wot's he do? What's 'is background? Where's 'is dosh come from?'

'I don't know,' snapped Parlando. 'I don't bloody interro-
gate my customers when they come here.'

'Maybe it's time you started, then,' grunted Erskine, with
a hint of menace. 'We can conduct this interview down at the
station, if you require. Things have a funny way of getting
sorted out quicker at the station.'

'Hold on, hold on,' said the inspector. 'No need for that.
This man is just helping us with inquiries. Voluntarily. He's
not under arrest.'

''Ee's a suspect, though. Inni?'

'Did I say that?'

'Yeh. Didn't you?'

'Not in his presence, no.'

'Yeh. Well—'

'So perhaps you should apologize to the gentleman. He's
a member of the public, after all, and we rely on them a lot.
For their co-operation.'

'Suppose, yeh. Sorry, squire. Got a bit carried away. No
hard feelings, eh?' Erskine offered his hand to Parlando, who
took it and replied, rather absently:

'None at all.'

Erskine looked round as if he wished some of the girls from the salon had been present, to see he could be decent and reasonable as well as tough.

'Ju-jube?' inquired the inspector, returning to the book. 'No surname?'

'She only has the one name, Inspector. I don't believe that contravenes any law.'

'Perhaps not, but it makes me think she – or he, as the case may be – might have something to hide.'

'I think not. Some people just have one name. They think it's enough. Even you must have known people with just one name, Inspector.'

The inspector thought. 'Well, the neighbour had a cat once, name of Topsy. Died of the dropsy. He got another one and called it Turvey. It went down with scurvy. He called the next one Pongo and it lived for donkeys' yonks. Had to be put down eventually. Yes. Nice old thing, but got a bit scabby at the end. Both ends, actually, I seem to recall.'

'I'm put in mind of old Sir Pitslimer, late of the Manor,' said Sol. 'Kindest of men, but wholly unsentimental. You remember? He had three dogs. Mumbo and Gilboa were two. There was a third, Swelker, but it had to be eaten in the hard winter of '63, along with a horse and the ostler's youngest.'

'We seem to have strayed,' observed Parlando.

'That's my way, actually,' replied the inspector. 'Let people talk, they'll hang themselves.'

'You are an old sly-boots, inspector,' said Sol, a touch uneasily.

'That's been said. And worse.' He looked at the hair-dresser. 'You were saying about people with one name?'

'It's the same', continued Parlando, 'as when people say *moi* instead of *me*. It's all to do with self-importance.'

'I see,' said the inspector. 'And this . . . ' he consulted the book once more. 'Ju-jube. Would you say she was self-important?'

'Let me put it this way,' said Sol. 'She once told me she had a Leo Moon, with Sagittarius rising.'

'Ah!'

'That suggests to me an exaggerated sense of self-worth.'

'Does it?' The inspector returned to the book and flicked through some pages in a desultory fashion. 'I can see this is going to take some time and you're—'

'A busy man? Yes,' prompted Parlando.'

'Indeed. So to avoid taking up any more of your—'

'Valuable time? Yes.'

'I'll take a photocopy, if I may. Oi, Erskine! See if you can find a photocopier.'

'We haven't got one,' answered Parlando.

'It's broken,' said Sol simultaneously. 'That is,' he added hastily, 'we don't in effect have one. Because it's not working.'

'In that case', sighed the inspector, 'we'll need to rely on traditional methods and put our pencils to paper. So we needn't detain you gentlemen any longer, if you have business to be about.'

As they walked from the office Sol remarked:

'It'll take them all day to transcribe those names. You're better having them in there, out of the way, than poking around the place.'

Parlando was silent.

'They're not going to find anything in the book, are they?'

Parlando remained silent.

'I mean, it's exactly what it appears to be, isn't it? A list of customers and appointments?'

'Of course. What else would it be?'

'*I* don't know, Parlando. But your reticence is enough to make *me* suspicious, never mind a nosy policeman.'

'I'm just on edge, that's all. I can't abide having those two idiots in the salon. It's like having a worm inside you. You know?'

Sol replied that he didn't. He had never knowingly played host to a parasitic worm.

'They're disgusting,' Parlando assured him. 'Listen. I could use a drink. You fancy one?'

Sol looked at his watch. 'It's a bit early but, seeing as how I'm on holiday, why not?'

In the office the inspector and his locum DC set about copying names from one book into another.

'Right,' said the inspector. 'Let's get things working efficiently here. One reads out a name, the other writes it down. I think as the junior man you should, as it were, be the secretary and take down what I say.'

'Better at reading, actually, Guv.'

'What?'

'Not got me notebook neither. It's in me other coat.'

'And you've not got a spare?'

'Na.'

'They supply you with two coats, but not a spare notebook! They must have money to burn down at D Division. I suppose I'll have to write, then.'

'What about a DNA on the ink, Guv?'

'DNA? On the ink? What are you talking about?'

'Nah, not a DNA. What is it they do on ink again?'

'We're not worried about the ink. Just read out the first name.'

Erskine scrutinized the words and spoke them to the best of his ability, running a short, thick index finger along the width of the page. The inspector, perplexed, asked him to repeat what he had said, which he did, and an entirely different sound emerged.

'Tut. Give it here,' said the inspector. 'COOMB BAASE. Right.'

'Yeh, well, it's a fuckin' nignog name,' complained Erskine.

The inspector wrote it down in his notebook.

'What you best at then, Guv? Readin' or writin'.'

'I'm modestly accomplished at both, if you must know.'

'Yeh? That's clever, that is.'

'Have to be, lad. I'm an inspector. Now what's the next name?'

Once more Erskine addressed it with screwed-up effort, and a strange chain of syllables dribbled from his mouth. Once again the inspector took the book from him.

'Fetta Brattatat,' he enunciated.

'Blimey!' exclaimed Erskine in awe.

'And you're better at reading, you say?'

'Yeh.'

'I don't think anyone's discovered what you're really good at.'

'Lot of ladies 'ave.'

'I don't wish to hear about that, thank you. Try the next one.'

To his credit Erskine tried very hard with the next one, and after each failure he returned with renewed vigour to the refractory words. He scratched his head as if this might catalyse things, just as to scratch the side of a beaker containing a supersaturated solution of chemical salts will sometimes induce instantaneous crystallization. But in Erskine's case nothing happened. He might have continued trying had not the inspector taken the book from him.

'Buist Llollinbaugh,' pronounced the inspector.

'Well done, Guv. I think you've cracked it.'

'It's possible I may be quicker doing this myself.'

'Right you are, chief. I'll just ask around a bit, shall I? See if any of the girls know anything?'

'I suppose you might as well. You're doing bugger all in here.'

As Erskine skipped along the corridor that linked the office and the main salon he whistled a popular tune of the time, 'Wicked Willie's Withered Stump', the tale of a disease-ridden old roué reflecting, with pride and pleasure, on his sordid past. The song was widely played on local radio, television, in lifts and supermarkets, and even over the telephone during those interminable waits to get the attention of some harassed clerk weighed down with complaints. It had plainly forced its way into Erskine's consciousness. The words 'pump' and 'hump' featured strongly in the chorus, obviously to rhyme with 'stump.' 'Jactitate' and 'masturbate' fell well enough together, but at one point the lyricist appeared to have painted herself into a corner and was forced to rhyme 'cludgie' with 'budgie.' To her credit she avoided pairing 'disco' with 'Frisco' and instead plumped boldly for 'Nabisco', that prosperous purveyor of popular breakfast brands, although this necessitated an extra four verses to create any sort of meaningful context. Not that Erskine knew many of the words. He *la-la'd* and *da-da'd* as he danced happily along the corridor, fists clenched, elbows cocked, stepping back, forwards, left and right, kicking left, kicking right, just like a pearly king. The inspector watched on the television screen in the office. He shook his head, but had to admit that for a big man Erskine was very light on his feet.

'Na then,' said Erskine to himself, surveying the salon filled with tight-trousered, nubile young hairdressers. 'Let's see what we've got 'ere.'

At first he pretended to be looking for clues. He would stop and examine things, look them up and down, and then nod knowingly. But all the time his real attention was elsewhere. He stood observing one of the girls at her work. She quickly became aware she was being watched, and grew embarrassed.

'What?' she said finally, a faint blush filling her cheeks.

'Nuffin,' replied Erskine. 'Just lookin'.'

'Well, don't. Makes me nervous.'

'Ah, but I bin watchin. You're really good!'

'Shut up!' she said, plainly pleased. She returned to her client, but her interest was aroused, and after trading a few platitudes with the man in the chair her attention turned once more to Erskine.

'Here, you're Old Bill, ent yer?'

'How'd you know?'

'Sticks out a mile, dunnit?'

'I know. Can't 'elp it.' And he looked at his crotch and laughed.

'Nah, not that! Shaddup!' She flushed.

Erskine continued to watch while she worked. 'Do you have to be like, taught at college and that?' he asked.

'Course we do.'

'I been to college too, yeh? Old police college up at Hendon. 'ere, can I 'ave a go?'

'Don't be daft!'

'Go on!'

'I'll get into trouble.' She looked around to see if they were being observed.

''ere! You missed a bit,' said Erskine, pointing.

'Shaddup! You're putting me off!'

Erskine chuckled.

The haircut was reaching its conclusion. The girl asked her client if he wanted, 'Anything on it?' He replied no, and

98

stood up. She brushed the hair from his shoulder and asked, 'All right then?'

Erskine answered for him, saying:

'Yeh, looks great. Reckon you got a good haircut there, mush. 'ere,' he said, addressing the girl. 'I wouldn't mind a cut.'

'Sorry. Only by appointment. Anyway, it's me lunch break, innit?'

'Yeh? Fancy a drink?'

'Not really.'

'Spot o' lunch then? Go on, I'm buying.'

'I'm on a diet, ent I?'

'Come off it! You ent fat.'

'I wish.'

'Well, just in the right places, like.'

'Shaddup!' she said, a coy smile on her face.

'Tell you what. See, my guvner told me to poke around a bit, see what I can come up with. On account of this crime.'

'What's that then?'

'Can't really say at this stage. But I thought you could show me around, like, seein' as how you know the place.'

The hairdresser thought about this for a few seconds. 'All right. What, downstairs and stuff?'

'Yeh, downstairs. And stuff!'

'Come on then.'

As they walked towards the stairs Erskine asked:

'What's your name, then?'

'Sandy.'

'Randy Sandy, eh?'

'Nah, don't say that,' she giggled.

She then took Erskine down the stairs and showed him store rooms and stock rooms, the staff room, a kitchen, the laundry and a place where things were disposed of. As she made to walk past one room, Erskine stopped.

'What's in there, then?'

When she didn't answer he opened the door and looked in. The room was cold and white-tiled. There were a number of slabs and on two of them rested naked corpses. Erskine had plainly not expected to see this. He turned to Sandy. 'What's all this, then?'

Sandy looked at him and then back at the slabs. 'I fink it's where they keep the bodies.'

Erskine stared at her for a few seconds, then back at the corpses. 'Like a morgue, you mean?'

'That's it. The morgue.'

'I seen a few of them in me time.'

'Well, you gotta put 'em somewhere, ent ya? Stiffs.'

'Suppose. What's next?'

They went to the room where the cauldron continually boiled and was stirred by two men in white coats.

'Blimey!' remarked Erskine. 'Pongs in 'ere a bit, dunnit?'

The two men stopped what they were doing.

Erskine held up his ID. He studied one of the men. 'You got form, son? Your face looks very familiar.'

The man, alarmed, backed away.

The detective looked at the second man, then back at the first. 'All right, cock. Carry on. I got bigger fish to nick. What is this muck anyway?' asked Erskine, looking into the bubbling pot.

The two men looked at each other, but remained silent.

'What's wrong? Ent you got tongues in yer heads?'

'I think it's hair restorer,' said Sandy. 'That's what the boss told me.'

'Yeh?' Erskine looked into the pot again. 'There's a lot would buy that. Baldy-headed bastards, mainly.'

'It's for other bits as well. Like some men want to be hairy, for when they go on the beach. It's really masculine and that, innit? Hair.'

'I reckon. Got a bit meself, actually. You like a bit of hair on a man, do you?'

'Don't mind.'

'That's funny, that, 'cos some birds like their men smooth. I think a man should 'ave a bit of 'air meself.'

'I went out with a geezer once, I tell you, 'ee was like a bleeding gorilla!'

Erskine smiled. 'Listen gal, I shouldn't get so excited about gorillas if I was you. There not all they're made out to be.'

'Real ones, you mean?'

'Yeh.'

'How d'you mean?'

'Well, for a start their dicks 'ent that big.'

'Leave it out! There's ladies present.'

'It was in the *News of the Screws*, it must have been, with old Desmond Wotsit. Everyone thinks cos gorillas are such fucking big bastards they got ginormous cocks. But they are not as big as your average man's. That's true. And I'll tell you another thing about gorillas: they eat their own poo.'

'Oh, go on! That is *disgusting*.'

'I saw it on the telly. I was 'aving me tea too.'

'Absolutely disgusting. They shouldn't show that on the telly. What if kids watched it?'

'I know, it's terrible, if you ask me. Showing things like that.'

The two technicians had stopped their work and were listening in on the conversation.

'All right, you two. You got no work to do? Come on, gal. Nuffin to see here. Wot's next?'

Sandy led him to Bay 17.

'Ay-ay. This is very cosy, innit? What goes on in 'ere then?'

'Nuffin much, really,' replied Sandy shyly. 'People come in here for, you know, a bit of a massage.'

Erskine chortled. 'Just the job at the end of the day, eh? Nice rub down. And, er, are you handy, Sandy?'

'What do you mean, handy?' she replied indignantly.

'Nah, not that. Not a hand-shandy. Just a proper massage, like. Got a bit of a stiff shoulder, I have. Fibrositis, the old quack says it is.'

After some bashful hesitation, Sandy agreed.

Parlando and Sol returned from the pub to find the inspector sitting in the office.

'You're not still here!' exclaimed Parlando, irritably.

'Apparently. But I'll be out of your way soon. I'm down to the last three names.'

'And where's that buffoon of an assistant of yours?'

'The inspector inspected his watch and blinked. 'I sent him to poke around, right enough, but he should have been back by now.'

'I can't be sure,' said Sol, who was standing next to the bank of surveillance screens. 'But I would say that this here looks like the sort of arse that could belong to Erskine.'

The others joined him at the screen.

'What's he up to now?' asked the inspector wearily.

Sol watched in silence as Sandy peeled off her tight blue trousers, and then removed her meagre underwear. He wondered how a charmless, witless oaf like Erskine managed to pull members of the opposite sex at all, let alone one like Sandy who, whatever else, was physically attractive. The forces responsible for animal attraction were plainly not of the same order as intelligence and social polish.

'It's a great leveller, sex,' observed Parlando, as if reading Sol's mind. 'The same juices run through us all. Royalty and celebrities have no more pleasure than you or I, or Erskine there. The same with drink. A drunken king is as much the fool as a drunken beggar. Having said that, let's draw a veil over this.'

He pressed a button, and the image of Erskine's thrusting buttocks gave way to a general shot of the salon.

'Honestly, Parlando,' remarked Sol. 'I really don't know why you employ these dirty little trollops.'

'This one was down on her luck.'

'I imagine this one is down on anybody.'

'I felt sorry for her.'

'That's me finished,' said the inspector. 'I'm off back to the station. Perhaps you would be so kind as to inform Erskine, once he's finished his, er, investigation.'

'Did you discover anything?' asked Sol. 'From all the names, I mean.'

'That remains to be seen. I need to run some checks first. Down at the station. Then get down to some knocking on doors and foot-slogging. Yes, there's a lot of hard work involved being a detective. Crimes aren't solved by brilliant insights, you know.'

'Just as well, in your case,' murmured Sol.

'Quite so. Do enjoy your weekend. I wish I had them. Have you anything planned?'

'I'm off to the country, since you ask.'

'But not *leaving* the country, I hope?'

'No.'

'Good. I would advise against that. You may be needed for more questioning. Taking the train, are you?'

'There are no trains in these parts. All the lines were closed some years ago.'

'More's the pity. Ah, I remember as a lad! On the platforms. The old steam trains. Many a happy hour! The Sprat and Winkle line.'

'Ran to the coast, did it?' asked Sol.

'Actually yes, it did. Very clever! Tell me, have you ever considered a career in the force?'

'No.'

'Pity,' said the inspector, and left.

But it had been no brilliant deduction on Sol's part. He knew all about the Sprat and Winkle Line from his own childhood. It is not known why these two species were chosen to name it, as there were many others that were transported to the town from where they had been landed on brine-soaked quays. Plaice and haddock, of course, but also shad, little dabs, eels, the odd flounder – and skate, whole 15-pound skates, which 'Jock' McCrackery, the town's fishmonger, hung in the window of his shop in Fleam Street. Here they remained, suspended like kites, until they curled up at the edges and were no longer suitable for a dining table. None of the conservative town folk were prepared to buy anything so different from what they believed a fish should look like. Indeed, there were those who, observing the wing-like form, believed them to be creatures of the air rather than the deep. Even Sol's mother never bought one, saying, 'It would never fit in the frying pan, even if we folded it in half.'

And then they closed the old Sprat and Winkle line and the town was cut off from the sea. It should have made Sol happy but things, he thought, were never quite the same after that.

'I must be going too,' he now said to Parlando. 'To prepare for the Murder Mystery Weekend.' He flicked the button at the monitor.

Sandy bounced away on the amorous policeman while he pummeled her shapely, mobile breasts. Sol reflected that if people behaved in the normal course of life as they did when having sex they would be strapped into a canvas bag and hauled off to the asylum.

8

Friday dawned to a lingering mist, but by mid-morning this had lifted and the sun shone warm and strong from an azure sky. It put Sol in a buoyant mood as he packed his bag. He decided to leave earlier than planned and stop off somewhere for lunch.

Soon he was speeding along the town's bypass towards the country and the hotel that was hosting the Murder Mystery Weekend. He wondered what Parlando's two other cars were like – if he was prepared to lend him one as impressive as this without so much as a second thought. Because the car ran so quiet and smooth he thought he was travelling at about 50 mph, but when he looked down at the clock the needle hovered just beneath the 90 mark. He lingered here a little while before slowing down. Sol had never craved status symbols but he imagined the car he was driving was of a sort favoured by managers of small to medium-sized companies, and probably also standard issue to the likes of junior ministers of unimportant departments when on official business. When he arrived at the hotel he might well be taken for a successful businessman. He had dressed smartly, but casually, and owned quality leather luggage (received one Christmas from his parents, and little used). If that's what the others at the event wanted to think, that was fine. In unfamiliar public situations, Sol knew, it helped to have an identity, and it was often no disadvantage whatever to have one that was not a true reflection of the inner man.

Sol entered the restaurant section of the pub and looked up at the chalked blackboard above the bar. He was not usually an offal man, but the words 'calf's liver' jumped out at him.

'Yes, sir? What can I get you?' asked the landlord.

Before he could stop himself Sol replied:

'How's the liver today?'

He hated silly questions! As if the landlord was going to say, 'It's a bit ropey actually. I'd have the fish if I was you.'

'We've a special on fish,' replied the landlord. 'Nice bit of sea bass.'

'But there's nothing wrong with the liver? It's not putrefying, or anything?'

'Not when I last looked. But if we should leave it much longer . . .'

Sol scouted momentarily for sarcasm but discovered none. He smiled. 'I'll take it, then. Such a shame for a warm-blooded animal to have suffered all that trauma for nothing.'

'That's very caring of you, sir. If you'd like to take a seat.'

Lunch was most agreeable. The calf's liver was cooked to perfection and served with buttered new potatoes and green beans. He washed it all down with a large glass of sherbety New World chardonnay. He left a generous tip, much more than he might normally leave, because he was enjoying playing the role of a successful man of the world who could give freely in the knowledge that whatever he spent could be easily replenished.

On the last stage of the journey Sol discovered his map-reading skills were not well developed. More than once he took a wrong turning and had to stop and ask the way. But eventually he found himself at the beginning of a road which he could see led to the hotel, about 200 yards distant. There was a wooden sign attached to a tree affirming that this route gave access to the hotel (and only to that – others were told to keep out). However, the way was barred by a gate held fast by a chain and chunky brass padlock. He sounded his horn a couple of times, expecting someone to appear with a key. But no-one came. He waited a while and then drove on in search of another entrance.

The way grew narrower, the verges higher, and moreover he seemed to be travelling away from the hotel and its grounds. Soon the road's surface deteriorated into a rutted and pitted track. It seemed to go on and on, this track, and led, not to the main road, or to the hotel, but to a scattered collection of dilapidated buildings.

Sol stepped out of the car and looked around. He could see no way beyond this point. There were just fields, bounded by hedges and fences. He would have to turn back the way he came. Whatever this collection of ruined buildings had once represented, it was obviously the end of the road. A dead end.

Indeed, it was difficult to tell what might once have stood here, so advanced was the decay. As he walked toward the one structure that had kept some sort of shape he noticed two things. Firstly, that an unsettling silence hung over the area. The stillness was broken only occasionally by the sighing of the wind through long grass that lay on part of the periphery. He realized also that he was walking on a hard surface. Pools of asphalt showed through a covering of moss, dandelions and coarse grass.

'A playground?' thought Sol. 'Or a parade ground, perhaps.'

He stopped and looked about. He could make out the perimeter of the square, which was delineated by the break in the vegetation.

'Yes, quite possibly an army barracks,' concluded Sol. 'It has a military feel. Discipline, rigour, and coldness.'

He tried to picture soldiers marching up and down, but no images formed, no echo from the past of the rhythmic stamping of boots. Instead, there was just the sad sound of the wind, a weary, long-suffering sigh. He looked into the remains of what had perhaps been a dormitory. Thick-stemmed weeds had commandeered the interior space, sprouting densely from the earth beneath rotten floorboards towards a skeletal roof. He recognized the bright yellow flowers of ragwort, and giant hogweed, with its skin-blistering sap.

Sol's light holiday mood had evaporated. There was a sombreness about this place and it pressed upon him. It was as if the mute earth here had borne witness to things best left unsaid. He hurried back toward the car and returned the way he had come. Presently he found that the gate which had previously blocked the way to the hotel had been opened in his absence.

'Are you here for the Murder Mystery Weekend?' asked a woman in Reception.

Sol replied that he was.

'You must be Charles,' and she held out her hand.

'No. I'm his brother, Sol. Did he not say?'

She seemed puzzled. 'Is Charles with you?'

'No. He can't make it. That's why I'm here.'

'Oh,' she replied, displeasure evident in her voice.

'Is there a problem?'

She looked through some papers on her clipboard. 'Well, we were expecting Charles.'

'Well, I'm afraid he's not coming,' said Sol a little more firmly. And when this didn't seem to register with her, he wondered how he could say it again in a way she would understand.

Finally she said, 'I see.'

'He did say he'd arranged it all.'

'Did he say with whom?'

'No, he didn't. He said it wouldn't be a problem.'

'Well it probably isn't for him – or you. But then, you're not organizing it, are you?'

Sol noticed the name badge then for the first time. 'Juppy Candela. Committee.' He tried to think where he had heard that name before.

'Listen, if it's such a big problem, I'll leave.'

'What? No! No, you can't just go.'

'Oh? Why not?'

'We need a murderer.'

'What do you mean?' asked Sol, defensively.

'Charles was playing the part of the murderer. There always has to be a murderer at these weekends.'

'I see,' said Sol, beginning to understand.

'Charles is very good in that part. He often takes it on.'

'He didn't mention any of this to me,' said Sol, then thought perhaps Charles had. There was all that stuff at the end of the phone conversation when he had not really been listening. Then he recalled where he had heard the organizer's name before.

'I do like your hair, by the way. I hope you don't mind my saying so. I think I'm right in saying it's Parlando's work.'

Juppy looked puzzled. 'Parlando? No, never heard of him.'

'Oh.' It was Sol's turn to be puzzled. 'I was sure – never mind. I interrupted you, Juppy. What were you saying?'

'Well, I suppose as long as someone plays the murderer, it might as well be you as Charles. I take it you've learned the script?'

Sol looked blank. 'What script?'

'*The* script! How can you play the part if you don't know the script?'

Sol shrugged. He noticed that the organizer's lower lip had begun to quiver.

'I'm sorry. Charles didn't say anything about a script. He said it would be a fun, relaxing weekend.'

'It is. Of course it is, but there's got to be a story. You have to know what to say, and what not to. You have to give away little clues with the things you say. How else are people going to solve the crime?'

'I don't know,' said Sol, growing exasperated. 'I've never been on one of these things before. I just fancied something different. And to help Charles out. If I thought I was going to have to learn scripts, I'd never have bothered.'

The woman started to weep. 'I knew something would go wrong. I just knew it. It's the first one I've organized. I've waited so long. And it's going to be a disaster.'

She didn't say as much, but Sol could tell she thought he was to blame.

The hotel manageress arrived. She looked coldly at Sol, then Juppy.

'Something the matter?' she asked.

'I think', said Sol, 'that the lady here – Juppy – thinks I've put a spanner in the works by not being my brother. I'm sorry, but I'm not prepared to shoulder any blame for the situation.'

'We've hosted these things before,' said the manageress severely. 'And they've never been any trouble. Never. And then you come along.'

She glared at Sol, who glared back belligerently.

'Anything I can do?' she asked Juppy.

'Something has to be done,' interjected Sol. 'The situation is not going to resolve itself without the application of some intelligence.'

'What do you suggest?' asked Juppy, who appeared to have recovered a little.

'Well,' said Sol. He thought a few moments. 'Why don't I try to get hold of a script?'

'It would be a start,' replied Juppy, smiling.

'I'm sure I can get hold of one. And I'm very quick at learning. Let me see.' He looked around the lobby and then at the manageress. 'Where do you keep the phone in this place?' he inquired sharply.

Unused to questions being fired out at her in such a peremptory tone, she maintained an icy silence for a few seconds, then told him he could use the one in the office.

Charles was surprised to hear from his brother.

Sol got straight to the point. 'Charles! What's all this about a bloody script?'

'Didn't you get it? I posted it.'

'No. I don't know anything about a script. Why didn't you tell me.'

'I did! When I spoke to you.'

'It was a bad line,' mumbled Sol. 'Anyway, it didn't arrive. It's probably lying on my doormat as we speak.'

'Oh, Lord! What are you going to do? You can't play the murderer without knowing the script.'

'Make it up as I go along, I suppose.'

'No, you can't do that. It's all been very carefully worked out.'

'I'm very good at improvising, Charles. You never have been, but—'

'You have to play by the script, for goodness sake!'

'Fax me a copy, then.'

'Don't have one to fax, old man.'

'Just a minute, Charles.'

Sol left the office. He asked the organizer if there was

another script. She said that as far as she knew the one Charles had had (likely now lying on Sol's doormat) was the only copy. Sol returned to the phone.

'Honestly, Charles, this thing is so bloody badly organized. What's her name? Juppy Candela. Well, she's not so bright. She's not even bothered to make a copy of the script.'

'There must be one somewhere.'

'But *where*, Charles? That's the key word, isn't it? It's no good being *any*-where or *some*-where. It has to be *here*.'

'I see your point, yes.'

Sol sighed. 'Listen, this isn't my problem. This whole holiday I seem to have been plagued with problems not of my own making and that are nothing to do with me.'

'How do you mean?'

'It's a long story, Charles. I'll tell you another time.'

'Listen! I've an idea. What's the fax number there at the hotel. I can send something through. I've got a pretty good idea what the plot was. I can write that down. Yes, that'll work. You can muddle through on notes, at least.'

'It'll probably be better than nothing,' agreed Sol, and relayed the fax number to his brother.

Sol went up to his room and unpacked. He looked out of the window. There was a well tended lawn directly outside, and beyond that a pitch-and-putt, clay tennis courts, a bowling green, an archery range, and a small swimming pool.

'Good facilities,' murmured Sol. 'And the room's not bad. Pity about the staff.'

He pushed down the sash window the few inches it had been open. The room was quite well enough aired, he thought. He lay on the bed and closed his eyes, but his mind was too lively for a sleep.

He went downstairs to the bar. It was closed.

'We open at six.' The manageress was looking at Sol with an air of disapproval and suspicion.

'Hello,' said Sol.

'The rest of your party won't be here until six. No point in opening up just for you.'

'No, you're quite right. I'm far too unimportant. Nor would I dream of putting you out. I can wait until six, thank you. In fact, I might not even bother at all today. It's not as if I'm dependent on the stuff.'

'Yes, that's right. Six o'clock,' replied the manageress.

'Has that fax arrived yet?'

'If it had arrived, I would have given it to you. Please don't ask me again. As soon as it comes, I'll inform you.'

Sol wandered over to one of the windows and looked outside to where an elderly gardener was leisurely clipping the edges of the lawn with a pair of shears.

'That looks like hogweed taken root at the back there.' He looked over his shoulder at the manageress, who was writing something in a book. 'You need to be careful with hogweed,' continued Sol. 'Nasty stuff, spreads like wildfire.'

He walked back towards the desk. 'Just thought I'd mention it. In case you were interested.'

'Interested in what?' Again there was irritation on her face.

'What a cow,' thought Sol. 'Is there nothing between those purple-thread-veined ears of hers?' 'I was just asking', he said aloud, 'how many others are coming to this event?'

'Thirty-one, including you. That's about the right number for these things.'

'I prefer even numbers myself.'

'Well, some will have to double up.'

'It would be odd if they didn't. Is the organizer around?'

'Juppy?'

'Yes. The radiant Candela. Where will I find her?'

'Don't go disturbing her! She's resting ahead of tonight. I think you rather upset her, you know.'

'She upset herself. Some people just can't deal with the unexpected.'

'Don't be ridiculous! Why would she upset herself?'

'Just let me know right away when that fax from my brother arrives, would you?' said Sol, adopting an imperious tone once more. 'I'll be in my room.'

As Sol mounted the stairway the front door eased open and a small man laden with two large suitcases stumbled in. He put them down on the floor and pushed the door closed. He looked about him, rather nervously, until his eyes alighted on Sol looking down at him.

'Oh, hello.' He smiled. 'I'm not the first, then?'

'And you'll not be the last, I'm sure,' replied Sol.

The smile on the little man's face faded. He appeared uncertain and confused, and began to stutter. 'I'm sorry, I . . . I—'

'No, it's me who should be sorry,' said Sol. 'I've no idea why I said that. Too many crossword puzzles, I expect. You'll be here for the Murder Mystery jamboree?'

'That's right,' replied the man, once more bright and smiling. 'Looking forward to it.'

Sol descended the stairs and introduced himself.

'I'm Shad,' replied the newcomer. 'Shad Yeazleby.'

'Pleased to meet you, Shad,' said Sol. 'Let me help you with your luggage. It seems a lot of baggage for a weekend, if you don't mind my saying so.'

'I suppose so. But it's okay, I'll carry it. I'm used to it. It's easier to carry two, isn't it? Question of balance.'

'As you wish. This way. I'll show you where to book in.'

'Thank you. Thank you so much. You're very kind, Sol.'

* * *

The manageress was standing at the reception desk studying some accounts. She continued to do so when Shad and Sol stood before her, even though the noise of the suitcases being dumped on the floor must have intimated that someone required her attention. When after six seconds she had not looked up, Sol took a coin from his pocket and rapped it on the surface of the desk. It had the desired effect. She looked up, stared at Sol and then at Shad.

'Can I help you?'

'Oh, hello. Yes. I'm here for the Murder Mystery Weekend.'

'Name?'

'Shad. Shad Yeazleby.'

'Shap . . . ?'

'I don't think he could have said it any plainer,' interjected Sol, with some venom.

The manageress looked coldly at Sol, then picked up a file and began to study it.

Sol turned to Shad, rolled his eyes to the heavens, and indicated the manageress with a histrionic nod.

Shad smiled uneasily. He was thrilled that someone had taken his side. No-one had ever done that before, save as a deception so that he would fall further and land harder when the carpet was eventually pulled. At the same time, something in him recoiled from a show of spirited disrespect against someone in authority.

'If you're busy,' said Shad timidly, 'I can always come back.'

The manageress ignored him and continued leafing through her folder. 'Ah yes, here you are. Yeazleby. Room 18.' She handed him a key.

Shad picked up his cases and he and Sol walked towards

the stairs. When he judged he was out of the manageress's earshot he said:

'Phew! That was close.'

'What was close, Shad?'

'She was getting very angry. I thought she was going to throw us out. You were rather rude to her, Sol.'

'You have to be with some people, Shad. It's all they understand.'

'She was probably very busy, what with the Murder Mystery Weekend to organize, and everything.'

'There's a form in these things, Shad. If what she was doing was so pressing as to keep her from the guests, she merely had to smile and say, "Would you excuse me a moment? I'll attend to you shortly." But she didn't do that. She didn't think us important enough.'

'Oh, I'm used to people not thinking me important enough.'

'I used to put up with it, but I don't now. Here's your room. I'm next door. Room 17.'

'Really? Oh, splendid! I'm so pleased we'll have rooms close to one another.'

'I am too,' said Sol, who had quite taken to this inoffensive little man.

'I might as well tell you,' said Shad confidentially. 'I'm playing the *victim*.'

'The victim? Oh, yes. In the – your role, you mean?'

'Yes. I often get cast as the victim. Well, always, actually. Nobody else seems to want to do it.'

'Do you?'

'I don't mind. I mean, well . . . if I'm honest, now and then I wouldn't mind *not* being the victim. You know, maybe once.'

'I'm playing the murderer. I suppose I can tell you that.'

'Oh, then it's so strange us meeting like this. It must be

116

wonderful to play the murderer. I'd really like – no, no it's silly.'

'What do you do as the victim?'

'Well, I have to disappear, sometime between drinks and dinner. And someone will discover my "body". And they look for clues and—'

'Yes, but what do you do once you've been, as it were, bumped off?'

'I have to make myself scarce, and once everything's resolved I can join the land of the living again.'

'Doesn't sound like much of a weekend, Shad. Just keeping out of the way. Stuck in a room somewhere.'

'Oh, it's not so bad. Of course it doesn't compare with being the murderer. Or one of the sleuths. Or the organizer. But *someone* has to do it.'

'Yes, but it doesn't have to be you. People could take turns.'

'People don't want to be the victim, though. I did once get to be a sleuth. Well, when I say . . . I mean almost. The person who was the victim didn't show up, so on the day I had to fill in.'

'Listen, Shad, I would offer to buy you a drink if the bloody bar was open.'

'Oh dear. Is it closed? I wouldn't have minded a small sherry, or something. I've an idea, though! Why don't we go for a walk together instead? In the grounds. It's turned out rather nice, hasn't it? Oh, do say yes, Sol! Walking with someone else is twice the fun, isn't it?'

As they walked across the lawn Shad pointed, and exclaimed:

'Oh, crikey! Giant hogweed! That takes me back.'

'I was telling the manageress about that,' said Sol. 'She wasn't bothered. She hasn't a clue, which wouldn't be so bad if she wasn't such a cow to go with it.'

117

Shad laughed, but then looked over his shoulder towards the hotel, just in case she was watching them from a top window – through field glasses, perhaps – reading their lips as they talked. Because the afternoon sun hit the windows he could not see if anyone was watching, and he grew anxious.

'Why does it take you back?' Sol asked him. 'The hogweed?'

'Oh, you know. School and things. Some of the bigger boys once threw me into a patch.'

'That wasn't very nice.'

'Just a bit of fun, really. They meant me to land in the nettles, but there was hogweed as well.'

'You shouldn't be so forgiving, Shad.'

'No. Okay. Sorry.'

'Nor is there anything to be sorry about.'

'No. Sorry.' Shad fell silent and seemed a little morose. He had picked up the slight note of irritation in Sol's rebuke. He thought his new friend, the friend he never had at school, or anywhere, was tiring of him and at any second would make an excuse to leave. And perhaps not even make an excuse. Instinctively he adopted a diffident stoop and walked a little behind Sol.

They stood by the swimming pool, which looked rather inviting, with the sun's rays dancing off its surface.

'That takes me back,' said Shad. 'We had a pool at school rather like this one. Yes, just like this one. Those of us who were useless at rugby – well, just me actually – had to swim lengths in the games period.'

'What? During the winter?'

'Oh, it wasn't too bad once you were in. As long as you kept moving. I imagine it was the same at your school, wasn't it?'

'No, actually it wasn't. My school had its faults, but on the whole it was quite civilized. In fact, after the fourth year, you weren't obliged to do games at all. You could study, instead. Or work in the art room.'

'How wonderful! I wish I'd gone to a school like that. But they say they're the best days, don't they?'

'I'm glad they're over, Shad.'

'I went to school in these parts, actually.'

'Did you? And are you going back to visit it while you're here?'

'No. It's not there any more. It was knocked down.'

'Developers, you mean?'

'No. Nor did they ever find out who did it. So sad. I've a good idea who it was, though.'

An image of the ruins he had stumbled across earlier in the day came into Sol's head. And he told Shad about it. 'We've got an hour. I'll take you there, if you like?'

Shad seemed unable or unwilling to speak for a few moments, then said he doubted it was the same site, but even if it was he didn't want to visit it.

'Oh look!' Shad had spotted the archery butts. They walked towards them.

'Did you have archery at your school?' asked Sol.

'Oh yes!' replied Shad, smiling.

'And did you enjoy archery?'

'I was useless at sport. Hopeless. Except for archery! I don't know why, but from the first I could do archery. I could make that old arrow go exactly where I wanted. It seemed so easy. I couldn't understand why everyone couldn't do it. The games master used to say, "Come on, you useless buggers! If that little twat Yeazleby can do it, anyone can." But they couldn't. Five times out of six I'd hit the bull. But they couldn't. Not even when they cheated and moved closer to the target. Of course, they got me back when it came to boxing. I could never box. I just stood there and tried to . . . '

'Look, there must be some bows at the hotel. Why don't we—'

'I don't think there are, you know.'

'Why not? Seems silly to have targets if there's nothing to shoot at them. People aren't going to bring their own, are they?'

Shad sighed and looked troubled.

'What's the problem?'

'It's just . . . well, I gave up archery.'

'Why? If you were so good. And enjoyed it.'

'I don't know. People resented my skill. It seemed to upset people, and I don't like to upset people. I tried to miss on purpose, but couldn't. It was like something took over. Something that wasn't me, and guided my hand. But anyway, one day at the end of gym, some of the bigger boys got hold of me and pinned me to the big target.'

'Pinned you?'

'Yes. With metal stakes. From the gym store, where they kept the OTC tents. I remember it like it was yesterday. They put the target flat on the ground, held me down on top of it, then hammered the stakes through my clothes. Quite a lot of them. I mean, I couldn't move, not even when they lifted the target.'

'And they shot at you?'

'No, no. Nothing like that. They wouldn't do that. No, they just rolled me along, like a big cartwheel. They took me to the brow of the hill and pushed me down the slope. Picked up a lot of speed, actually. They couldn't keep up. They just watched and shouted and jeered. Luckily there was a tree, so it didn't roll all the way to the bottom. It was quite a big hill. I think I must have fainted or something, because when I came around everyone had gone. I managed to free myself and hurry back to class.

Just my luck! It was Latin with Old Cacknacker, and I got a good thrashing. But that was par for the course, if you were late for lessons. Rules are rules. Can't complain about that.'

At the mention of Cacknacker, the scene of a film set, with a graveyard, was triggered in Sol's mind. 'That's a name I've heard before. Cacknacker.'

'He was the headmaster,' confirmed Shad. 'Old Cacknacker, we called him. Don't know if he had a first name. If he did, we certainly weren't allowed to speak it.'

'Yes, that's what I saw written down. Inscribed. Yes, that would fit. I wonder. And I imagine those who . . . ' Sol briefly described his experience as a film extra, omitting to say why he was really there, but including his encounter with Choy and Clowsie. 'They must have been at your school too – were they? Dreadful fellows.'

'Oh, they weren't so bad. Not once you got used to them. The big one sounds like Clowsie Doenitz. I suppose he was a bit of a rotter. And the other was Choy Chevers.'

'That's them, then. Coarse fellows with a rather strange idiom?'

'That's right. But you know, I don't think they could help it. There were some awful bullies in the Upper Remove. 'Scar' R'Dodo, 'Breakneck' Breary – a lot of them had nicknames. 'Graiae' Grizling—'

'Deformed, was he? Old Graiae?'

'Yes, he was. How did you know?'

Sol explained his line of reasoning and then added:

'Funny, isn't it? "Bullies" used to mean something quite different.'

'Did it?'

'Yes. A bully was a friend. Someone you liked a lot. A fine fellow. From the Dutch, *boele*, lover. Remember in

Shakespeare. The rude mechanicals refer to "Bully Bottom".'

'We didn't do English at school, I'm afraid. I would like to have done. But thank you for telling me.'

'The word probably came across with the Dutch weavers. A lot of them came across the North Sea in the sixteenth century. Fleeing the Spanish and religious persecution. That's where we get the f-word. *Fokken.* Means to beat. I imagine English soldiers might have picked this up when they fought in the Netherlands.'

'Gosh! Did you learn that at school too? I wish we had done history. It's so nice to be able to talk about – you know, decent and clever things. I hope we can have some more talks like this, Sol.'

'I don't see why not.'

The two men walked silently for a while, then Sol asked:

'What about the Umbelishas?'

'Ah! The twins! Yes. That was so sad. So very sad. And they were such a credit to the school.'

'Pup Mordecai?'

'Poor Pup. Poor, poor Pup. He was so sweet, Sol. You've no idea. He expired one afternoon on furnace duty. In the hard winter of '63. I did miss him. He was too delicate for this world, Sol. Just too . . . ' Shad's words tailed off as the sadness welled up in him.

'Oh dear,' said Sol. 'I'm sorry I brought it up.'

Shad shook his head to indicate that it didn't matter.

'Still,' said Sol, attempting to lighten the moment. 'I imagine it wasn't a bad place to be during that hard winter. The furnace room?'

'It was okay,' agreed Shad.

'And this Choy, and his brutish friend, I imagine they made your life a misery at school?'

'Just a bit, yes,' replied Shad, once more a picture of

anxiety. 'Sometimes.' He looked round apprehensively. 'I hope they don't come here and spoil my weekend. They didn't say anything to you, did they, when you saw them? About coming here, I mean?'

'Nothing like that. But they sound a real pair of shits.'

'Oh, they weren't so bad,' said Shad mechanically.

9

After Shad parted from Sol he made his way to the site of the old school. He did not go the way Sol had, along the road and track, but used a shorter route through the woods. Even where the path was overgrown Shad knew where it ran, because it formed part of the old escape route from the school, where he, the Umbelishas, Squib-Diddly and a number of others had come to grief one stormy night. (That there was no safety in numbers was a lesson Shad learned early in life.)

He had been to the site of the old school before. Always alone. There was a spot sheltered from the elements close to where the old perimeter wall had once been. Shad sat here silently looking out over the weed-choked ground, the rubble and the dilapidated shells of buildings. The wind stirred, first sighing, then moaning like the sick and dying in a fever hospital. Then it grew agitated and formed into little vortices that scuttled across the earth sucking up dry leaves and spitting stinging dust into Shad's eyes, before losing form and energy and merging once more with the air around it. But it didn't deter him from his vigil, which was an attempt to exorcize the memory of Cacknacker's School. Even though the bricks and mortar had perished, the day-to-day foulness of his years within those cold walls still lived on in Shad's spirit.

Old Cacknacker stood six foot eleven. When he walked, his head moved from side to side, his elbows pumped the air, and at each step he brought his foot down with great force and deliberation, as if stamping on cockroaches. To witness this on the first day at a new school was disturbing.

Cacknacker, who was called Old even when he was young, was as strong and powerful as a force of nature. Cacknacker didn't spare the rod. In his prime it was a point of honour that neither his victim nor he himself should remain standing at the end of a thrashing. It was fear that kept order in his school. What curbed the dreadful excesses of his unruly pupils? Fear of something mightier than themselves. Fear of Cacknacker in his fury: stern lawgiver, judge and strong-armed executioner, wielding a cane of whippy ash.

The prefects in Cacknacker's School carried poles of polished wood about four-foot long. Cacknacker knew of the Spartans and their laws and of the Old Babylonians and their code, in which it was decreed that a man was free to beat his wife, children and female relatives on both sides of the family, his servants and animals, wandering mendicants, insolent or importuning hawkers, and so on – so long as the implement used was no thicker than a man's thumb. He adopted this law as his own. In a school where quips were rare, humour frowned upon and frivolity proscribed, it became known as 'Cacknacker's rule of thumb'. Once a week, on a Tuesday, there would be a ritual in the open air. The prefects would parade in front of the whole school, their poles resting on their shoulders. Then they would form up and one by one present their poles to Cacknacker for inspection. And the measure of the thickness was his own thumb, which was twice as thick as any other man's. When a pole was gauged to his satisfaction, he would touch the prefect on the forehead, as if in blessing, and say:

'Thy rod and thy staff comfort thee!'

Cacknacker's School could make or break a man. Most it broke; some it destroyed. In the world at large, those employers who saw the school's name on an application form would immediately throw it in the bin.

But there came two in Yeazleby's day whose strength and cunning would see them through. Choy and Clowsie, by chance, started at the school on the same day. Once more against the odds, no surname fell between 'Chevers' and 'Doenitz'. So, in a school where everything was done strictly by the alphabet, Choy and Clowsie were always put together. Their beds were side by side in the dormitory, so that back to back, bloodied but unbowed, they could fight off the marauding bullies from the Upper Remove. The animosity of the Upper Remove was not personal and the bullies turned to easier prey, weaker or less spirited boys who could or would not fight back. And in due course Choy and Clowsie grew large and strong, and themselves became the bullies.

Hogweed was rampant in the grounds of Cacknacker's School. The Headmaster had great admiration for the plant. Its vigour and strength pleased him, and its size too. It pushed aside lesser plants, occupied more than its share of God's space with its huge leaves, spoked blossoms and sturdy stalks. He told his gardeners to:

'Let it grow where it will.'

Those boys who damaged it in their mischief he punished. When Shad was thrown into the weeds, and crushed some of them as he landed, he was thrashed. Cacknacker also admired the weed because even when it lay broken and dying its sap could still injure. And when boys cut the hollow stalks to turn into pea-shooters they became ill with its poison. Even as they lay in the sickbay they were thrashed by Cacknacker, while Matron looked on in stern approval.

In Cacknacker's School, everything being done rigidly by the alphabet, Shad Yeazleby soon learned that he was always last. Being always last, he would sometimes stay hungry at the end of the day because all the food had been eaten by those who came before him. Being last, his bathwater was always grey with the dirt of fifty boys, and the showers had run ice-cold. If it was a game, everyone had grown bored and was drifting away by the time it came to Shad's turn.

Shad Yeazleby's name was also last on the school roll. Once a week, on a Tuesday, at the rule-of-thumb ritual, the roll would be read, from beginning to end, in the open air – which was not so bad on a sunny May morning, but an ordeal in winter, when the fields were frozen and the sleet was blowing in on an easterly wind. Every pupil, even the first, had to remain standing in rows on the asphalt playground until the last name, which was Yeazleby's, was read out. Cacknacker had decreed it.

And naturally enough, when it was cold and wet and the list seemed interminable, the school grew restive. The pupils, with their warped schoolboy logic, blamed Yeazleby for keeping them there. By the time the names of the Umbelishas and Calli Umpaat were read out, they were ready to riot and the prefects walked the ranks, now and then lashing out with their poles, or dragging someone to the front to administer summary punishment. And when finally all were dismissed, they vented their anger on the hapless Yeazleby.

* * *

Shad wished that things weren't so, that he did not always have to be last. He had read somewhere that the day would come when 'the last shall be first'. It was like a shaft of dazzling light illumining his world. He learned the words by heart and repeated them to himself on long dark nights when he was too frightened to sleep. Until, one day in morning assembly, the words fell from Cacknacker's lips.

'"The last shall be first."' There was a silence before he thundered:

'THEY—WILL—*NOT!*'

That terrible sound shattered Shad's hope as if it had been a delicate wine glass. He sat rigid and paralysed with terror as Cacknacker continued, first in a small voice:

'"The meek will inherit the earth."'

And then, once more, like a great battery of guns:

'THEY—WILL—*NOT!*' Old Cacknacker surveyed the sea of faces before him, scanning for a movement, an expression, that might spell dissent or rebellion.

'Can day be night!?' he boomed. 'Or black be white?'

In the classroom such silly, rhetorical questions were met with a barrage of profanity or rasping mouth music. But no-one answered Cacknacker.

As he continued, his tone took on a note of anguish. 'How can last be first, how can one thing be another? And not just another, but its opposite. If a thing has a name we must not give it another, for verily that is the road to confusion. In my school things must be – and remain – what they are and nothing else.'

And he brought his fist down on the old oak lectern, extending the split that ran across its face:

'IN MY SCHOOL THE LAST WILL BE LAST. THE LAST ARE LAST BECAUSE THAT'S WHERE I PUT THEM, AND THAT'S WHERE THEY BELONG!'

Poor Shad. Anguish filled his being. His bowels boiled,

129

and he chewed on his knuckles over words that seemed intended for him and him alone. As he sat there, crushed and humiliated, anxiously chewing, a prefect leaned over and prodded him sharply between the shoulder blades with his pole.

'Oi! You know the rules. No chewing knuckles in assembly. Shag fucking Weasle-bum. Report to me afterwards! Upstairs, in your gym kit!'

Old Cacknacker, for all his power, had a bad memory. He could not remember many of his pupils' names. Yeazleby was one he could, and he always spat it out like some bitter bile that fouled his mouth.

'Yeazleby! My office! Now!' How often did that happen, when it was some other wretched boy with a common, unremarkable name who was the miscreant. But it was not for the likes of Shad to tell Cacknacker he had made a mistake.

Yeazleby. Shad hated that name. His mother had spurned Moir Berlingo, just because he was a notorious pederast. A certain Ned Boynynge, a haberdasher by trade, had also proposed. What happened to him? Why hadn't she married him? Shad tortured himself with that question. 'B' was so close to the beginning! So close! In a school where everything was done by the alphabet, life would have been so, so much sweeter.

Each term Shad scrutinized the noticeboard for the names of new arrivals. Surely, he thought, there must come someone, sometime, with a name to succeed his own. Perhaps a ridiculous foreign name, such as . . . Zingalongadingdong? Perfect! Not only would that person be last, but with a name like that he would draw the fire of the bullies in the Upper Remove. But there never did come anyone with that name. More than once it came tantalizingly close, with

Yealing, Yarer, and later the bumptious Yahootie. When the mysterious Xenophon arrived, and Shad heard his name spoken, he cried, *Hallelujah!* But when he saw he was still last, and protested, the housemaster clouted him round the ear and told him he was an imbecile.

One day, when the school returned from the long holiday, Cacknacker *was* old. His mane of shaggy hair had turned white. He was no longer as strong and fearful as a force of nature. A beating had barely begun when he grew confused and disoriented. Far from being prostrated, the miscreant would walk away whistling and gesticulate crudely behind the Headmaster's back. At the weekly rollcalls Cacknacker would nod off and the silence would grow and grow until one of the bolder prefects would approach and strike him firmly across the side of the head with his pole, sending up puffs of powdery snow from the layers that covered his thick eyebrows. The Headmaster would awake with a start and a stertorous intake of breath. The roll would continue, though probably not from where it left off. Sometimes his finger would slide back to Nick Borbyganimus (or thereabouts) when before falling asleep it had advanced to Eyrie Slinker. At such times a loud and profane protest would issue from the Upper Remove and they would leave in droves, followed by many of the lower school. Only the meeker boys remained and for them the day was long. For there were now great gaps in the roll, and whenever a name went unanswered Cacknacker would wait and wait, and wait again, before finally entering a shaky cross against the name. Now and then he would lift his head, until it was imperiously erect, and survey the ground before him. And though he saw only a scattering of boys, he could not remember how many there were supposed to be. It was not long before most of the boys stopped attending the weekly roll-call, and the prefects wielded poles that were thicker than any thumb.

No-one can be sure why Cacknacker's fury waned so quickly and the fear-based order of the school disintegrated and the forces of the id came to the fore. Some say the rot had taken hold when he married. The day before the wedding Cacknacker was summoned into his father's study to be instructed on his marital duties. It was a sombre occasion in that room of dark, tobacco-stained wood, as befitted the oner-ous duty to give and take instruction on such matters. After much embarrassment and circumlocution the father rested a hand on the son's shoulder and said in a sorrowful voice:

'It boils down to this. The man covers the woman and effects a coupling. Should a second child be required, the act must be repeated.'

Meanwhile the bride's training for life did not extend beyond the lapidary arts and feather work.

Nevertheless there came a babe.

More so than most boys, the minds of the pupils at Cack-nacker's School were full of filth, yet it was beyond even their prurient imaginations to conceive of their Headmaster in a carnal embrace. Some opined that the child could not be of his loins, but had one day appeared mysteriously in the flower basket that swung outside Cacknacker's front door.

And Cacknacker was moved by the boy child, and was kind to him. When he cried, hungry or full of wind, or from anguish at being thrust into the cold world, Cacknacker did not reach for his rod. He simply watched bemused as his wife coddled the infant, and with love and affection caused it to smile.

As he aged, Cacknacker grew more uncomfortable with large numbers. He was a man who liked a sense of proportion in all things. Long strings of digits alarmed him, but nor was he fooled by the shorthand mathematicians employ to express numbers of great magnitude. One day he put a limit on the size of number that could be used at his school. He would creep along the outside of the buildings and peer through the windows of the classrooms to ensure that his rule was not being broken. And sometimes he would interrupt a maths lesson and demand to see the exercise books. If he thought the numbers had grown too large, perhaps by multiplication, he would order all the books burned and beat the maths master about the head and ears. Finally he drove out the mathematicians. Some of those masters, hoping to be reinstated, hung about the gates for weeks, where they were jeered at and spat upon by boys of all years. Long after the event, people would recall in awe the day Cacknacker drove the mathematicians from the school.

When Cacknacker was young and vigorous the school had marched to a military beat and, as the pupils practised at the snare-drum, their jaunty paradiddles would ring out through the school. But in his dotage he was moved only by mawkish melody and simple sentiment. An old hymn, 'God Made all the Corncrakes', became the school anthem and each morning was given a dreadful and disharmonious rendition during the school assembly. Cacknacker's mouth would open and close like that of a codfish, and the tears would roll down his cheeks.

In the days of Cacknacker's dotage, as they came to be known, the sleek Don Drongo arrived from Madrid to teach dancing and Spanish. He stayed for a time – a day and a half, to be precise, most of it spent hiding – before disappearing, never to return.

* * *

The time came when liberal sentiment prevailed throughout the land and it was forbidden to beat boys with rods at all, let alone rods the thickness of Cacknacker's thumb. The older boys particularly were bitter, those who had come up through the ranks thrashed by masters and prefects, but who, now that it was their turn to dish it out, were going to be denied.

'Damn pissing liberals!' they exclaimed. 'What's wrong with the stick, anyway!? A few scars don't hurt. Something to show the grandchildren.'

And such punishments as were allowed failed to deter, and disorder prevailed in Cacknacker's School.

Shad passed all his school years in Cacknacker's School. Each holiday he would implore his parents not to send him back, but they remained unmoved by his pleas.

10

As Shad left to return to the hotel he was unaware he was being observed through a pair of field glasses. Two figures watched from the far side of the old school grounds, obscured behind vegetation and the piles of rubble.

'What's that bloody twerp doing here?' asked Choy as he handed the glasses to his comrade.

Clowsie stared through the binoculars for a few seconds. 'You're right, Choy. I recognize him. Pissing tick! Plenty of trouble he gave us. Damn squirt.'

'Damn right he bothered us,' answered Choy, taking back the binoculars. 'But we made him pay. Eh, Clowsie?'

'Right, Choy.'

'He got a bill all right, and we made him pay it. Cash on the nail and fuck the taxman. He got the full audit, and I don't think he liked the receipt we left him.'

'That's right, Choy. We striped him up a few times. Made him howl a bit.'

'Why's he back here, Clowsie? That's what I want to know.'

'Maybe he wants some more, Choy. I'll land some on him, if that's what he wants.'

'Those stinking chits in the Juniors! They all looked the same bent and screeching.'

'You're right. Let's get him.'

Choy put the glasses away.

And the two set off purposefully in Shad's direction.

Just like Shad, Choy and Clowsie sometimes returned to this place, although this was the first time their paths had crossed. They had built a shelter out of stones and branches well hidden in the undergrowth. Here they stored a small stock of food: tins of beans and sardines, and bottles of beer, which Clowsie opened with his teeth. The beans they cooked in their tins at the side of the fire, puncturing them first with the big knife. And when they sizzled and the ochre-coloured sauce came bubbling out of the holes they took the scorched tins from the fire and peeled off the tops with a Swiss Army knife. Clowsie would pour some of the steaming contents down his large throat, then hand the tin to Choy. They also learned how to lay snares for birds and rabbits. The butchering came naturally. When they had carved open a rabbit, its entrails and furry skin were thrown on the fire, where they crackled and hissed as they were consumed by the flames and gave off a smell that both men came to love. The pink flesh was roasted over the flames on sharpened skewers of green stick until it was dark and oily, and streaked with black char. That was a good meal, beans and rabbit washed down with beer.

There was sometimes good reason for them to go to ground: when the heat was on, and it was better to be out of the eye of the constabulary. But there was another reason too. For this was a scene of triumph and victories; one where they felt their power renewed. Although it was a place, for Shad, where terrors had to be exorcized, and where Sol sensed evil, to Clowsie and Choy it was a haven in which to revitalize their strength – just like the bulls in Spain that find a spot in the ring which they are reluctant to abandon, because it seems to act as a conduit for the

Bull-sign earth energy that will give them new strength to fight off the tormenting matadors.

Choy and Clowsie came here sometimes for just a day, sometimes for two weeks. Cold or storm didn't worry them. They had their shelter, they had fire, they had food and drink. Sometimes they would sit and talk about old times, but there were also long periods of silence. At least once on each visit they would walk the bounds of their domain, swiping and prodding the undergrowth as they went, as they used to – still thinking, perhaps, they might find a Junior or a sodomite cowering there.

As Shad hurried along the path through the wood, he feared he was being followed. Stopping to listen only confirmed his fears. He recognized that sound of wooden poles beating the undergrowth, and it sent a spasm of fear coursing through his innards to the very pit of his groin.

A tiding of magpies burst into loud bickering in the tree-tops and startled Shad.

He was small and nimble and made good progress through the trees and bushes. He knew the woods, and the paths that led nowhere but back on themselves: where the nettles and thorns made the way impassable, and where treacherous roots crossed the path. He knew the short-cuts. But then, so did the hunters know all this.

He came to the edge of a steep embankment. He knew it was a risk, but he had to take it. He hesitated and then stepped over the edge. He controlled his descent for a while, but then slid and tumbled the rest of the way to the path below. He lay dazed at the bottom for a few seconds then picked himself up and hurried on. He looked around once more. They would have heard him falling. They couldn't have failed to. He listened and was sure the thrashing sounds were closer. He cursed himself for having taken the short-cut down the precipice. If they caught him now, it would only be his own fault and he would deserve whatever they did to him, for being so foolish.

At last the trees and undergrowth began to thin and he could run unimpeded until he came to the hole in the fence that bounded the hotel. He squeezed through, gingerly skirted the curtain of nettles and hogweed, and walked across the lawn, just once looking behind him.

Choy and Clowsie were not far behind. When they poked their heads through the gap in the fence, Shad was just disappearing around the side of the hotel.

'It's this damn pissing place,' said Clowsie. 'They wouldn't serve us the drink we wanted. Said we were too young, school caps and everything.'

'That's right. And when we didn't go, they sent for the dogs.'

'Ridgebacks, I remember. And a damn German shitter.'

'No ridgebacks hereabouts, Clowsie. But right, a big-bast-ard German shitter it was.'

'Don't worry about the dogs, Choy. I'll sort them. A few bites never hurt anyone.'

'When dark comes, Clowsie!'

'We'll get him all right, Choy. I'll land a few stingers, then you can have him.'

11

Sol was coming down the stairs as Shad, still agitated from the chase, entered the vestibule.

'Shad, old stick,' he called out. 'What's wrong? You look a little put out.'

Shad looked up. 'Oh, hello. Er, no. I'm . . . I've just been for a walk, actually.'

Sol stood next to Shad. 'You're out of breath. A little flushed.'

'Am I? Oh. Well, I, um, ran a bit of the way. Yes.' He nodded. 'I like of bit of running,' continued Shad, his breathing settling down now. 'Got used to it at school.' He glanced anxiously out of the window.

'Been to see the old school?' asked Sol.

'*No!* I mean, no. Nothing like that. Just in the woods and round about. You know.'

Sol glanced at Shad's white trousers, which were stained with grass and mud.

'Ah yes,' said Shad. 'Had a bit of a tumble. Lost my footing on a steep bit. Silly, really. Better go and change, eh? Can't turn up to drinks looking like this.' He forced a laugh and then hurried up the stairs to his room.

Sol rang the bell at the reception desk, but it summoned nobody. He went into the office and saw a red light winking on the fax machine. It was out of paper. He cursed the manageress for her inefficiency. There was one sheet sitting on the machine. It was from Charles. Most of the text was inconsequential. Just Charles babbling on about nothing much. Only the last eight lines on the page related to the Murder Mystery plot. The rest of it remained invisible because some stupid woman was not doing her job properly. Sol looked around for more paper and found some in a cupboard. He imagined the remainder of the script lay embedded in data stored in the fax machine and that printing would begin anew once the paper tray was replenished, just as it did with his printer at work. And indeed, it did begin. And he enjoyed a brief moment of triumph before the red light started to wink once more and a message informed him there was a paper jam.

One sheet had been spat out. It contained four more lines of plot, some gibberish, and some smeared toner. Sol once more cursed the hotel's management. He opened all the parts of the machine that could be opened, but could detect no paper jam. He switched it off, and then on again. This seemed to right the problem. The machine hummed away quite happily and informed Sol, in the only way it could, it was:

'Online/Ready.'

What it couldn't tell him was that the information he was awaiting was lost. The incredibly complex, yet transitory, arrangement of electrons that represented the script for a weekend's entertainment had been jolted into chaos when he switched the machine off. Sol phoned Charles but was answered by a machine. He left a message asking for the script to be re-sent, then stapled together the two sheets of information he had salvaged. It didn't amount to much, but it was something to work on.

* * *

The bar was still closed, hidden behind a rolling aluminium shutter. Sol looked at his watch. There were sounds coming from the dining room, so he went to investigate. He discovered a young woman with her back to him, setting a table. She continued at her task but then sensed she was being watched and turned around.

'Hello,' said Sol.

'Hello,' she replied, observing Sol with an expression of impatient irritability, as if about to chide him. It seemed to correspond well with the brisk, no-nonsense way she moved. Looking past that, though, it was an attractive face, a delightful retroussé nose its focal point. She waited for Sol to say something more, and, when he did not, she thoughtfully rubbed the fork she was holding with a white cloth and placed it carefully on the table.

Sol remained where he was. He was finding it pleasant just watching her work. She turned around to face Sol once more.

'If you want the bar, it's closed,' she said, a rustic burr to her voice.

Sol laughed. 'Why does everyone think I'm desperate for a drink?'

The woman shrugged. 'Buggered if I know.'

'I mean, do I have the blue-bulbous worm-eaten nose of a sot? A drunkard's tremor?' He held out a hand and set it trembling, as if in alcoholic spasm.

Her eyes looked him up and down, sharp and disapproving. She seemed ready to respond, but then walked away with brisk strides.

Sol retired to his room. He looked out of his window but saw no sign of any other guests. He wondered if he should look in on Shad, perhaps play a hand or two of cards, but a fatigue came upon him quite suddenly, like a sea mist. He lay on his bed and fell into a deep sleep.

When he awoke, it felt as if he had been asleep for hours. He couldn't even remember at first where he was. He had risen too quickly from black depths of sleep and it took a few seconds for his conscious mind to catch up. He looked down from his window. There were plenty of cars parked outside now. The most impressive was a big Bentley of gorgeous midnight blue. There were a couple of sleek sports cars and some ubiquitous off-road vehicles. The rest were run of the mill. His own (or, rather, Parlando's) vehicle stood distinguished enough in motley company. A flash of light from the edge of the grounds caught his eye. He thought he saw shadowy movement too, but his eyes were not yet quite focused. He looked again but this time there seemed to be nothing out of the ordinary. He didn't doubt that he had seen a flash of light, but it could easily have been a ray of the early evening sun striking some broken glass. He caught his reflection in the mirror. His clothes were crumpled. He removed them, and, as he had nothing on, thought he might as well take a shower.

Afterwards he dressed in black trousers and the white dinner jacket he had purchased in a charity shop. He looked at himself in the mirror once more.

'Oh yes. Much better.'

These days Sol had his trousers made at a bespoke tailor's, where his measurements were his own and where his legs were not compared with everyone else's and labelled 'short'. In the big stores, when you selected a pair of trousers from the rack and took them to the cashier, invariably she would study the label and read aloud: '34-inch waist, short leg,' presumably for the benefit of customers who could not themselves read, or who did not appreciate that garments came in different sizes. As soon as the words 'short leg' were read out, Sol could feel the eyes of other shoppers upon him.

Once he had countered in a sarcastic vein, asking if they stocked 'extra short' leg to correspond to the XL category at the other end of the spectrum. When the assistant replied that the store did not, Sol said he had suspected as much. There were, after all, shops that catered for the larger man or woman, measured either by height or girth, but none that dealt with dwarfs or midgets. Sol suggested the store might be in violation of human rights, as defined by interfering European courts. The woman, who was plainly tiring of the conversation, suggested he should try the children's department if he wanted something smaller.

At his bespoke tailor's they would not dream of passing judgement on his inside leg measurement, let alone broadcasting it to all and sundry. And when they asked, 'On which side do you dress, sir?', and he replied, 'In the middle, actually!', they always feigned amusement.

As Sol walked past the desk in the lobby on his way to the drinks reception the manageress called out to him.

'You'll need one of these.' She held up a name badge and waved it about. 'Everyone has to wear one,' she added brusquely.

Sol strode across and took the badge from her hand. He glanced at it, then threw it down on the reception desk. 'Well if you'd like to give me one that's got my name on it then I might deign to wear it. But I've no intention of spending the whole evening explaining to everyone I talk to that I'm not my brother.'

She read the name on the badge. 'Well, if you will go changing things at the last minute you have to expect a little inconvenience.'

'Where's Juppy?' he asked, abruptly.

'If you must know, she's not very well. All that nonsense earlier on. I think it's a touch of quinsy.'

'Quinsy?' exclaimed Sol.

'That's what I said.'

'Have you sent for a doctor?'

'Of course not! It's just a touch of quinsy.'

'Just a touch of quinsy?' said Sol, heavy with sarcasm.

'Juppy said she didn't want a doctor.'

Sol knew that was a lie, and he could see that she knew that he knew.

'I hardly think the patient is the best judge in these cases – do you? Did it not occur to you that Juppy, old trouper that she is, was just being terribly British and not wanting to be a bother to anyone?' Sol walked off in the direction of the drinks reception, but stopped and turned:

'I imagine there might be a doctor in our distinguished company. I suggest you find out and then ask if he wouldn't mind having a look at poor old Juppy. I mean, let's give her a fighting chance and have the attention of someone who knows what they're talking about. Don't you think?'

The manageress was obviously unsettled by Sol's confident bluff. She looked at the desk and muttered something to the effect that she would 'look into it'.

Sol stood on the threshold surveying the company. Everyone was formally dressed, save one: Shad Yeazleby, who wore a sports jacket and trousers of an appalling shade of brown. He was standing on his own like a lost little boy. His eyes lit up when he saw Sol.

'I wondered where you'd got to. I was a bit worried, actually.'

'I've just had another set-to with that damn stupid manageress. Had to put her in her place. I like the outfit, Shad! It's very you.'

'Do you? Thank you. Nice of you to say so, Sol. You don't think it's a bit, you know, casual?'

'Not at all. You'd think someone had died, all this bloody black in here.'

The young woman Sol had seen earlier stood before them. She wore the black-and-white livery of a waitress and held a tray.

Sol leaned forward and read the badge pinned to her bosom.

'Hello, Rosie,' he said.

'You want a drink?'

'Love one. What do you have?'

She seemed surprised at the question. 'Well, there's wine, ent there?' And she indicated by nodding. 'Red and white.'

'I see. In that case, red.'

As he took the glass she gave a little token curtsey, a drop of the knee, as if they had just finished a dance. (Or were beginning.)

'Thank you, Rosie. Nicely done.'

She appeared a little uncomfortable with this aspect of her job.

'I'll call you when I need another.'

'Oh, I'd like one too,' said Shad. 'Thank you.'

They both watched as she walked away. 'She's awfully pretty,' remarked Shad once she was out of earshot.

'I suppose so. In a bucolic sort of way,' agreed Sol.

'I'd like to see her with nothing on.'

'What?' Sol laughed.

'I'd like to do it with her.'

'Steady on, Shad!'

'Do you think she'd let me?'

'There's a certain form to these things.'

'Is there? Oh. Sorry.'

'You can't just drag her behind a bush and mount her, you know. We're not agents of the id, are we? Not like two we could name.'

'Oh, gosh, no. Sorry. I don't know what gets into me sometimes.'

'There's no need to be sorry, Shad.'

'Oh, no. Sorry. I mean, no. It's just . . . I've never been very good with women. Well, I say that, but I sort of got on all right with Matron, you know. I mean, would you put in a word for me? Or something. With Rosie?'

'What I will do, Shad, is offer you some gratuitous advice. When you're knocked off balance by a woman just think of the whole picture. A woman is not just pleasing curves and sensuality. Think of her in the throes of dysentery, or having a baby – you know, a stomach like an igloo and a slimy, blood-streaked head poking out of her splayed crotch. That'll cool the ardour a bit.'

Shad blanched and exclaimed:

'Oh, crikey! That's horrible.'

'That way they don't have power over you. Desire is power. You desire a woman, she has power over you.'

'Have you ever seen a woman having a baby, Sol?'

'Yes, once. On television. I was having my tea.'

'Oh dear.'

'Do you still want to "do it" with this servant woman?'

'Um . . . yes, please.'

'Okay. Well, if the opportunity arises, I'll let slip in the presence of said Rosie that you are, how shall I put it, somewhat smitten.'

'I say, Sol, that's—' Shad broke off as a couple who had just arrived walked past. Then, lowering his voice, he said:

'Listen, Sol. We shouldn't really be talking like this. People are getting suspicious. I've seen them looking at us. You know, I'm the victim and you're the . . . '

'Ah, I see what you're saying now. I was forgetting. The Murder Mystery.'

'We don't want to make it too easy for people.'

146

'You know, I think I could quite enjoy this weekend if it weren't for this silly game.'

'Oh no, Sol. It's great fun! Honestly.'

'Well I'm glad you know what you're doing. I've only the vaguest idea of my part. Let's hope it all works out, eh? I'll see you later.'

Sol drifted away.

Shad approached a tall, haughty-looking man. 'Ah, hello. We met at another of these things not so long back. At the Appledore? Remember? It's Andrus, isn't it?'

The man looked at Shad as though he was something that had dropped from a dog's bottom.

'No, we've never met,' he sneered, and walked away.

'Oh. Sorry,' replied Shad. For a while he stood alone, looking uncomfortable and finishing his drink. 'Time for me to disappear,' he then murmured to himself. 'So people can start looking for a body.'

12

Sol had gleaned little from the fragments of script he had pieced together, and Charles – it seemed – had not received the message about faxing another. He decided he would have to operate in a responsive mode, answering questions as he saw fit and letting circumstances dictate his movements, actions and answers.

He downed the last of his wine and looked around the room for the waitress. She wasn't to be seen, so he strolled to the lounge, thinking she might be there. But the room was empty. He was about to return to the drinks reception when a door opposite the one he had entered creaked open a few inches. Sol watched to see who would emerge, but when no-one did he concluded it was just a draught, a sequence of doors opening and closing elsewhere in the old building. However, when once more it creaked towards him a few inches, then back again, the feeling grew that there *was* someone there after all, staying out of sight, but watching him. Sol called out, but there was no reply. He walked across the room, and pulled the door towards him.

It opened directly on to a short but steep stairway.

Sol checked his step. 'That's not so great,' he remarked. 'That's a death trap. Bloody stupid manageress! Why isn't there a warning sign?'

Cautiously he descended the twisting stone steps, which

ended as suddenly as they had started, in a small, low-ceilinged, gloomy room. There were a couple of gas cookers, an old-fashioned refrigerator as tall as a man, racks of saucepans, and other implements of cooking hanging from the wall. The place bore all the signs of a kitchen and yet it puzzled Sol because it was so at odds with the rest of the hotel and seemed so inadequate to its needs.

There was a solitary man dressed in jeans, tee-shirt, and a floppy chef's hat. On the bench in front of him was a large tub, from which he pulled a wriggling eel. The man held it a few inches in front of his face and looked it in the eye.

'Ahhgh!' he yelled, and let the fish drop back into the tub. 'Bloody thing bit me!'

Sol smiled.

The man, suddenly aware that he was not alone, looked up. 'It's not funny! You wouldn't laugh if it was you.'

He held up his thumb, but Sol could see nothing wrong with it. There was no blood, hardly a mark. Sol peered into the tub of writhing eels.

'This is dinner, is it?'

'Yes.'

Sol looked about the kitchen, observed some grey liquid bubbling away on the stove, but otherwise no sign of preparations. 'I'm Sol, by the way.'

'I'm Eustace.'

'Eustace?'

'Yes,' he replied, defensively. 'If you must know.'

Sol looked at his watch. 'You'll need to get a move on, won't you, Eustace?

'The trouble is, I never really cooked eels before. I'm not sure what to do.'

'Is there no-one to help you?'

'No,' he replied, looking pained. He waited for Sol to offer, and when he didn't, he added:

'Will you help me?'

'I don't know how to cook eels.'

'I've got a book that tells you.' He looked around, then hurried to a table where he swept aside some dirty pots. 'Damn! I had it just—'

'This it?' said Sol, picking up a soiled brown tome from beside the sink.'

'Yes, yes! Good. Turn to the bit on eels! Go on! Read what it says!'

Sol hesitated, then flicked through some of the sauce-stained pages.

'Look under fish! It's a fish. Why are you looking at puddings?!' The man was shaking with impatience, flapping his hand in imitation of turning pages. 'Yes, look! There! "How to cook eels." See!'

'Well why don't *you* read it . . . follow the instructions?'

'No, I can't,' whined the man.

'You can't read?'

'Of course I can bloody read! I did, but it didn't work. Hopeless! Bloody useless book!'

Sol studied the page for a moment. 'Seems straightforward to me.'

'Will you cook them, then?' pleaded Eustace.

'I'm not a chef. I'm a guest. I'm not cooking my own dinner.'

'Please. You said you'd help me.'

'I didn't.'

'You – you didn't say you wouldn't, when I asked.'

'Look! I'm not dressed for working in a dirty kitchen'.

'That's not a problem. I'll get you an apron.'

Sol sighed. 'Look, I tell you what. I'll read the instructions – you do the work. And if you get stuck, maybe I can offer advice. I don't know how, though, because I'm not a chef.'

'That's okay. Neither am I.'

Sol looked puzzled. 'Then what are you doing here? In a hotel kitchen? Cooking dinner?'

Eustace appeared alarmed. 'That came out all wrong! I am a cook. I am. Yes. Definitely.' He clapped his hands. 'Come on. Hurry, hurry! Tell me what to do!'

Sol sighed. He read out the instructions, slowly and simply.'Right. First you have to kill the bloody things. Then you skin them, then you cook them, then you serve them.'

'Okay,' said the man. 'That's easy. Let's do it.'

'It also says it's advisable to let the fishmonger perform the first two operations. That is, the killing and skinning. But you didn't do that.'

'No.'

'No,' agreed Sol peering into the tub.

Eustace nodded vigorously and his ill-fitting hat fell off.

'Right, start killing the eels.'

'How do we do that?'

Sol thought a moment. 'I think a bash on the head might do it. Do you have a suitable implement?'

The question seemed to stump Eustace.

'Have you a rolling pin?' prompted Sol.

'Don't know.'

Sol pulled one from a rack.

'Ah, I wondered what that was.'

'Use this to kill the eels. Hit them on the head.'

Eustace appeared horrified. 'No, you do it. You're better at it.'

Sol grasped his wrist and slapped the rolling pin into his palm. 'Here! I'll get one out for you. Uggh! They're slimy aren't they?'

'See! It's not so easy, is it?'

'There you go,' said Sol allowing the creature to slide

from his hand on to the bench. 'Quick! Whack it before it gets away.'

Eustace swung with the rolling pin but his feeble blow missed the fish by about a foot.

'Come on!' chided Sol.

Eustace swung again, but again was well wide of the target.

Sol lost his patience. He hated seeing anything being done badly. 'Christ! Give it here.' He snatched the rolling pin, took aim and landed a solid blow.

Eustace cried out and covered his eyes.

The eel was not dead; not even stunned. If anything, perhaps angered by the assault, it was moving with more vigour. Sol was forced to grab it as it was about to squirm off the bench top.

'For God's sake kill it quickly!'

Sol concentrated and landed a second blow.

'Oh, that's horrible!' wailed Eustace, as once more the rolling pin found its mark.

'There,' said Sol. 'I think its dead.'

'Ahhgh! No, it moved.'

'Just nervous electrical discharge. I'm told it happens with people as well.'

'It's horrible.'

'One down,' said Sol. 'Now do the same with the rest. Better get a move on.'

'What's all this bloody noise?'

It was Rosie, the waitress.

'All this bangin' and shoutin'.' She stared into the tub, and then at Sol. 'What you doin' in here anyway?'

'I wish I knew, but I'm about to leave.'

'No!' exclaimed Eustace. 'Don't! Rosie'll help us, won't you, Rosie? We've got so much to do.'

Rosie picked up one of the eels. It did not seem to protest at her touch, but adopted a gentle sinusoidal rhythm as it hung there in her fingers. She looked it up and down and then at the two men, rather archly, and asked:

'Now what would I know about eels? Can't see what all the fuss is about eels. Give me a nice bit of Dover sole any day.' She let it drop back into a tub. 'Some old bugger wants a bloody egg in 'is drink,' she announced, walking to the refrigerator.

As she was leaving Eustace called after her: 'Come back when you've done that Rosie. Come back and help us.'

'Bog off! I got me own work to do.'

'Thank you so much Rosie! You're so bloody helpful!'

'I'll get you started,' said Sol, 'then I'm going. We'll skin one together, then you can do the rest.'

Sol picked up the book and reread the instructions. 'You need to have the eel suspended. The dead one. Tie some string tightly just below the level of its head, then hang it from something. Okay? You get a sharp knife and make a shallow cut around the circumference of the body, just beneath the head. Then you get a pair of pliers – yes; pliers it says – and pull away the skin from the cut. You ease it all off, using the pliers and your fingers. Slowly. Don't yank it, or you'll probably break the string. Okay? Think you can do that?

'No,' replied Eustace.

'I see what they mean, it would have been better to let the fishmonger do this bit.'

Rosie came bustling in once more. 'They *all* wants bloody eggs in their drinks now.'

'Rosie, I need some dill,' announced Eustace suddenly. 'Look. It says on the recipe. Dill.'

She glanced at it. 'Well, you'd better go and get some, 'adn't you?'

'Where from?'

'The garden, stupid.'

'There's none there. I had a look.'

'Go and buy some from the shop, then.'

'Yes, okay. What shop sells it?'

'No good goin' to the village, is it? Gone six! Shop'll be shut. Try the Paki place in town. Better 'urry, though, I think they wants fed tonight sometime.'

'Right! I'll take the bike! Where is it?'

'No good lookin' for the bike. It's got a puncture, and it was you bloody done it and didn't bother to get it fixed.'

On that note she scooted away with her eggs.

'Damnbuggerblast!' exclaimed Eustace. She's always leaving me to do everything.' He hung his head and seemed ready to cry.

Sol made to leave.

'Unless . . . ' He looked at Sol.

'What?'

'You must have driven here.'

'Yes.'

'I'll borrow your car. I can be there and back in no time, in a car.'

'It's not actually mine.'

'But you drove it here.'

'Listen, it's not even my weekend, I—'

Eustace's imploring look continued

'This is getting ridiculous. How about if *I* go to town to get the dill and *you* can get on here?'

'No, no, no! I'm hopeless here. You've seen how bad I am. It's much better if you stay. I expect you'll have it done by the time I'm back, won't you? You're so much better at cooking than me.'

'I am not – here – to – cook,' replied Sol, who was growing increasingly exasperated.

'I'd be ever so grateful.'

'I don't want your gratitude – oh, what the fuck!' Sol took the car keys from his pocket and thrust them into Eustace's hand. 'Just take the car and get back here. Quickly. The white Sierra. Right? Then just leave me in peace. Okay?'

'Yes, yes. Fine.' He fondled the keys and smiled. 'Thanks very much. You've been really helpful.' He threw his hat off and ran out of the door.

Sol looked around at the gloomy, untidy kitchen and shook his head. He glanced at the eels in the tub, and at the dead one lying forlorn on the bench. He placed some dirty plates on the draining board and was about to turn on the tap when Rosie appeared once more.

'Look, I don't want to worry you but I just seen 'im getting in your car.'

'Yes, I said he could use it. For going into town.'

'Oh, you bloody didn't! You know he can't drive?'

'What!?'

'Did he say he could?'

'No, but I assumed—'

'If you want to see your car again you'd better go and stop 'im.'

The two of them rushed from the kitchen, and through the lobby, from where they could hear the grating of gears, the sounds of an engine over-revving, and of spinning wheels churning up gravel. Once outside they saw the car bouncing along the driveway in fits and starts. Sol waved and shouted. He ran after it, but could not catch up, although he followed far enough to see the car pass perilously close to the concrete posts of the main gate and then shoot straight out on to the road without stopping.

He was panting and sweating a little by the time when he returned to the front door, where Rosie had remained.

'You didn't catch 'im, then.'

'No. It's not even my car.'

'Whose is it then?'

'Parlando's.'

'Who?'

'See, the answer doesn't mean anything to you, does it? You shouldn't ask pointless questions.'

'You shouldn't be lending it to Useless Eustace, if it's not yours. Bloody pest he is!'

'How did a get a job here? I can't understand it. He hasn't got a clue.'

'His mum's in charge, 'ent she. That's 'ow.'

'The manageress. Ah! All falls into place.'

'I suppose I'll 'ave to do the cooking now,' said Rosie. 'Bloody last thing I need. Don't suppose you fancy 'elping, do you?'

Sol was about to turn down the request, but the longer he thought about it, the more appealing became the prospect of her company, and certainly a better option than mingling with the pretend sleuths.

Back in the kitchen Rosie picked up the grubby book of recipes. 'Bloody eels!' she exclaimed disdainfully. 'And look what 'ees written 'ere! Stuffed quails! Eustace wouldn't know a quail if one flew up his arse.' She tossed the book to one side. 'Bugger that for a game of soldiers. I'm not cooking no quails or eels.'

'What about the guests, Rosie? They'll be expecting it and I don't think the manageress will—'

'Guests?'

'Yes.'

'Did you say *guests*?' She laughed a sardonic laugh. 'You didn't think Eustace was cooking for the guests, did you?'

'Well, yes. I mean—'

'Useless Eustace, cooking for 'otel guests!? Don't be daft. You've seen what 'ees like.'

'I did see. And I had grave doubts, but—'

'This place has got stars for its food!' She laughed again.

'I can't understand why he was pretending. He said he . . . ' Sol hesitated as he tried to recall exactly what Eustace had said.

'Come 'ere,' said Rosie. 'Let me show you somethin'.' She beckoned with her finger and Sol followed.

They passed along an ill-lit corridor and when they came to a door Rosie opened it and stood aside to let Sol inspect what lay within. It was another kitchen. And it was clean, spacious and throbbing with activity. People worked with a calm concentration, so much so that they did not even notice the two faces staring in at them. A chef put finishing touches to a large, pink, quivering blancmange. The starter was already prepared, with greenery and fruit sauce, on clean white plates, rows and aisles of them. A plump salmon lay on its platter, next the steamer from which it had recently emerged. A chef of Oriental extraction, perhaps brought in especially for the occasion, was garnishing it with lemons, and vegetables that had been carved into the shapes of stars, leaves and flowers. Another stood at a stove tenderly turning a sauce, now and then adding a pinch of green herb.

Sol turned to Rosie, a puzzled expression on his face.

She beckoned him out and closed the door behind him.

'Why are there two kitchens?' asked Sol as they returned along the corridor.

She explained that the smaller of the two belonged to an earlier era of the hotel's history, but had proved unsuitable for providing gourmet meals for large groups of guests. It was as simple as that.

They were back in the other kitchen. 'We just use this one for the staff meals now. Quite 'andy actually. This 'ere is all the staff quarters. That's my room. Up the stairs. There.'

'So old Useless Eustace was just preparing the staff meal.'

'That's right.'

'Or rather, wasn't.'

'Well that's what we gotta do now. C'mon let's get busy, or they'll be in 'ere moaning.'

She went into a larder that lay off the kitchen and emerged with a 28-pound bag of flour, which she placed heavily on the central work bench.

'Never mind bloody quails and eels. Stew and dumplin's. And beer. That's good enough. How are you on dumplin's?'

'Not bad.'

'There's some suet in the larder. Salt too.' She pointed. 'Water's in the tap. Here, use this to mix.' She placed a ceramic bowl on the table, white, except for where the glaze had worn away. 'Bloody eels! Here give us a 'and.'

Together they lifted the tub on to the floor. 'Just leave it there for now. Can't be bothered. Bloody Eustace can sort it out. 'Ere!' She blew and brushed the dust from a smooth wooden board and placed it next to the bowl. 'You can use this – mind you puts flour on the board though.'

'Yes, I know how to make dumplings.'

She had a bossy tone, did Rosie, but Sol didn't mind. In fact, he found it quite endearing.

There was a small alcove in the kitchen. It had probably at one time held a bed, or bunks, where weary kitchen hands had slept after a long day's drudgery. Now it contained metal lockers. Rosie opened one of them. She unzipped her dress and slid it down her body. At the sound of the zip running its course, Sol looked up. His mouth dropped. Had he been a man of less self-control no doubt drool would have rolled from the edges. But he just stared in wonderment at a woman transformed. His eyes roved over the black underwear, and the white flesh in between. He admired the buoyancy and symmetry in her breasts. Her behind, too. Sol hated Hottentot buttocks and dimpled cellulite, and the starved, emaciated cheeks some vain-foolish women sported on the beach or catwalk, yet which have no rightful place outside the realm of human atrocity. Rosie's was neither of these extremes. There was ample marble-smooth flesh but formed into shapely firmness by the quick purposeful strides that made up her long working day.

She lifted her head suddenly, saw she was being observed, and smiled the coy smile of one flattered but a little shy.

'Don't want to go getting my nice dress all dirty, do I?'

'No. No, indeed,' was all Sol could say.

She slipped on a white smocklike garment, not unlike those used in a surgical theatre. A tall, floppy hat completed the outfit and did much to dispel the feminine allure that had so magnetized Sol.

'You should be wearing an 'at too. Don't suppose it matters. Stick your jacket in 'ere.' And she indicated a locker. 'Pity to get that all messed up.'

Sol rolled up his shirt sleeves. He measured out some of the flour into the bowl and poured in a proportionate amount of suet. Then he began to blend the small greasy pellets with the fine powdered flour. His mind connected the blending motion, the gentle but firm squeezing between thumb and the first two fingers, with stimulating a woman's nipples. He imagined himself performing this arousing act on Rosie. He thought of her near-nakedness of a few moments ago, and a wave of excitement coursed through him. He looked from the mixing bowl toward her. She was very focused on her work, chopping an onion, with the sharp knife clacking out a staccato rhythm on the bench top. She swept the cut pile to one side with a dismissive gesture and began on another onion. The tears streamed down her cheeks. He wanted to say something touching and witty but all he could think of was, 'Don't cry Rosie! It might never happen,' and was immediately ashamed at having come up with something so trite.

She looked up, a little piqued, it seemed, at being interrupted. 'What you sayin'?'

'Oh, nothing,' replied Sol.

'How you gettin' on there?'

'Pretty well,' he lied.

She was cutting carrots now, with impatient frigging-like movements. She seemed very capable. He knew if he took a pair of callipers and measured the thickness of each slice, they would be the same to within a millimetre.

Once more Rosie broke off from her task. 'What you lookin' at me with googoo eyes for? Have you done?'

Lost in reverie, Sol's work had slowed right down.

She looked in to the bowl. 'Come on! You're as bad as old Eustace. Get a move on! Here let me show you.'

She pushed him gently aside, began to blend vigorously and had done more in ten seconds then he had in ten minutes.

'Got to put some *effort* into it. See!'

'You're a hard taskmaster, Rosie. That's all I can say.'

'I am 'ard,' she affirmed and returned to her own task. 'Got to be in this bloody life.' She looked up at him and with a coquettish little smile added: 'I can be soft sometimes, though.'

Finally the dumplings were ready for the pot. Rosie examined one of the doughy balls and nodded approvingly. Everything was cooking nicely. The big pot of vegetables and meat was boiling and there were potatoes baking in the oven.

'You'd better 'urry up if you're goin' to eat,' said Rosie

'I'm not getting stew, then?'

'Nah. You're getting' the bloody good stuff. You're a guest.'

'I'd almost forgotten. Such a strange turn of events. Yes. Um, perhaps see you later?'

'You might,' she answered, casually.

161

13

The amateur sleuths lined both sides of a long table in the wainscoted dining room of the old hotel. The brass and crystal of chandeliers hung over their heads, oil paintings adorned two of the walls while on another hung a large mirror with an elaborate gilded frame. In two corners of the room stood suits of armour. The curtains were heavy and royal purple, the floor of polished wood that resounded loudly to the fall of leather-soled shoes.

The salmon Sol had watched being prepared in the kitchen was greatly enjoyed.

'Beautiful fish,' everyone said at some point in the course of the meal, nodding to those next to them and opposite.

It was enormous. No matter how much they ate – and most had at least two helpings – there always seemed to be plenty remaining. It lay on the platter, its unseeing eyes and gaping down-turned mouth creating an impression of unmitigated dismay, as if at the moment of death it saw clearly for the first time that life was just one great upstream struggle that ended in being boiled and eaten. Eventually, of course, as more of the pink flesh was consumed, it did lose its distinct piscine form, so the bones lay exposed, and in places silvery blue-grey skin lay like parchment on the chrome platter.

'Ask the chef where it's from, would you?' one diner said to a waiter.

On learning it was from the Tay, he announced:

'I thought as much. You can tell, you know. When they've swum that little bit further, the flesh is that much firmer. Can't beat a Tay salmon – though the Tweed's not bad.'

'Mind you,' added another, 'you can take things too far. It can't be said extra mileage makes the Norwegian variety superior to all its cousins.'

'There are limits to everything,' agreed the first. 'Because something is good, it never follows automatically that more is better. No, the Norwegians can keep their fish. Give me the Tay every time.'

Others nodded their agreement.

'The Dee's not bad,' volunteered another, though a fraction too late, for the conversation had flowed on and no-one bothered to acknowledge his remark.

Sol did as he often did at formal functions such as these. He leaned towards the person sitting opposite him, made a show of reading his name badge, and said:

'Don't tell me! You must be . . . '

In this case it was Catchpole Ragoon, who just happened to be the owner and editor of the newspaper Sol read most days. He was in his early sixties, tall, silver-haired and patrician. Some at the table might have judged Sol's flippant forwardness to be unseemly and disrespectful. But Catchpole had a fond regard for young people and was not at all put out by Sol. On the contrary, he quickly warmed to him.

'I'd say you were a newspaper editor,' continued Sol.

'Lord! You're not psychic, are you?'

'No. I read your paper.'

It seemed to surprise Catchpole that anyone did.

'Your name's in it,' Sol informed him. 'On the left-hand side of the letters page.'

'Ah.'

'I see you've changed your crossword compiler recently.'

'That's right.'

Sol was about to voice his complaint about the fall in quality, when the editor continued:

'My wife does it now.'

'Really?' said Sol. 'Interesting.'

'Yes, she "fancied a go," as she put it. Hate crosswords, myself. Bloody waste of time. What d'you think, though? Her crosswords. Any good?'

'How shall I put it . . . ?' A tight smile formed. 'They do display a woman's touch. They're very, er, different.'

'Different?'

'Challenging.'

'That's good, isn't it?'

'Exactly. It's the whole point. If you're not challenged, there's no point to a crossword. Yes, do please pass on my congratulations to your good lady. I assume it's just modesty that prevents her putting her name to her work.'

Catchpole nodded absently and took a sip of wine. 'Have you any ideas?' he asked Sol. 'I mean, about the murder?'

'A few, actually. Now you mention it.'

'Do you indeed! Well, I wouldn't jump to any conclusions if I were you. Although I'd be interested to know what you and that little man in the tweed jacket were nattering on about.'

'I bet you would, Catchpole. Classified, I'm afraid. But I will tell you this: he plays his part wonderfully. Wonderful acting. Marvellous.'

'Talking of acting,' said the man sitting next to Catchpole, 'how's your sister getting on?'

'Butters? Oh, well enough, I think. Still getting parts. She was in the town the other day. Making a film. On location, I think they call it.'

Butters? thought Sol, who then said:

'Oh, that is extraordinary! I was there too. I was an extra in the film. Butters Nicobar?'

'That's right,' replied Catchpole. 'Married an actor. Sam. Charming man – unusual name, though.'

Sol's own views on the acting ability of Butters Nicobar revolved around the conjecture that she must have a curtain rod inserted into her back passage before going on camera. But it was the diplomat in Sol that spoke:

'She's a wonderful actress,' he chimed, with all the false conviction he could muster. 'She must be due an award soon, surely?'

Catchpole laughed. 'I really can't imagine why.'

'How do you mean?' said Sol.

'She's wooden! There's no getting away from it. *Wooden.*'

'No, not wooden,' countered Sol, feeling obliged to defend his original position. 'There's so much emotional excess on the screen these days that when someone comes along who's restrained, and dignified, we—'

'Oh, don't get me wrong, she's a lovely gal and a pleasure to be with. But she's wooden, and I've told her that. You know what would be the perfect part for Butters?'

'No,' replied Sol.

'A railway sleeper. A bloody railway sleeper.'

Sol protested once more, as did a few others.

In a sense it gratified Catchpole that others jumped to his sister's defence, but he held his ground. 'There's no point pretending, is there? Not at my age. Mind you, I should be a little more discreet. That's her nephew at the end of the table.'

Sol looked where Catchpole indicated, to four young men in earnest conversation.

'That's Bowker. My brother Bernard's boy.'

At the mention of the name Bernard the image of an aquiline profile formed in Sol's head.

'Is Bernard a dentist, by any chance?' asked Sol.

'Good grief! You *are* psychic!'

Sol smiled. 'No, I met him recently. He was standing in for my usual dentist.'

'Now there's a case in point. My brother Bernard. Was ever there anything more ridiculous? I ask you. A blind man insisting on being a dentist. You didn't let him near your teeth, did you?'

'Of course not,' lied Sol. 'But again, and forgive me for saying so, you judge him harshly. Surely we must admire his courage and tenacity?'

'It's a fine line between determination and pig-headed stupidity, and I know on which side Bernard falls. For example, he spent every day for four months, one summer, in a hot-air balloon over Alaska.'

'Whatever for?' asked the company, amused and intrigued.

'Looking for the North-West Passage. Yes, that's right, *the* North-West Passage. The one they realized three centuries ago didn't exist. "Oh, I know you can butt a way through the ice with these modern ships, but I ask you. "Commercial possibilities," he said. "Open up the dried-fish trade with Johnny Eskimo."'

'Good for the heart, dried fish,' remarked Sol. 'Perhaps he was on to something.'

'But what's the point of living a long life in the frozen wastes? And the women! Let me say this to you, Sol. Never take an Inuit for a wife. They smear themselves with rancid whale fat and don't get out of bed for six months of the year.'

'Thanks for the advice, Catchpole. I won't.'

Sol glanced down at Bowker, who seemed oblivious of the fact that the follies of his father were being discussed. Observing his modest, smoothly contoured nose, Sol said:

'He takes more after Hetty, doesn't he?'

'Well, it's Hetty I feel sorry for,' said Catchpole. 'What she has to put up with. It's all rather awkward, you know. Bloody difficult for all of us. Having to send her cheques all the time. But what can you do when it's your own flesh and blood?'

Sol noticed Rosie. It appeared her duties were limited to the far end of the table from where he was sitting. He tried to catch her eye, but she seemed never to be quite looking in his direction. He watched in the mirror as she walked away from the table. Rosie didn't realize she was being observed and, as she walked, looked over to where Sol was sitting, an expression of critical curiosity on her face. She almost paid for her inattention when the dining room door opened just as she approached. There was a clatter as a pile of plates slipped, but they remained on her tray. A few items of cutlery fell to the floor, and she rested the tray on the buffet table while she retrieved them. It could have been much worse. Sol turned to admire her shapely crupper as she crouched down, and then smiled when their eyes met.

And he continued to observe her from time to time.

Towards the end of the meal Sol took a break from conversation. He was staring into his glass, reflecting on how well matched were the colours of the wine and the curtains, when he heard from afar, very clearly through the fug of well oiled chitchat, the sound of howling. He glanced around him, but no-one else seemed to have heard. Then once more, the same sound: distant but distinct and unnerving in its strangeness. It sounded human, or sub-human, and it seemed to signify triumph and victory, rather than pain or fear.

Sol turned to the man next to him. 'I say, did you notice that howling sound just then?'

The man smiled and answered, in a dramatic tone:

'*I must warn you, Sir Henry, under no circumstances venture out on the moor alone.*' Then he added, 'No, I can't say I heard anything.'

'That's because', interjected the man sitting opposite Sol's neighbour, 'you were talking and not listening.'

This fellow was stout and fair, and spoke with a Teutonic accent. He wagged his finger playfully. 'And, you know, it is a far, far better thing for a sleuth to be a listener than a talker.'

'I see,' answered the man who had been chided. 'So you heard something, did you?'

'Oh yes,' answered the German. 'And I saw that my friend here' – indicating Sol – 'did too.'

'And have you formed an opinion as to its cause?' asked Sol.

'Well, you know, it is now the time of the new moon, and animals have always howled when the moon was dark as well as when it was full.'

'Syzygy,' said another, eager to display his astronomical knowledge. It was he who had championed Dee salmon and who was having a hard time making an impact on proceedings. When no-one even looked to see who had spoken, he withdrew into his shell once more.

'Our primitive ancestors,' continued Klaus, 'who were not so far removed from the animals, after all, they also felt very unsettled at the time of the new moon. Naturally enough, for where there is no light, there is danger and fear. As for the hound our friend alluded too with his amusing mimicry? Well, I have already in the afternoon explored the grounds, and there are no signs of canine life.'

'Used to be, though.' It was Catchpole. 'Used to be dogs. Yes, I've been here before. Few years ago now: damn great beast of an Alsatian. Never mind its bite, the bark used to terrify the wits out of the guests. There was talk of putting it down, but someone – or something – saved them the bother. Yes, very strange. The dog was found dead at the edge of the grounds. Every bone in its body broken, I'm told. Lord knows what could have done that. All kept a bit hush-hush, I recall. Not the sort of thing you want bruited about.'

Everyone agreed; it was very odd.

Sol read the German's name-badge. 'Well, Klaus, if not dogs, then what?'

'I know it is a common thing to do, but sometimes we should not look beyond the obvious. And so I ask you, aside from dogs and wolves, and others of the canine family, what other beast is noted for howling?'

People puzzled, but no-one offered an answer.

'The answer is quite simple,' continued the German. 'The howler monkey, of course! Now, I can see you smiling and saying to your selves, "He must think we're all *dumkopfs* here." But that is because you are assuming I am talking about wild monkeys. And of course I am not.' He excused himself, and blew his nose before continuing:

'I am sure all of you are aware that the residence of the distinguished, but eccentric, anthropologist Sir Vyvyan P'hucks – I think that is how you say it – lies not ten kilometres from here in a south-westerly direction.'

Sol for one hadn't known that, but indicated that he had.

'Sir Vyvyan spent a lot of time in Madagascar, you know, and when he returned to this country he shipped many wild beasts over here. Howler monkeys are amongst them. And he keeps them all in a little zoological garden. And of course for much of the time you cannot hear them, but at night, when the wind is coming from that way – which presently it is; earlier I felt it on my cheeks, warm and moist – then that is a different matter. And then too the dark moon and fear amplify the sounds of the big males. I expect, if we all listen, we will hear some more howling before the night is out. But I am not sure it will lead us to the murderer.'

'Well done, Klaus,' said Catchpole. 'You always did have an original line on everything. And your homework's as meticulous as ever.'

'Not quite,' offered Sol. He recalled an insult of a cross-word clue from one of the previous week's papers: *Amazonian ape makes gaffe*. 'Howlers are found in South America, not Madagascar.'

'Oh well,' said Klaus dismissively. 'Perhaps it was Brazil of which I was thinking. Would you excuse me, gentlemen? I have some more detective work to be doing before the night is out.'

'Yes. Suppose we'd better get on,' said Catchpole, and signalled to Bowker and his three friends. 'We're going for a poke about the grounds. Like to come? Beat about the undergrowth for a while, see what we can find?'

'Thank you,' replied Sol, 'but I've a few leads of my own to follow up.'

'Of course. Well, good luck.'

'Thank you. And do mind out for the hogweed. There's a lot of it about.'

'The whatweed?'

Because the newspaper proprietor was a city man, Sol had to describe what the plant looked like, and why it was a hazard.

The diners left the table and gravitated towards the lounge. There, in pairs, or groups of three or four, they began to discuss in earnest the Murder Mystery that lay before them. Sol, of course, had no idea what he was supposed to do. He stood alone by a table bearing cups, silver coffee pots, and plates of mints and petits fours. There were also glasses of wine left over from the drinks reception. A portly balding man with nervous flitting eyes approached the table and nodded at Sol, who returned the greeting.

'I think I saw who did the murder,' said the man. 'It was the strangest thing.'

'Quick work,' remarked Sol.

The man picked up a glass of red wine in either hand, and downed each in a single motion. He returned the glasses and gazed despairingly over the table.

'You think there'd be some brandy, wouldn't you?'

'Try the bar,' replied Sol, pointing.

'Roderick, by the way.' He held out his hand. 'Will you join me?'

'Thank you, no.' He watched Roderick hurry toward the bar with a peculiar waddling motion.

'*Hello!*'

Sol looked round and saw Eustace standing in the doorway.

'I've forgotten your name. Can I come in?'

Sol indicated that he was free to do so.

Eustace stood next to him and looked around nervously, as if he shouldn't really be here.

'Better give me the car keys, while I remember,' said Sol.

'I wouldn't mind a drink, actually,' said Eustace, turning to address the wine on the table.

'Where's the car?'

'It's all right. Just get me a drink first.' Once more he surveyed the room shiftily.

Sol looked worried, but handed over a glass of wine. Eustace took a sip and looked pleased to be hobnobbing with the dinner-suited guests.

'Keys?' Sol reminded him.

'I haven't got them.'

'What! Where are they?'

172

'I don't know. I think they're still in the car.'

'Well, go and get them.'

'I can't.'

'Why not?'

'I . . . It's, er—'

'Bloody hell! *Where – is – the – car?* Come on, what's going on here?' Sol struggled to contain his anger and keep his voice down. Some of the others looked across, no doubt imagining this little unfolding drama to be some sort of clue to the Murder Mystery.

Eustace put a finger to his mouth and said:

'*Shh!*'

'Just tell me what you've done with the fucking car!'

'It's stuck.'

'What do you mean, stuck? *Where?*'

'In a ditch.'

'How did it get into the ditch?'

'I don't know. It just went in. I was pushing it. I was trying to turn it round and it—'

'*Why* were you pushing it?!'

'It was pointing the wrong way and I couldn't get it to go backwards.'

'You don't push cars, you halfwit. You use gears. You do a three-point turn.'

'Don't shout at me! I don't like it.'

'And you left the keys in the car?'

'It's all right for you,' whined Eustace. 'I had to walk back.'

'What the bloody hell you doin' in 'ere?' It was Rosie.

'He's only gone and put my car in a ditch.'

'Oh, you stupid pillock!'

'Shut up,' said Eustace, looking pained and raising his hand, as if to shield himself from the harsh words. 'Leave me alone!'

173

'I did warn you, didn't I?' she said, addressing Sol. She looked sternly at Eustace. 'Where's this ditch then?'

'Up round Enham.'

'Enham! What was you doin' up there? Nowhere near the bloody town!'

'Shut up, Rosie! Just shut up. You've always got to go sticking your tits into everything.'

'Don't talk to her like that!' shouted Sol, and pushed Eustace, spilling some of the wine from his glass. The rest of the company were observing curiously. One or two took notes.

'You're bloody in for it when your mum 'ears about this.'

'What do you mean?'

'You'll get a right bum-basting.'

'I won't! Course I won't.'

'Drinkin'. Drivin' a car. You're in for a good hidin'.'

'She won't know unless you tell her, Rosie.'

'Why shouldn't I tell her? You're a bloody pest!'

Rosie stormed out. Eustace looked after her, and then at Sol. He appeared anxious.

'I don't know what she's talking about.' He laughed unconvincingly. 'My mother doesn't hit me. Huh. I'm far too old for that.' He put the wine glass to his lips, hesitated, then put it back on the table, even though it was still half full.

Rosie reappeared.

'I was just going,' said Eustace, and hurried away.

'I wouldn't wish his mother on anyone. Not even him,' remarked Sol.

'He'll catch it all right. I've seen 'er when she gets goin'.'

'Whereabouts is Enham? I'll need to sort out the car.'

'About four mile away.'

'I see, and it's marked on the maps, is it?'

'I dunno. Suppose so.'

Sol took from his wallet the AA card Parlando had

174

given him. 'I'll go and phone them now. See you later, Rosie?'

'You might.'

'And whereabouts in Enham is it?' asked the girl at the AA HQ.

'Um, not sure about that. But I imagine there's only six hovels and a church in a place like Enham.'

'We need to know exactly where your car is if we're going to retrieve it.'

'It'll be the only white Ford stuck in a ditch thereabouts, if that's any help.'

There was a sigh followed by a silence at the other end of the line. 'Don't worry. I expect the mechanic will find it,' said the woman.'

Sol asked if he needed to be there to meet the pick-up truck, and she said there would be no need. The AA man would tow it to the hotel and leave the keys at reception.

14

In the staff kitchen Rosie, having finished her waiting duties, was clearing up after the staff meal.

'Hi, Rosie!' chimed Sol as he descended the stairs.'

She looked up from the sink. 'It's you, is it? Well, now you're 'ere you can stay and 'elp me clear up all this mess.'

Sol surveyed the greasy clutter of the sink and draining boards. 'You make it sound like a chore, Rosie. Of course I'll stay and help you. What shall I do?'

'Give me an 'and with these perishin' eels for a start.'

They each took a handle of the tub and walked along a corridor to a back door. It was slightly ajar and Rosie pushed it open with her foot.

'Have you got some place for them to go, Rosie? A pond, maybe?'

'No pond 'ere. Used to be. They filled it in though. 'ere we are.'

'Where?'

They put the tub on the ground and she pointed to a rusting drain cover, a little over two-foot square.

'But you can't just tip them down the drain.'

'Course I can. They's just eels.'

'But they're alive!'

'I can see that. And they can swim, cain't they?'

'But this is a sewer.'

'And where do sewers go?'

'I don't know. Sewage works, I suppose.'

'This one don't.'

'How do you know?'

'Cos it bloody goes into the river, then to the sea. Always has. And that's where eels comes from, the sea. They swims up the river and gets caught. The men puts nets out for 'em. It's a storm drain too. Gets filled up when it rains heavy. They'll get carried off all right.'

Sol shrugged. He looked sympathetically down into the tub of oblivious eels.

'Honestly! You town people with yer daft ideas about animals.'

'And which daft ideas might these be?'

'Listen, it says in the Bible we got dominion over the animals. And birds, and fishes. And eels is fishes, of sorts. It says that, in the beginning bit.'

'Does it?'

She looked at him severely. 'Yes, it do. And that means we can treat 'em how we want. Now, you gonna help me, or not?'

At each end of the drain cover was a hand-sized hollow with a thin metal bar that could be gripped between fingers and palm. On Rosie's command they raised the heavy cover a few inches and laid it on the grass to one side. Sol grimaced at the weight, and the escape of foul air.

Although the sun had set, where they stood was well enough lit by the hotel's floodlights, which shone down above the level of the surrounding bushes. The shaft of the drain descended about five or six feet. There were iron rungs set in the concrete to facilitate access.

Rosie grabbed one end of the tub and instructed Sol to grab the other.

'Hang on,' said Sol who was peering into the shaft. It was dark, but a small area was lit up by one of the floods.

'What is it now?' said Rosie, impatiently.

'There's something there. I can see—'

'Don't be daft!'

She crouched down next to Sol, who pointed. 'See.'

'There is n'all. It's a body!'

'Don't say that, Rosie,' groaned Sol. 'I've had my fill of bodies this past week.'

'Blimey! It's 'im! What the bloody 'ell's 'ee doin' down there?'

'Who?'

'The jacket. That's 'is tweed jacket.'

Sol leaned as far as he could into the shaft. 'It *is* a jacket. I can – Shad! What are you up to?' He laughed and said to Rosie:

'It's the game, the Murder Mystery. Shad! Really this is taking things too far.' Sol laughed again, but there came no sound from the drain, save the brittle note of water flowing over uneven stone.

Sol and Rosie looked at one another uneasily.

'Don't like the look of that,' said Rosie. 'He 'ent right, is he?'

'He might just be unconscious. Fell, maybe. Banged his head.'

'Don't think so, do you? How's he goin' to get the lid back on, for a start.'

Sol pondered this point. 'Well. Um, let's see—'

'Couldn't even lift it. Squirt like 'im.'

Sol removed his jacket and handed it to Rosie. 'I suppose it'll be me who goes down there.' He peered into the dark shat. 'Got any matches?'

'Don't go bloody lightin' a match down there! Get gas in sewers. Burnin' gas.'

'Yes,' replied Sol, a touch irritably. 'It's called methane. Well. Go and find me a torch then.'

179

Rosie returned presently with a heavy-duty rubber-bodied flashlight. Sol descended the shaft, flinching as some cobwebs caught his face. His foot landed on part of Shad and he swore and apologized. He shone the beam. Shad's face was turned sideways so his cheek was resting against the filthy, sewage-stained stone. It wore an anguished expression. The eyes were dull and not quite closed, the lips parted. He looked closer and saw that Shad's teeth were false. The upper plate had slipped so that the incisors protruded between and beyond his lips. As like as not, mused Sol grimly, the natural ones had been extracted by Upper Remove bullies determined to discover where Shad hid his tuck.

Sol rested the back of his hand on Shad's forehead.

'What's 'appening?' called out Rosie.

'He's not cold,' said Sol. But he knew all this meant was that he was not long dead. He felt for a pulse at the side of the neck but didn't really expect to find one. He looked the body up and down and saw no obvious signs of foul play.

Sol sighed wearily. 'He is dead, Rosie. We'll need to get him up.'

'No! Leave 'im!'

'What?'

'Just *leave* 'im. Ent nothin' you can do for 'im now.'

'That's crazy. We can't just leave him in a stinking sewer.'

'Leave 'im be! Honestly, you bloody soft-headed . . . People dies all the time. What's so special about it? We all gotta go sometime.'

Sol heard a scratching sound and saw scurrying dark shapes. 'Come on, Rosie. Give me a hand. There are rats crawling over him.' He shone the torch up the shaft and saw Rosie looking down at him. She appeared quite sinister lit from beneath.

'No! I wants nothin' to do with it. You want 'im out of

there, get 'im up yourself. Or get your bloody posh sleuth friends in there to 'elp.' And with that, she walked off.

Sol called after her, but to no avail. He looked down at the body. One of the bolder rats was sniffing around Shad's ear.

'Fuck off!' shouted Sol, and swung at it with the torch. The rat darted away, but not very far, and turned to await another opportunity.

Sol wondered how he might get the body out of the sewer. It wasn't heavy, but it was still cumbersome in the confined space. He would need to try to get it across his shoulder in a kind of fireman's lift. He got a grip on an arm and leg, but as he stepped back his foot slipped in something soft. He pointed the torch downward and the beam picked out turds and toilet paper. He suddenly felt nauseous, and a little faint. He climbed up the shaft and sat on the grass, happy to be breathing in sweet air. He sat for a while, just looking at the grass in the warm evening. Then he became aware of someone standing behind him. He turned.

'Thought you might want this,' said Rosie gently, as she handed him his jacket.

He took it, and she sat down beside him.

'What was 'is name again?'

'Shad Yeazleby. Good lad, Shad! He was so easy to please. You only had to direct a scintilla of human warmth towards him.'

'How long d'you know 'im?'

Sol thought. He looked at his watch. 'About six hours.'

Rosie seemed surprised. 'Ee weren't an old friend, then?'

'No.'

There was a silence before Rosie continued:

'I'm sorry too. But you get this body up, and you got to bring in the police. The proper police, I mean. Then you'll 'ave to go down to the station. Me too, and I 'ent got the time. Now I know you didn't do it, but when they get stuck into you down there, you'll admit to it. And six other crimes, most like.'

'I've heard all this before – it's a long story. I'll tell you sometime.'

'People goes missin' all the time. Most of 'em never turns up.'

'Well, I don't suppose anyone will miss Shad. Thing is, Rosie, the days are getting warmer. He's going to start to stink.'

'That's my problem, 'ent it. You won't even be 'ere.'

'I suppose not.'

Once again they lapsed into silence. Then Rosie asked:

'You want me to say a prayer, or somethin'?'

Sol looked at her, smiled, then said:

'That's a nice thought.'

She closed her eyes, put her hands together, and looked very solemn. 'Ashes to ashes, dust to dust. If God won't 'ave you, the Devil must. Amen.'

Sol looked askance. 'What liturgy's that from?'

'Dunno. Just read it in a book once. Right! One more thing to do.'

She dragged the tub to the shaft and tipped the contents into it. Sol didn't protest.

'Come on,' ordered Rosie. 'Up off your arse and 'elp me with this lid.'

Together they dragged the cast-iron cover to the drain shaft and put it back in place. Rosie stamped on it a few times, then took some dust in her hand and let it run into the fine gaps between the edge of the cover and the surrounding ground. Then, as if playing cymbals, she smacked the residual dirt off her hands. She took Sol's arm and slowly they walked towards the kitchens.

15

After leaving the drinks reception Shad had gone upstairs to his room to eat sandwiches bought at a railway station earlier in the day. He re-read his script, even though he knew it by heart, and took from one of his cases the items that would serve as 'clues'.

Just as the guests were starting on the salmon, Shad left quietly by the front door and set about distributing the 'clues'. Once or twice he was required to venture beyond the bounds of the hotel, but mostly he kept within them. He ended up, just as the sun was setting, close to the door that led to the kitchens. The last item had to be laid in this area. He looked for a branch, a foot or so above eye level, from which he could hang a single strand of coloured thread. As he did so, two figures, one large, one long, emerged from the shadows.

Shad froze. His mouth fell open and he stared in horror. He felt a savage jolt of pain through his chest and left shoulder. He gasped once or twice, attempted to speak, then fell down dead.

Choy and Clowsie stood over the body and with their poles turned it over, so Shad was facing up at the sky.

'Damn stinking chit,' said Choy. 'What's he dying for? We didn't even do anything.'

'Let's land him some stingers anyway, Choy. Just to show him.'

'Save it, Clowsie. Too late for that.'

'What we going to do with him? Can't leave him here.'

'Don't know, Clowsie.'

'This damn little pisser always gave us trouble.'

'That's right, Clowsie. He wouldn't lie down, this one, and always screamed blue murder.'

'Shall we put him with the other ones?'

'I think the answer's here! Look at the sewer hole. That's the place for him. Open it up.'

Clowsie lifted the cover as if it were the lid of a biscuit tin and threw it to one side. Choy grabbed Shad's corpse by the ankle and dragged it to the edge of the shaft. Then, using their poles, they levered him into the sewer. The cover was replaced.

The waddling drunk, Roderick, had left the dining room and wandered into the store rooms adjacent to the kitchen in search of strong drink. He heard sounds from outside and peered through the dirty pane of a small window at what was taking place. He saw Choy and Clowsie tipping the body down the drain and then, poles over their shoulders, walking off into the rapidly fading light. He was wondering what to do about it all, when an unnerving howl rent the air, closely followed by another.

16

On returning to the kitchen area the first thing Sol did was rid himself of the stench and stain of the sewer. He cleaned the filth from his shoes and at the rest-room sink removed his shirt and washed his face, hands and torso. He examined his shirt and trousers. There was some dust, which he brushed away, but otherwise his clothing had come out remarkably unblemished from the descent.

He returned to the kitchen, where Rosie had broken the back of the washing-up. He joined in, and they were soon finished.

'Well,' she said. 'I reckon we earned a drink.'

Sol followed her into the wine cellar, where she plucked a bottle at random from a rack. As an afterthought, she took another.

'One for luck. Face-ache'll never know, and even if she does she'll blame Useless Eustace.'

'Does she really beat him?'

'Not 'alf! I wouldn't like to be on the end of it.'

'Maybe it was Eustace I heard howling, then.'

'When?'

Sol told her about the sounds he had heard while at the dining table.

'Don't sound like it were 'im.'

'Have you heard of Sir Vyvyan P'hucks, Rosie?'

She thought a moment. 'Yeh, I 'ave. Used to own the big

house t'other side of Wherwell.'

'Used to?'

'Well, ee's dead now. And 'is animals too. Used to have this little zoo in the grounds.'

'With howler monkeys?'

'Yeh, there was monkeys. Suppose they're all dead. They gets old too, don't they? We got to go and see it, when I was a little girl. It was lovely. 'Ere, c'mon! We can go up in my room, if you like. Be more cosy.'

Rosie collected a couple of tumblers and they ascended the winding stairs to her small room with its skylight and sloping ceiling. She took a multi-function pocket-knife from a drawer, flicked out the corkscrew, adroitly opened the bottle, and then filled the tumblers almost to the brim. She took a good mouthful then sat on the bed, leaning against the headboard, legs out in front, knees slightly bent.

'Nice to get the weight off the old pins, eh Rosie? Well, here's to absent friends. Nice knowing you, Shad.'

Rosie appeared solemn and took another gulp of wine. 'Yeh, he ain't comin' back, that one.'

Sol was not the most forward of men when it came to seduction. He had neither great charm nor great confidence in this area. He hated being rebuffed and more often than not this prevented him taking the first step towards his desired goal, which in this case was the fellowship of Rosie's upper thighs. He looked about the room, then studied the surface of his drink, hoping all the while a suggestion from Rosie would carry things forward. He glanced up at her. When she looked up at him, he returned his gaze to the wine glass.

'What?'

'You've got nice legs,' answered Sol.

''ave I?'

'Yes. They're, um, quite long.'

She looked them up and down. 'Are they? Don't know. Never much thought about 'em.'

'You shouldn't take your body for granted, Rosie. I knew a woman once who married her dentist. Said she liked a man who was interested in her body. It didn't matter what part.'

This remark may or may not have been an attempt to catalyse things, but from here on in progress became exponential. Sol sat on the bed. Rosie adjusted her position a little, to give him more room. He leaned forward and kissed her lips. Her response was encouraging, so he placed his hand on her smooth white thigh and slid it up towards her crotch. It all seemed a blur as they pulled their clothes off, but as she lay naked he paused to focus on her sacred region. Up until this point in his life Sol's fumbling forays into sexuality had taken place beneath duvets in dimly lit or dark rooms so his experience of the woman's parts had been tactile rather than visual. As he studied the object, he was put in mind of an exotic fruit or vegetable swollen and split by the power of its own ripeness.

They quickly became as ravening beasts, and for the first time in his life Sol plunged willingly hand-in-hand with another into the sea of abandonment.

'That was all right,' said Rosie when she had got her breath back.

'Yes,' agreed Sol, equally breathless.

'Reckon I could use some more o' that.'

Sol looked down at his member, which had taken on the appearance of a toiling prizefighter whose flagging white body glistened with sweat and had been pummelled to a blotchy purple-red, yet still he was game for more, because the sense to know better had long been battered out of him.

'Yes, well, give me ten minutes and I'll see what I can do.'

187

Sol lay with his arm about Rosie, her head on his chest, each savouring their own state of being.

It was Sol who broke the contented silence. 'What about Eustace, then?'

'What about 'im?'

'Does he satisfy you?'

'None o' your business.'

'You needn't be coy. Just interested to know who's ploughed a furrow before me.'

She lifted her head from the pillow and looked at him. 'It's none o' your bloody business.' But after a pause she relented and said: 'If you must know me and 'im don't 'ave it off.'

'Why not?'

''is mum won't give us 'alf a chance, that's why. Says we got to be married first.'

'Married!' Sol sat up. 'Marrying Eustace? Oh come on, Rosie, you can do better than that.'

'Not round 'ere I cain't.'

'Go to the town or city. There are plenty of men there that'll have you.'

'Na. You wouldn't get my old Mum to move, and she needs me to look after 'er. Besides, if I marries Eustace then I gets the 'otel, don't I?'

Sol thought a moment. 'Um, how does that work then?'

'The Old Cow ent goin' to be around for ever, is she? When she goes, I'll be in charge. We runs the place together, me and Eustace. I'll get some other girl in to be the dogsbody.'

'I'm not sure how to put this, Rosie. But . . . Eustace's mother, she's the manageress here?'

'Yeh.'

'Not the owner.'

'Same difference, ent it?'

'Not exactly. No.'

'What do you mean?'

'Well, although she's in charge, and the boss, she doesn't actually *own* the hotel. She runs it *for* the owners.'

'Why she live 'ere then? And tell everybody what to do?'

'She lives here as a benefit of the job. She's just basically employed to do a job.'

'You shut up,' snapped Rosie, suddenly agitated. 'You're just makin' it up.'

'No, I'm afraid not.'

'Well who *do* it bloody belong to, then?' demanded Rosie hotly.

'Some large company. Some chain that owns hundreds of other hotels and pubs.'

'So what 'appens when she dies? What 'appens then?'

'They'll employ someone else to run it, that's all.'

'What about inheritance and stuff?' continued Rosie. 'Her son should get it. That's the law.'

'It's not hers to bequeath. It doesn't belong to her. So they'll advertise in the papers. For someone experienced in managing hotels. I suppose Eustace could apply, but I don't think he'd make a good manager.'

'Oh, bloody 'ell!' Rosie was close to tears now.

Sol tried to comfort her. 'There's no need to get upset, Rosie.'

'Ent there? Half an hour ago I 'ad a dream. Ent got nothing now!'

'It wasn't much of a dream, was it?'

'You bloody shut up! It was mine. Come in 'ere with your fancy bloody talk. Don't know where I am now. Get out my room! Go on. Don't want you 'ere. Get out!'

Sol was stung by her outburst, feeling himself an innocent party wrongly accused. But once more she told him to get out. She pushed him, and he slid off the bed, banging his elbow painfully on the floor.

'Go on, leave me be,' she shouted. Swiftly she gathered his clothes and threw them out into the corridor. She picked up his shoes and threw these too.

'For Christ's sake, Rosie, give me a chance—'

'*Out!*' she cried, pushing him doorward.

He protested, but she forced him into the corridor. She slammed the door and locked it. Sol knocked and demanded entry.

'Come on, Rosie! Don't be like that,' pleaded Sol, turning the handle and pushing against the locked door. 'Look on the bright side. At least you don't have to marry Eustace now.'

But there was no reply from within.

Sol sighed and gathered up his clothes. He had no time to fulminate against the fickleness of women for at that moment he noticed Catchpole Ragoon standing at the head of the stair.

'Hello there!' he said. A refined man, he affected not to notice that Sol was stark naked.

'Hello, Catchpole,' replied Sol. 'Nice to see you.' He began to dress. 'These are the staff quarters. What brings you up here?'

'Well, I wandered into the kitchen by mistake. Then I heard all this kerfuffle going on and thought it might be a clue of some sort.'

'I see. And how did you get on in the grounds? Any joy there?'

'Drew a blank, I'm afraid. You had any luck?'

'In a manner of speaking.'

'Ah! Hot on the trail are you?'

'Certainly hot, yes.'

'Excellent! That's the stuff. Oh, congratulations, by the way, for spotting the flaw in Klaus's tale. I was going to mention it, but it's better coming from someone young like yourself. Damn Germans! Think they know everything.'

'It was pretty transparent, if you ask me. Never mind the monkeys, Catchpole. I happen to know Sir Vyvyan died five years ago, and his zoo with him.'

'Ah! There's a thing.'

'Tell me, do you think Klaus is the guilty man?'

'Not ruling him out at this stage.'

'Me neither.'

'Ah well, catch you later. In the bar?'

'Look forward to it.'

Sol, who was once more dressed, knocked gently on Rosie's door. Then again, a little louder. When there was no answer he put his ear to the door and heard a faint sound of snoring within, as of a motorbike in the distance.

In the bar a few sleuths had stopped investigating for the day and were sitting together, drinking and chatting. Sol nodded in their direction but did not feel like joining them. He looked around, but could not see Catchpole. Roderick was in his element. He sat on his own looking quite florid, but happily cradling a huge brandy which now and then he swirled and savoured. Sol waved in his direction, but received no acknowledgement. This didn't surprise him. He imagined that the world beyond the brandy glass would be well out of focus by now.

The manageress was serving behind the bar. She was chatting to the tall, arrogant-looking sleuth who had snubbed Shad. Andrus. Sol knew if he went to the bar and asked for a drink she would ignore him and carry on talking. She was hard-faced, not to put too fine a point on it – a feature which she unwittingly accentuated by sweeping her straw-coloured hair back in a bun. She was big for a woman, too; not fat, but with a large, big-boned frame. Sol imagined that at school she won the prize for throwing the discus every sports day. If he were a film director he would not cast her in the role of hotel manageress, but as a female guard in a concentration camp, terrorizing the hapless inmates, and sweetly complimenting the commandant on his 'pretty lampshades'. Sol knew you had to be strong with women like that. If not, they would simply crush you. So what chance would someone like Shad stand against a woman like her? Poor Shad.

Sol went to the desk to collect his key. There was no-one there, but he saw his car keys hanging on the peg next to his room key. He retrieved the car keys, and went outside. It was dark, but the parking area was floodlit and Parlando's car had indeed been returned. Sol examined it. There were a few small scratches that appeared to be new, but overall it was in better shape than he had hoped. He patted the bonnet and returned to the lobby. As he plucked his room key from the board his eye was drawn to the one for Room 18. Shad's room. Sol looked around him, then took Shad's key from its hook and slipped it into his pocket.

Sol switched on the main light and observed that Shad's room was much like his own. One of the suitcases was on the floor, the other lay flat on the bed; closed but, judging by the position of the brass clasps, not locked.

If Shad had been murdered, Sol quickly concluded, there was no evidence of it in this room. No signs of a violent struggle, or even of a break-in. He looked under the bed, but found nothing there.

Sol drew the curtains together and then examined the contents of the case on the bed. There were clothes, as might be expected, but also a number of thick hardback diaries and an A3 folder. Out of respect Sol hesitated, for a man's private world does not necessarily die with him.

He flipped through the pages of one of the volumes, too quickly to read properly, although he could see that it was an account of school life. Finally, curiosity got the better of him. He opened the volume towards the back and began to read:

I do wish I could have gone to the Alps with mother and father. I think I would have liked it, despite what they said. I know my health isn't good – at least that's what I am told – but isn't mountain air good for you? Ah well, I imagine they had lots of things to do that didn't require a 'little boy' around. But I suppose Christmas at school isn't so bad. The season even seemed to mellow Cacknacker a little. We were excused lessons on Christmas Day, although Matron had us polishing the desks and the floor in the classrooms. At chow time there was a whole lot of food – I think it was the stuff the big shops couldn't sell, and it would go off if they left it over the holiday. Choy and Clowsie took it all. They said there was some oranges I could have, and, of course, I 'fell for it', like I always do! There were about half a dozen in a mesh bag, and boy did they 'let me have it' with this. I think it was just a lark at first, but Choy and Clowsie just don't know when to stop. There weren't too many bruises, but it was sore afterwards, and I was quite groggy for a while. And later on, in the evening, I couldn't go to the toilet properly. I went to see Matron, who looked at me sternly, wagged her finger (as she does!) and said: 'I've told you before about playing with the rough boys. You don't listen, do you, Shad Yeazleby? I've a mind to send you to the Headmaster.' But then she softened and said as it was Christmas she imagined Cacknacker didn't want to be bothered with disobedient boys. She looked me over and said it was nothing a good cold bath wouldn't put right. Three cheers for Matron! A heart of gold beneath that craggy exterior.

Sol noticed a little telling slip on the word 'gold' which
had been written first as 'cold' before the 'c' was crossed out
and replaced with a 'g'. In another section was written:

> Arrived early in class today for the Latin test, only to discover
> someone had dropped an anvil on to my desk. (I wonder
> who!!!) What a mess it was. Put me out a bit, if I'm honest,
> and I didn't do as well as I might have. Cacknacker wasn't
> much pleased either. (Ouch!)

Sol turned the pages and read further accounts of toil,
crushing discipline and terrifying cruelty, mostly recorded
in a stoic, matter-of-fact, at times, cheery, tone.

> Furnace duty today – what a bore! What a horrible, tedious
> bore. When I arrived poor Pup was doing his stint, stripped
> to the waist with his tie knotted about his middle. How fragile
> he looked with his pale torso smeared with coal dust and his
> puny arms as thin as the shaft of the shovel he wielded. It's
> so awkward to shovel the coal. The heat's terrible when you
> open the furnace door, so you can't stand close enough to
> make sure all the coal goes in – and the opening is at such
> an awkward height for any of the Juniors. Isn't it just typical
> of this cockeyed school! Once you're big and strong enough to
> do the job properly, you no longer have to do it.
>
> I called down to Pup and almost lost my footing on the
> steep iron stairs in my eagerness to relieve him. And even
> though his poor arms must have been aching so, he smiled
> and said, 'Just one more load, Shad. Get you off to a good
> start. It's really hungry today, this old thing. It must be cold
> out, is it?'
>
> It told him it was. Freezing. But he's right about that furnace.
> It has a gluttonous appetite, and there is a real malevolence
> about it. Sometimes it's like it's just waiting for you to swoon

in the heat and fall against its searing hot plates. And I'm sure it would be just as happy with Juniors in its belly, as the black coal we shovel in!

Poor, poor Pup. I fear for him in this horrid place.

'Shad was a survivor,' murmured Sol. 'At least, up until now.'

He picked up and opened the A3 folder. Inside were a number of drawings, some in pencil, but most in pen and ink. There was quite an elaborate one of two youths, bearing a strong resemblance to Clowsie and Choy, heading a band of thugs armed with chains and clubs. They were drawn as giants trampling on buildings and pupils. All that stood in their way was a begowned figure that Sol assumed was Cacknacker. He was sketched as large as the leering youths. He carried a rod of whippy ash and wore an expression of great resolve. Other members of staff stood behind Cacknacker, somewhat less resolute, while more pupils fled toward the safety and protective arm of the Headmaster. In silhouette against the background of the evening sky Shad had sketched, in his goat form, the Devil. It was very impressive, thought Sol; reminiscent, in feel rather than detail, of the apocalyptic works of certain of the Dutch Masters. And he reflected that artistic talent had probably counted for nothing in Cacknacker's School.

Another drawing was a cartoon of a boxing match. One of the fighters was enormous, and portrayed in the time-honoured way with cropped hair, scarred face and crushed nose. His opponent was scrawny, with shorts that reached almost to his ankles. He was about the size of one of the bruiser's gloves. In the picture the big man had just delivered an uppercut to his puny opponent's chin which had lifted him about five feet off the ground. At the ringside was a row of grinning schoolboy faces, their caps set at jaunty angles.

There were photographs too. One, according to a hand-written note on the back, was of Shad, aged three months, being dandled by his parents. There was one also of a happy two-year-old sitting on his mother's knee, and another of a family group taken when he was older. Here everyone was rather stiff and unsmiling. Shad looked very serious, and a little apprehensive in his school uniform. Perhaps, wondered Sol, this was him just before he left for Cacknacker's School for the first time?

There was a pencil sketch of an attractive young woman who bore a resemblance to Shad's mother in the photographs. She wore a flower in her hair and there was a hint of ample cleavage before the clear outline diffused into shading. Another sketch portrayed a plainly wishful-thinking Shad as a teenager in playful wrestle with his father.

Sol froze. He could hear someone in the corridor outside. He watched as the brass door-handle slowly turned and then was released. A few moments later the person's footsteps receded down the corridor. Sol put the diaries and folder back into Shad's case and closed the lid.

'Why on earth', he asked himself, 'would a man carry a past like that around with him?'

Sol went down to the reception desk and, when no-one was looking, returned Shad's key to the Room 18 hook. Then he went upstairs to bed – and to reflect upon an extraordinary day.

17

Sol's eyes opened with a startled blink. He could tell from the quality of light filtering into his room through the chink between the curtains that much of the morning had already passed. He rose from his bed, and, after showering and dressing, went downstairs to reception.

The manageress's head poked out of her office as Sol approached. 'You'll not get any breakfast now,' she snapped.

'Don't want any of your stinking breakfast,' he replied, and continued past the desk into the dining room, where he hoped to find Rosie. But she wasn't there. He went down the stairs he had taken the day before and looked first in the staff kitchen, which was empty, and then in the main kitchen. Here it was busy – lunch was being prepared – but there was no sign of Rosie. He went to her room, knocked, and, when there was no answer, turned the handle. The door was locked, and there was no sound of life within.

He returned to the staff kitchen then made his way back up to the hotel lounge. There he discovered Eustace, who had the sullen air and stiff walk of one who might indeed have been recently thrashed. He seemed alarmed at Sol's appearance, and turned to walk away.

Sol decided on a chummy approach. 'Hello, Eustace!' he chirped. 'And how are we today?'

Eustace stood still but didn't turn.

Sol stood next to him. 'I'm not annoyed, you know. These

197

things happen. We've all put a car in a ditch before. Part of growing up, really.'

'It wasn't my fault.'

'Course not. Tell you what. Later on, if you fancy it, I'll take you out in the car. Give you a go behind the wheel.'

Eustace brightened. 'I wouldn't mind,' he admitted. 'We could go to the old airfield.'

'Well, maybe this afternoon.' Sol made to leave, but then turned to Eustace again. 'By the way, I was looking for Rosie. Any ideas?'

'She's at her mum's. It's her day off.'

'Where's her mum stay?'

'Gowkthrapple. She went on the bike.'

'Must have fixed the puncture, then, eh?'

'Why do you want to know where Rosie is?'

'No reason, really. Just making conversation. Oiling the wheels of social intercourse. Um, and might you know when she's expected back?'

'Tomorrow. She's got to do the breakfasts, so I don't. Else people always moan and my mother gets annoyed.'

'Your mum give you a hard time, does she?'

'No!' replied Eustace defensively.

'Don't worry. I won't tell. Now, what about the rest of the guests? You know, the "sleuths". Where are they?'

'How should I know? Don't keep asking me questions!'

'Okay. Please forgive me.'

'Some of them said they was going to the quarry, if you must know.'

At that moment an unnerving bellow rent the air.

'Oh, Christ! That's my mum wants me,' said Eustace.

'Ah! So it isn't a rhino on heat, after all?'

Eustace looked puzzled. 'No, it's my mum. I better go and see what she wants.' And he hurried away in the general direction of the dreadful sound.

18

As Sol walked out of the hotel's main entrance, Shad entered his mind for the first time that day. He made his way around the back and stood close to the drain cover. There was a cloud of flies circling lazily above it. Not frantic bluebottles, but the delicate long-legged things that draw trout to the surface of chalk streams, are buffeted by the gentlest of breezes, and inspired (we imagine) various scientific models of the motion of gas molecules.

Sol sniffed the air.

There was a faint odour of sewage, but nothing more. Lying on the metal cover were some hogweed blooms. These troubled him, as they had not been there the night before, and their ordered disposition suggested human intervention.

Sol looked about him and then kicked the blooms to one side. He sat on a garden seat from which he could observe the drain without seeming to be particularly interested in it (just in case any 'sleuths' were observing him). He wondered if Rosie had let sympathy override common sense and was responsible for the floral tribute. If so, it was a foolish thing to do, and he would tell her so later. He felt a strange compulsion to lift the lid and look down the dark shaft once more. But he resisted it. He grew reflective, wondering at this strange turn in his life, this sudden intrusion of death, and his rather detached reaction to it. He had carried a corpse – he didn't even know the man's name – down the stairs at the hairdressing salon but felt no sense of horror or outrage at what he had done. True, he had felt sadness at the loss of Shad, but half an hour later it was far from his mind as he and Rosie lay locked in carnal embrace. Shad's life had been miserable, nothing could change that. But it was in Sol's power to grant him a dignified death, and to try to bring to justice those who had murdered him. So he went to his room and dialled his home town's police station.

He recognized the voice at the other end.

'Erskine?'

'Yeh, who's that?'

Sol informed him, and told him he was phoning from the country. 'There's been a crime . . . ' began Sol.

'Can't help you, mate. Going off duty. Got a date.'

'Ah!'

'Listen, what d'you reckon about shagging skinny birds?'

Sol replied he had no firm opinion on the matter.

'Me, I like an arse on a woman.'

'Better with than without,' offered Sol, wondering what he had done to win the policeman's confidence in such intimate matters.

'What about old birds?'

'Well,' reflected Sol, 'they've got everything the young ones have, only they've had it longer.'

'Right. Can't be doing with old birds.'

'I guess, then, that old-skinny ones are right out. But listen, I'd like to report a suspicious death.'

'What's your local nick down there?'

'Don't know.'

'Why don't you give them a ring? Can't stop. Cheers mate.' And he hung up.

Sol looked through the information folder that had been left on his bedside cabinet and discovered a number for the local police station. He dialled it but was informed by a recorded voice that there would be no-one in until Tuesday afternoon.

Sol went outside once more and encountered a gardener trimming the edges of the lawn.

'Morning!' said Sol.

'Mornin',' replied the gardener.

'Lovely day.'

The gardener stopped his clipping, took a handkerchief from his pocket and mopped his brow.

'It is that,' he agreed.

'Tell me,' said Sol, eager to push on the conversation. 'You been here long? I mean, at the hotel?'

'Few year now. My dad afore that.'

'The grounds look really good, actually. I was saying that to some of the other guests. You do a good job.'

'They'd soon get rid o' me if oi didn't.'

'You didn't by any chance also work at the school when it was going, did you?' asked Sol.

'What school would that be?'

'You know . . . ' Sol pointed vaguely in the direction of the ruined school. 'Cacknacker's School, I think it was called.'

The gardener looked puzzled. 'Nothin' o' that name round 'ere. Only school in these parts is over in Gowkthrapple. The bigger kids, they 'ave to get the bus up to town.'

'The ruined place over the other side of the woods?' said Sol, pointing again. 'Wasn't that once a school?'

'That place! Weren't never a school.'

Now it was Sol's turn to look puzzled. 'That's odd. Someone I knew – know – told me it . . . I have to say, though, at first I thought it was a barracks, or something.'

'Weren't no barracks neither.'

'What was it then?'

'It were a *madhouse*.'

'*Madhouse?*' repeated Sol.

'Sent folk there from all around, they did. From the town, the city. Everywhere.'

Sol remained perplexed.

'Some terrible things went on there,' continued the gardener darkly. 'At least, that's how the stories went. Everyone were glad when it got shut. Some of 'em used to escape. We took to keeping dogs 'ere to keep 'em away. I'll tell you! I wish it 'ad o' bin a school.'

'What sort of terrible things?'

'I'd like to tell 'ee, but I got work to do. The Old Bag'll be out here soon, yellin' at me, if I don't get movin'.'

'Yes, of course. I'm keeping you back. Well, perhaps we could have a chat later? Over a drink?'

'I never says no to a drink.'

'This evening, perhaps. Goodbye for now – oh, and I meant to ask: which way's the quarry?'

'T'other side o' the village,' the gardener pointed: 'Thataway.'

In the centre of the village was a green, with a cricket pitch and pavilion. Sitting on a bench just outside the boundary line was one of the local inhabitants. In appearance he resembled the gardener Sol had not long left, but he was older. Sol scanned the deserted cricket field and asked when the game was due to start.

The old man took a fob watch from his waistcoat pocket, flicked open the lid, studied the dial for a second or two, then returned the watch to his pocket.

'Just about now, I'd say,' he said.

'I see,' said Sol. He sat next to the man, and, shielding his eyes from the sun, looked over towards the pavilion, which was all shut up. 'Can't beat it, eh? Smack of leather on willow on a sunny summer's day in the country.' Sol looked over at the pavilion once more. 'Be, er, coming out soon, will they?'

The ancient looked at Sol as at a cretin. 'They 'ent playin 'ere. Be over at Gowkthrapple.'

'Ah! Now I understand. I know someone there, actually. Might wander over later on. Take in a few overs.'

The local man seemed supremely uninterested in Sol's intentions.

'That'll be the pub?' remarked Sol, pointing to the village inn, opposite the church.

Once more there was no reply.

'A glass of good country ale is never amiss on a warm sunny day,' Sol continued in a vein of forced bonhomie. 'I'll bid you good day, sir.'

As he lifted the latch on the pub door and stepped in, all eyes turned to him. There were perhaps thirty men, in rustic attire, seated two, three or four to a table.

'Afternoon!' said Sol brightly. The locals returned to their mumbled conversations without acknowledging his greeting.

'Ah, good day, mine host,' said Sol, maintaining his cheery mode. 'I'll have . . . ' In vain he scanned the bar top for pump-handle badges indicating what was on offer. ' . . . lager?'

'Ent got none of your fancy city drinks 'ere,' replied the landlord.

'You were going to say that whatever I said, weren't you?' said Sol, smiling and wagging his finger. 'Well then, what can you offer me?'

'Pint o' Flat. Or we got Old Execrable.'

'Not sure about the Flat. Call me a philistine, but I like my beer cold and full of gas.'

The landlord leaned confidingly towards Sol. 'I don't

normally offer advice, but I'll make an exception in your case. I wouldn't touch the Execrable, if I were you.'

Sol pondered the options. 'Flat it is, then.'

The landlord disappeared around the back and returned with a slopping tankard.

'The old ways die hard, don't they?' remarked Sol, tapping the end of his finger against the dimpled pewter. He peered into the dark brown brew and sniffed. 'Doubtless this will leach out some of the lead.' He raised the tankard and nodded to the landlord:

'Your health, sir. Probably not mine.' He took a swig, shuddered, and turned around to survey the pub. There was no pool table, no dart board; no fruit machines, no juke-box. There were no carpets on the floor; no pictures on the nicotine-stained walls. Sol walked to a door in the back wall, thinking it might lead to a beer garden beyond. There was indeed a patch of grass, but it was occupied by a small flock of sheep, kept in check by two alert, crouching dogs.

Sol returned to the bar.

'Wouldn't mind some lunch,' he announced. 'Possibly a ploughman's?'

The landlord nodded and disappeared through the back once more. He returned shortly bearing a wide shallow bowl, which he put down on the bar in front of Sol, along with a spoon.

'What's this?' asked Sol. He looked at it closely. 'I mean, I can see potato and cabbage mixed together and reheated—'

'That's right. Bubble and squeak.'

'I did ask for a ploughman's.'

'That's what our ploughman 'as for lunch. You ask 'im. There 'ee is, over there.'

The ploughman identified himself and confirmed that this indeed was what he often had for lunch. Bubble and squeak. Sometimes it was fish cakes, especially the salmon variety.

'An' I suppose', said the landlord, 'you think ploughing goes on all the time in the country.'

'Can't say I'd ever thought about it,' answered Sol.'

'I said that because that's what the last person from the town who came 'ere thought.'

'Fine,' said Sol and began to eat, for he had no aversion to the dish in general and this particular example of it had been prepared and cooked well enough. And having had no breakfast, he ate it all.

He picked up his tankard, put it to his lips, then put it down again without imbibing any of the cloudy liquor.

'None of you playing cricket this afternoon, then?' said Sol in an attempt to integrate. 'Over at Gowkthrapple, I understand. I, er, may go over myself later.'

Again, no-one seemed particularly agog to know what Sol might do that afternoon. Presently one of the company stood up, cleared his throat, cupped his hand over his ear and started to sing. It was nasal and dirge-like, but with a steady beat that the rest of the company marked with stamping feet. After a while others chipped in with verses they had obviously learned by heart.

> Cows in the parlour,
>> Sheep's in the pen;
> Pigs in the boghouse,
>> Eight nine ten.

> Flies in the buttermilk;
>> Shoo, flies, shoo!
> Vicar's in the choirboy;
>> That won't do.

And so on.

Quatrain after quatrain – opaque as Nostradamus, much of

it – in a seemingly never-ending paean to rustic life. For a while Sol tapped his fingers on the bar and pretended to be enjoying it, but after some eighty verses he unobtrusively settled his bill and left the premises.

Outside, the old man was still sitting on the bench staring out over the deserted green. He looked up as Sol walked by.

'I meant to tell 'ee, afore 'ee went in,' he said.

'Tell me what?' wondered Sol.

'Leave the Execrable well alone.'

'I did,' said Sol sitting down beside him. 'I pretty much avoided the Flat as well, as it happens. Is it as bad as your warning implies, the Execrable?'

The old man, in a talkative mood now, enlightened Sol.

The Execrable recipe, he said, was a closely guarded secret, although it was understood hogweed and wormwood gave it its astringency, while a sprinkling of the fungus known as avenging angel, in powdered form, accounted for much of the disorienting effect (not to mention the lingering pain emanating from the region of the liver which even small amounts of the brew were known to produce). Old Execrable appeared in at least two seventeenth-century pharmacopoeias, recommended in one as a lotion for treating boils, and in the other as a suitable anaesthetic when sawing through bone.

It was widely held that the original recipe had been the work of monks whose monastery once stood at the edge of the village, improbable as it might seem that anyone with even a shred of Christian charity would inflict such a liquor upon the world. But if these monks had, then they most surely deserved their fate – which was to be beaten and reviled by Henry VIII's troops, before twitching away their last minutes in this vale of tears at the end of a hempen rope. The monastery was looted of its plate, liquor and animals, desecrated, and a bonfire made of its relics, precious manuscripts and books (but alas, not the recipe for Old Execrable). Finally the buildings were set on fire. The local landowner, a Protestant, carted away most of the stone for his own building projects. The land lay fallow for a while, then was used for growing parsnips, and mangel-wurzels for the cows.

The yokel pointed with his stick to a towering chestnut tree across the green. 'That was where they 'ung them monks,' he said. 'From one of they branches.'

'Fascinating,' commented Sol.

The man nodded. He beckoned Sol closer and disclosed in conspiratorial fashion:

'I 'ave it on good authority, that when a man's 'anged, his tadger goes stiff.'

'I've heard that too,' said Sol.

'You'd think that'd be the last thing on their minds! Bit o' rumpy pumpy.'

'Nature's strange in her ways,' offered Sol. 'And doesn't always get it right, in my view.'

'They also say tadgers was much bigger in them days. And sturdier. Used 'em to flail the corn.'

'I see. And where did you learn this?'

'My old dad told me.'

'If olden tadgers were so huge as to flail corn,' countered Sol, 'the race would have died out. So much blood would have been required to engorge them that it would have drained from other parts of the body, particularly the brain. A man would faint before he even had a chance to effect penetration. Like the mule, believe you me, the man with a truly enormous organ is doomed to sterility.'

The local ruminated on this for a while, then remarked:

'You's probably right. Now I think about it, my dad did speak a lot of tosh most days. I blames the Execrable.'

Sol bid him good-day and set off for the quarry.

19

Catchpole Ragoon and the four Young Turks had parked their off-road vehicle at the end of the track that led to the quarry and then made their way on foot to the site of the old school. One of the Turks seemed to know exactly which area they should be searching. They spread out into a line, with about five yards between one person and the next, and moved slowly along, closely scrutinizing the earth as they went, now and then prodding with the sticks they carried.

The man at the end of the line drifted towards a clump of long grass and, as he swatted some of it aside, a dense cloud of flies shot noisily into the air, and dispersed in ever-increasing spirals.

'Oh Lord!' said one startled Turk, and pointed to the ground. The others hurried to where he stood.

'Country ways,' said Catchpole. 'That'll be someone's supper.'

The rabbit's eyes were still as bright and shiny as any that enchanted a child, but they had been jolted from their sockets by the force of the steel trap, and its head was almost severed from its body.

The group continued searching and it wasn't long before one of the young men called out and crouched down to examine something. He picked up three small objects and placed them on the palm of his hand. The others gathered round.

'Teeth,' said one, stating the obvious.

'Human,' said Bowker, and they all agreed.

'Ancient or modern?' asked Catchpole.

The man holding the teeth turned them over in his palm. 'Ah, yes. A filling. Definitely modern.'

'To whom do these belong?' mused Catchpole. 'And would it tell us anything germane to the Murder Mystery if we knew?'

'One doesn't imagine there was ever a dental clinic here,' said Bowker, looking about. 'It's likely these teeth were detached from their owner by violence.'

'Quite probably,' said Catchpole. 'But frankly I think we've caught a red herring here. Dental records have a place in solving crime – but not this one, I fear.'

From their lair Choy and Clowsie observed the group of 'sleuths'.

'Damn more rozzers,' said Choy as he looked through the field-glasses. 'They're on our case, Clowsie. Saw some this morning too.'

'Must be rozzers, Choy. Poking about like that. Somebody called them out all right. What we going to do?'

'Not our worry this time, boy. What have we done to anyone?'

'Nothing, Choy. Not this time.'

'That chit, he just dropped dead. We never touched him.'

'Never touched him.'

'We put him in the drain, but there's no law on that one.'

'No law, Choy. It was just a lark.'

'We stuffed plenty of stinking juniors down the drain. Some down the chimney. No law about it.'

'Never hurt anyone, Choy, being stuck down a drain. Just larking.'

'Hold on! They're off, those pissing snot-gobblers. What's their game now?'

'Damn spunk-monkeys. Let's take them, Choy. '

'Put the brakes on, Clowsie. I think they're off the trail. Better to act normal.'

'Okay, Choy. Let's open a bottle and not worry about it.'

The quarry, which was well beyond its working life, and had been flooded, appeared very blue as it scintillated in the strong sun. The pool was almost circular and about seventy metres in diameter. For most of the perimeter there was a steep rock-face rising out of the water to a height of about thirty feet. But where Sol stood, and for some yards either side, the higher ground dipped more or less to the level of the water.

When Sol arrived he saw first the off-road vehicle, and then on the water a rubber dinghy containing Bowker and two of his companions. Sol climbed a little way up the slope to his left, so he could see what they were doing. They each had a viewing tube and were plainly searching the bottom. He could also see a man in the water, with a wet-suit top, snorkel and fins. He too was searching. Now and then those in the inflatable would direct him to a particular area and he would dive down, his webbed pale legs appearing vertical for a second or so before sliding beneath the water.

'Hello, old man!'

Sol looked away to his right and saw Catchpole sitting under a tree. He waved back and made his way towards him.

The older man was dressed very informally in cotton trousers, a loose shirt and a panama hat. He was sitting on the ground, his back against a shady tree, wicker picnic hamper at his side.

'Have something to eat,' he offered. 'These fellows', and he indicated the men on the water, 'are far too busy to stop for lunch.'

'Your offer's most kind, Catchpole. But I've just had some.'

'A drink, then?'

'Be glad to. Lovely day.'

'It is splendid,' agreed Catchpole. He reached into the hamper and pulled out a bottle of wine. He showed the label to Sol, who nodded sagely:

'Very nice.'

It was uncorked, poured and the two men chinked glasses.

'That's more like it,' said Sol, savouring the claret. 'A proper drink.'

To put the last remark in context, Sol described his visit to the village and the pub.

Catchpole was quite tickled. 'Lord, it's true what they say, isn't it? About country people,' he chuckled. 'Flat or Old Execrable. I ask you! And how did you manage to shovel down the bubble-and-squeak, for heaven's sake?'

'Oh, that wasn't so bad. It was the beer, so-called.'

'Yes, well, have some more of this.' And he topped up their glasses.

'What's happening here, exactly?' asked Sol, indicating the men on the water.'

'The Young Turks? Well, I've already told you about Bowker. The man in the water, that's Urqual. Then there's Challoner and Carden.'

'I have to say, they seem to take it all very seriously. Did they just happen to have a dinghy and these viewing tubes with them?'

'Oh, they come prepared.'

'And where are the rest of the sleuths?'

'Following up their suspicions and hunches, I imagine.' Catchpole explained that it was usual for fragmentation to occur early on in the course of a Murder Mystery Weekend. Individuals formed teams, which were very co-operative within themselves but quite closed off to outsiders. The Young Turks were an established team who attended events up and down the country, and even abroad. (Between them they were fluent in Spanish, German, Italian, and French.) It was highly competitive within the Murder Mystery fraternity and a lot of pride was invested in success. And this quartet wanted to be the best. They had invited Catchpole – Bowker's uncle – to be one of their number for this particular weekend, appreciating that an older head could form good ballast to anchor their energetic enthusiasm, which carried them far and forward, but sometimes in the wrong direction. He kept an eye on them. Advised. But also let them learn by making their own mistakes.

'Do you think they're on to something here?' asked Sol.

'I'm not sure, you know. But they seemed very keen to explore. I have to say, it's been rather an odd one, this. I mean, there's usually a much clearer pattern by now. Certainly a body. Have you any ideas?'

'Not really. I'm new to this game. I wouldn't know where to look.'

Catchpole took another sip of his wine. He seemed content.

'Such a hot day. And all this green.' He gestured to indicate the surrounding lushness of the woods. 'Reminds me of Malacca, in a strange sort of way.'

'Malacca?'

'You know it?'

'As it happens, yes. Family moved to the Far East when I was a youngster.'

'Really? Splendid! Best thing that can happen to a chap. Spend some time in the East. Tin or rubber?'

'Tin, actually. Yourself?'

'Diplomatic Corps. Bit hush-hush. Knew a lot of the

planters, though. They were my eyes and ears, in a manner of speaking.'

'This reminds me of the old tin mines,' continued Sol, pointing at the quarry. 'You remember, when they'd got all the tin out, they'd fill the hole up with water, form a little lake, and stock it with fish. I used to catch little perch-like things with spiny backs. Couldn't eat them, though. Gave them to the *amah* and she took them home and fed them to her dogs.'

'I remember the *amah* I had. Wonderful cook. Wonderful. In all these years I've never come across anyone anywhere who makes such a good chicken rendang. Not for lunch, though. Never liked a big lunch in the heat. Just some satay, with the little cubes of rice, and a bottle of Tiger beer. Sitting on the veranda. Marvellous! Take my advice, Sol, marry a Malay.'

'Any particular one?' asked Sol.

'Wonderful women,' continued Catchpole. 'They're modest, submissive and mysterious. What more could you ask for in a woman?'

'Yes, well, I'll keep that in mind. Thank you once more for the advice.'

They sat in silence for a while, then Catchpole said:

'I hope you don't mind my saying, but you've done rather well for yourself with that servant girl.'

'Rosie? How did you know about her?'

'Oh, word gets around. People are very alert at these functions, you know. Besides, I discovered you in flagrante delicto, more or less.'

'Ah yes. That.'

'Had a little chat with her at the table last night. Struck me as, mmm, phlegmatic.'

'Yes,' agreed Sol, 'but with some choler to spice her up.'

'Personally I think it's melancholy that most becomes a woman. I can't abide empty-headed giggling fizgigs.'

'I'm with you on that one, Catchpole.'

'Some people mistake melancholy for gloom or depression, but it's not, you know. Melancholy's a dark night from which a beautiful dawn emerges. Not sure where depression comes from. I think it's something the moderns invented. You don't find it in the classical philosophers.'

There was some excitement in the dinghy. The diver had come up with something from the bottom. They shouted to Catchpole and began to pull towards the shore.

'Right. Let's see what they've got,' said Catchpole, standing up and brushing some moss from his clothes.

'I think you'll find this interesting,' said Urqual. He held up a Gladstone bag.

Catchpole examined it and then, at Bowker's prompting, opened it.

Lying on a layer of mud was a rusty snub-nosed pistol.

Catchpole took the weapon, studied it for a few seconds, and told them what type it was, its calibre and range, how many had been manufactured, and where. 'There's a serial number.' He pointed. 'But someone's been at it with a file and acid. Plainly it belonged to some rogue and was used for nefarious purposes.'

'Forensics can still get the number, can't they?' asked Bowker. 'Even when it's etched like that.'

'Yes. The stamp for these mass-produced weapons would leave an imprint,' agreed Catchpole. 'If the etching has not gone too deep, then you can often pick it up under the right lighting. But I don't know if there is anything of significance here. I'd say from the state of it it had been in the water some weeks, even months. I don't think it's likely to have featured in our little weekend case, do you?'

Disappointment registered in the faces of the team. They had been sure they were on to something.

'Seems odd', offered Sol, 'that the gun was put in the bag and then thrown in. Made it less likely to disappear, I'd have thought.'

The Young Turks looked at Catchpole to see what he thought, and when he registered no interest in Sol's remark they too ignored it.

'I think', said the older man, 'you should take it along to the local constabulary. They might well be interested.'

'There's no-one there until Tuesday afternoon,' said Sol helpfully.

'Oh?' said Catchpole, raising an eyebrow. 'And how do you know that?'

'A recorded message informed me.'

'If it's not too much of an impertinence, might I ask why you were phoning the local constabulary?'

'Oh,' answered Sol, making light of it with a wave of his hand. 'Just a line I was following. It led nowhere, as it turned out.'

'I seem to recall', said Challoner, 'that at the drinks reception you were awfully chummy with the victim.'

'The victim . . . ? You mean? Not Shad, surely!'

'It was always very obvious who the victim was,' said Carden. 'It's just that we can't find the body, or anything that connects him with the perpetrator.'

'You know who did it? That's very quick work.'

'We've a good idea who the killer is,' said Urqual. 'But there's no point playing our hand just yet.'

'Old Shad the victim!' said Sol, shaking his head. 'Fancy. He's a wily one, all right. I've been following the wrong track all along. I was under the impression – no, I'm too embarrassed to even say who my suspicions fell upon.'

The Turks shortly packed up their gear and made to

leave. Sol cadged a lift with them, but Catchpole said he was happy to linger a while and finish the bottle of claret.

Klaus, the German sleuth, watched the off-road vehicle turn from the track on to the road, and then accelerate towards the hotel. He made his way to the quarry with a quietness bordering on stealth. There he found Catchpole fast asleep, the empty bottle of claret at his side. Klaus looked him up and down, then walked up the slope and along the lip of the quarry until he came to a point about 180° from where he had started. He stood a while looking out over the water, and at the still sleeping Catchpole. Klaus had already eliminated the quarry as having a part to play in this Murder Mystery and it surprised him that seasoned campaigners like the Young Turks (particularly with Catchpole at their head) thought there might be something to be found here. The so-called clues that pointed here were, in his view, so plainly spurious.

'Perhaps', thought Klaus, 'he was just humouring the Turks, who for all their arrogant confidence still have a lot to learn about murder mysteries. Or perhaps he's just an old man who needs a sleep after lunch.' Klaus smiled at his own musings and then headed off in another direction. The site with the ruins, now that was another matter; indeed, very interesting.

The German ventured far into the grounds, further than Catchpole and the Turks had gone. His attention was diverted by the various ruins and, just as Sol had, he speculated on what sort of place this might have been. He was drawn from his abstraction by the sound of heavy footsteps.

He turned and saw two men, each armed with a cudgel. The one with cruel eyes addressed him. 'What you think you're doing here? Wandering round like a dog looking for somewhere to point its piss.'

Klaus had no time to make sense of the situation before the blow passed between his imploring upraised hands and smashed into his skull.

'Nice one, Clowsie! A real lava-cracker, that!'

Choy and Clowsie buried him with the others, in the square plot near their lair where the red-and-white mushrooms grew thick in the autumn. Klaus's Audi, which he had parked in the woods, they transported to a high point on the quarry's perimeter. Clowsie rested his foot against the rear bumper and pushed. The car rolled slowly forward, then plunged to the water below – where it slowly sank, and would remain undetected for twenty years before being discovered by a couple from the village who came to swim one hot day. The young man, eager to impress his lover, dived naked from the lip of the quarry into the scintillating blue water, and the momentum of his plunge took him almost to the bottom, and within a few yards of the Audi. Credit to the marque, it was remarkably well preserved, with little evidence of rust. The registration plate was quite legible, but the young man neglected to note the number. He assumed it had been dumped there by joyriders from the town or city. On returning to the village the couple telephoned the police station, but were informed by a recorded message that no-one would be there until Tuesday afternoon – by which time both young persons were otherwise occupied and the matter of the car in the quarry was not the first thing on their minds.

As Rosie remarked, thousands of people go missing every year and many of them are never found. Klaus's disappearance was duly reported by relatives in Germany about six weeks after his death. He had no immediate family, and no close friends. He had chosen to focus his life's energy on work and contrived amusements such as murder mystery weekends.

Klaus's name was placed on a database and remained there for eleven years – until it was accidentally erased during a computer-system update.

20

In spite of some excellent food, dinner that night was a rather muted affair. A certain discontent reigned amongst the sleuths. No clear pattern was emerging. Order was not crystallizing out of disorder. The mystery was proving obdurate, and this unsettled the sleuths, who to a person abhorred mysteries and disorder and drew great comfort from banishing one and reversing the other.

As Sol was drinking his coffee he felt a light tap on his shoulder. It was Juppy Candela.

'A quiet word if you please,' she said, smiling, both at him and those round about.

'Of course, Juppy. It'll be a pleasure. Excuse me, would you?' said Sol, rising from the table.

The two of them walked to a quiet corner of the room.

Before she could say anything, Sol said:

'I'm so glad you've shaken off the quinsy. It can be such a distressing complaint.'

'I feel much better now. Thank you.' She looked to make sure no-one aside from Sol was listening. 'People are complaining. They're still in the dark. They say there are not enough clues, and that those there are lead nowhere. We're well past the halfway stage. People should know by now. Are you sure you're playing your part properly? I mean, where's the body, for goodness sake? It's not where it is supposed to be.'

'Hmm, is that right? Well, the only thing I can think of . . . I was talking to Shad yesterday,' replied Sol, lying, 'and he said – and I agreed with him – that he was "minded to improvise".'

'Improvise!? No, you can't do that. Not on a murder mystery weekend. You have to stick to the script. It'll be chaos otherwise.'

'I share Shad's view, Juppy. A little bit of uncertainty and chaos adds a necessary spice to the proceedings. Life can get very dull when you stick to the script all the time – there are no surprises.' Sol turned and surveyed the sleuths, most of whom were still sitting at the dinner table and engaged in casual conversation or earnest discussion.

'I don't know, Juppy. What do they want? They pay to be challenged, and when they are they complain it's not easy enough. Perhaps I should just hang a sign around my neck: see if they pick up on that?'

'No, don't do that. No!'

'I mean, of all the great detectives – and I'm sure you know them all, Juppy – of all the great detectives, who was the one that said, "This case is a bit vexing. I think I'll just pack it in." ?'

'I don't know if anyone said that.'

'I've been dropping clues all over the place, but no-one's been picking them up. Frankly, I think this is rather an obtuse bunch.'

'Oh, I don't think so!'

'Believe me,' said Sol. 'I think it's all moving, impercep-tibly, toward a fabulous denouement.'

'Do you?'

'Indeed.'

Juppy studied Sol for a few seconds, then said:

'I hope so.'

'It's just a short step from hope to belief, Juppy.' Sol

saw that she indeed believed what he had said. She was as credulous as the inspector was suspicious. He was a man who turned over every word as if it were a stone that harboured grubs and worms beneath it. For some reason – possibly the wine and country air – Sol found himself quite fancying Juppy. He wondered if there was a Mr Candela, and what he was like. Sol smiled. Juppy did too, an uneasy smile compounded of politeness and puzzlement. She was wearing an elegant evening gown and he let his eyes rest on her exposed shoulders. They were so white, smooth and unblemished. Their contours were perfect, as if constructed according to some sacred geometry, some architectural golden mean which made the surface an infinite everything and the underlying structure invisible. Sol's smile had become a satyric grin. He felt a strong urge to lick those pearly shoulders, indeed might have done so had his reverie not been interrupted.

'Ah, there you are!' It was Catchpole.

'Hello,' replied Sol. 'Have you met Juppy?'

'Yes, of course. Hello, my dear.' He kissed her cheek. 'You're looking radiant tonight. What a wonderful gown. Sets you off perfectly.'

'You've pre-empted me there, Catchpole. I was about to say the same thing myself.'

Juppy seemed flattered, and giggled.

'Listen, sorry for intruding on your conversation but, well, myself and the young fellows are going to try the village pub. Care to join us?'

Sol laughed. 'It would almost be worth it to see what the locals make of all the dinner suits and dickey bows. They'll think the place has been taken over by a magicians' convention. But, no, forgive me. One pint of Flat a day is enough for any man.'

'Oh Lord, yes. Must remember that. Flat. What was the

other one? Yes, bubble and squeak.' He returned to his younger friends and they set off for the village.

'He's a character, isn't he? Catchpole,' remarked Sol. 'Just what you need at events like this.'

'Charming man. A gentleman.'

'There are a few of us left, Juppy. But listen, much as I would like to have you all to myself for the rest of the evening, I know it's your job to circulate and talk to everyone. But not too much. You must give your throat some rest. We don't want that quinsy coming back.' Sol fixed her with a sympathetic look.

'No. I'll do as you say and . . . take it easy.'

Shortly after the conversation with Juppy, Sol retired to his room and went to bed. He quickly fell asleep and had a dream in which he and Catchpole were fishing at a lake in the country. Catchpole was dressed in waders, a tweed jacket and a hat festooned with feathered hooks. They had long whippy rods and Catchpole was trying to teach Sol to fly-fish, though without much success. The older man was not saying anything but it was plain he was losing patience. Eventually he packed up his gear and walked away. Sol followed suit but, when his mentor entered a large sewage pipe that opened out on to the lake, he hesitated. The pipe was of such a diameter that the dream-Catchpole, who was significantly taller than the flesh-and-blood one, could walk within it without stooping or removing his hook-bespangled hat. There was no odour or unpleasant debris issuing from the pipe but still Sol was reluctant to enter. He could make out noises within. These at first sounded like two men working at an anvil, then he grew convinced it was the rhythmic clanking of a train and he was standing in the entrance to a tunnel. He awoke to the sound of persistent knocking on his door.

'Who is it?' he called out.

'Me. Rosie.'

'Rosie! Great. I wondered when you were coming back.' He hurried to open the door. 'Come in.' He kissed her on the cheek.

'Come on. We ent got time for that.'

'What?'

'I gotta do breakfasts, ent I?'

'That's a shame. Can't someone else do them?'

'Ent no-one else.'

'What about Useless Eustace?'

'Sick, ent 'ee? Well, says he is. Gut-ache.'

'I bet.'

'Thing is, I'm really behind.' She looked at Sol. 'Don't suppose you fancy 'elpin'?'

'I'd much rather you threw your clothes off and jumped into bed with me.'

'Good. I knew you'd 'elp.'

In the kitchen, the main kitchen, two of the chefs were busy: frying, boiling, steaming and toasting. Mostly frying.

'Right. Cook fills the dishes 'ere,' explained Rosie. 'All you gotta do is put lids on 'em and take 'em up to the buffet. I'll need to get the tables set. Guess who should 'ave done that last night.'

Sol did as he was asked and soon the buffet was full of appetizing dishes. He looked at his watch. It was coming up to eight o'clock. He imagined people would soon be coming in to fill their plates.

Rosie entered, in a hurry, tying her waitress apron behind her.

'Right. I'll do the tables, you keep your eye on the buffet. Make sure nuthin' runs out. When it does, you go down to the kitchen and tell 'em, right?'

225

'Do my best.'

She made some adjustments on one of the tables and was on her way out of the room, when she turned, walked over to Sol and kissed him tenderly on the lips. 'Thank you for 'elpin'!'

'My pleasure, Rosie. I'll claim my reward later.' Sol glanced at his watch again, then strolled through to the lounge. Asleep in a chair was the bibulous Roderick, still dressed in a dinner suit. As Sol approached him he opened his eyes and looked about with a bemused expression. 'Must have fallen asleep!' he remarked.

'I think so,' said Sol. 'It's breakfast time.'

'Breakfast! Just what I need.'

'Come on through and we'll fix you up.' Sol stood in front of the buffet, lifting in turn the lid of each silver dish. 'There's bacon, scrambled egg, fried egg, mushrooms, tomatoes, sautéd potatoes, kippers, Cumberland sausage – very popular with the ladies – and this is? Devilled kidneys, I would say. There you are. What's it to be?'

'A large gin, please.'

'*Gin!*' queried Sol.

Alarm filled Roderick's face. 'Is there none?'

'Um . . . let me—'

'Cooking sherry will do!'

'I'll see what I can find,' Sol said, and he disappeared into the staff kitchen.

He returned two minutes later to discover Roderick banging rather feebly, with the base of a fire-extinguisher, at the padlock on the bar grille. When he spied Sol coming he let the extinguisher drop to the floor and hung his head in shame.

'No sherry, I'm afraid,' Sol announced. 'But there was a bottle of rum in the larder. Probably used for puddings. It looks a bit—'

Roderick snatched it from him. 'That will do nicely, thank you,' he said, caressing the dusty bottle. 'I'll breakfast in my room, if you don't mind.' And he hurried off.

Guests now began to arrive for breakfast in twos and threes. If they were surprised to see Sol assisting Rosie they didn't say so.

Afterwards Sol and Rosie sat in the staff kitchen, having prepared a breakfast tray for themselves. There was coffee, orange juice, scrambled egg, bacon and toast for Sol, and oatmeal and toast with lime preserve for Rosie. There were little beads of sweat on her forehead, and she smelled delightfully musky. It was hot work in and out of the kitchens, running up and down, and the day already felt warm. Sol sported damp patches on the underarm of his shirt.

'This is very pleasant, Rosie.'

She nodded and carried on chewing her toast.

'You know what I'd like to do? I'd like to go for a roll in the hay. Isn't that what you country folk do? I've often thought I'd like to do that.'

Rosie emptied her mouth of toast. 'Ent so much fun.'

'Oh?'

'Can be quite pointy and sharp, them bits of 'ay. You gets 'em pokin' in all the wrong places.'

'I hadn't really thought of that.'

'See, you got it wrong about us country folk. We 'ent so different. We does it in beds most of the time.'

'You mean, you weren't inducted into sex at the age of eight by one of your male relatives?'

'Don't be daft. First time I done it I were seventeen. With Reggie Plews. Didn't last with 'im, though. Ee went and wed Biddy Hobbs. They got seven kids now.'

'Seven! What's "Biddy" short for? Libidinous? – talking

227

of which, I'd like to claim my wages for helping you with breakfasts.'

Rosie was generous in her remuneration and it was mid-morning by the time they dressed. Sol watched her, admiring her shapely form. They say in modern times the sexes have become less differentiated, more epicene. Not like in biblical days, when the men were muscular and hairy with sperm that swam swiftly and in great number, while the women were broad-hipped and heavy-breasted and strong enough to give birth squatting on the ground, under a scorching sun, amongst flies and sheep ticks, and to do so again and again, for the survival of these Semitic tribes depended upon a host of strong sons to attend the flocks and fight off marauders from the desert kingdoms. To Sol it seemed Rosie was of the same, vital, earthy stock.

'What you staring at?' she asked.

'What do you think? Here, let me help you with your zip.'

But Sol struggled with it.

'Yeh, I know, I'm gettin' fat in me old age.'

'You're not fat. You're Feminine, with a capital 'F'.'

'Feels fat.'

Sol patted her behind. 'You'd be surprised how many men like an arse on a woman. See you later, I hope.'

'You might.'

21

Many of the sleuths spent Sunday morning finalizing their investigations. Five who didn't were Catchpole and the Young Turks. They lay in dark rooms suspended in that unsettling space between life and death – at least, that's how it felt to them. The previous night, in the village pub, encouraged by mischievous locals, they had each ordered not one, not two, but *three* pints of Old Execrable. To a man they passed out before they were halfway through the third. They were transported back to the hotel on the body of a combine harvester and tucked up in bed by dutiful night staff. By midday on the Sunday they were still in no fit state to attend the lavish lunch enjoyed by the other sleuths, and which also marked the conclusion of the investigations.

At the end of the meal, as the company retired to the coffee lounge, Catchpole and two of the Turks did appear, looking very pale and drawn. When Juppy Candela clapped her hands to call for order, they all winced and rested their palms against their foreheads.

'If we can all settle down?' said Juppy, a little tense and shrill. 'It's time for the denouement. I'm sure some of you have worked out who committed the, er, dastardly deed. Would anyone like to take the floor?' She looked around, hopefully. '*Anyone?*'

No-one seemed anxious to begin. There was a restless distraction about the company. They fidgeted and seemed irritable. It had grown very warm and uncomfortably humid. People were loosening ties, removing jackets, and mopping brows with handkerchiefs. Someone signalled to Rosie and asked for a jug of iced water. The manageress sent Eustace to fetch a couple of electric fans from the storeroom. She opened the windows, but the air that flowed in was more oppressive than that which hung in the room.

'Now then,' said Juppy once more. 'Who'll kick us off?'

A hand went up.

'Yes,' said Juppy. 'It's Roderick, isn't it?'

'I saw who did it. There were two. A big fellow, and another with a cruel face. I watched through the window in the back. They had big sticks and threw him down a hole.'

'I don't think so,' said Juppy. 'Not according to the script.'

'Yes,' he insisted. 'The little man in the sports jacket. He fell, and they put him down the drain. I tried to get him out, but the cover was too heavy to lift.'

'Nice try. Anyone else?'

'Oh, very well. It was *me* who did it,' continued the stout little drunk.

'No, it wasn't you.'

'Yes, *I*'m the guilty one. I need to be *punished*.'

'Thank you, Roderick. But it's not that sort of week-end.'

The man appeared abashed. He excused himself and made for the bar.

'Now, anyone else like a stab?'

A snigger went up from the company.

Juppy smiled. 'No, that wasn't intended as a hint.'

'I think it was Klaus,' offered another. 'I mean, he's not here, and his car's gone. I think that's what I'd do if I was the killer. I'd scarper. I wouldn't stick around waiting for people to finger me.'

Juppy looked around the gathering. 'Well, you're right. He doesn't seem to be here. And his car's gone, you say?'

'Doesn't prove he's the killer,' said another sleuth. 'Maybe his old mum's ill back in Bremen and he had to rush off.'

And a laugh went up when it was suggested that Klaus might simply have disappeared in a hurry to avoid paying his bar bill.

One of the Young Turks, Carden, stood up, wobbled a little, focused, and pointed to Sol. '*That*'s our man. *He*'s the killer.'

All eyes turned to Sol. He appeared surprised and looked left and right to see if anyone else could be implicated by Carden's accusing finger, which in truth was shaking and drifting quite markedly from side to side. The accuser sat down again and took a sip of cold water.

'And what chain of logic brought you to that conclusion?' asked Sol.

'You were seen naked in the servants' quarters,' came the reply.

'That was a tad embarrassing, I admit,' replied Sol, 'but nothing sinister, surely.'

'It suggests to me you might have been in the process of disposing of your clothes. Which begs the question—'

'It suggests', said Challoner, who had at last regained the power of speech, 'that there were incriminating stains upon them.'

'Mere speculation,' pointed out Sol.

'But it is not speculation', interjected Catchpole, 'to say you were seen in the room of the victim, and also returning his room key – number 18, I believe, – to reception. Can you explain that?'

'Yes,' replied Sol, thinking furiously. 'Yes, I can. Shad – the victim – as you know, suffered terribly from asthma, and related conditions. I can see you didn't know that, but

I assure you it is the case. I'm no physician, but I think it might be related to his oppressed childhood. But certainly it is triggered by pollen, of which there is much in the country, especially at this time of year. He was particularly susceptible to hogweed, I understand. Anyway, the victim and I were sitting on a seat in the garden when he began to experience difficulty breathing and soon became distressed. I suggested we went inside, but he said he needed his inhaler. So I ran up to his room and fetched it for him.'

'And did you stop to return the key?' asked Challoner.

'I took him his inhaler first, left him to recover, *then* returned the key.'

The Turks and Catchpole drew together in a whispering confab.

Outside there was a rumble of thunder and the curtains in the room billowed inward on a sudden swelling of breeze.

Challoner stood up. 'In many ways this is an infuriating case,' he said, with an exasperated gesture. 'There has been so little you can get a hold of, and without a body and a weapon, it's very difficult. *Very* difficult, particularly when the killer—'

'Alleged killer,' corrected Sol.

'Particularly when the alleged killer is so – what's the word? Unco-operative.'

'And is that the sum of your detective work?'

'There are one or two other things,' Challoner replied, referring to a folder. 'And the fact that the car you arrived in does not belong to you only tends to increase our suspicion.'

'You're right. It's not mine. I borrowed it from a friend. For the weekend. No buses out this way.'

'According to our information, it was stolen two weeks ago in North Wales.'

'Don't be ridiculous! I borrowed it from my hairdresser,' insisted Sol.

The Turk shrugged. 'Facts are facts.'

'Besides. Even if it were stolen – and it isn't – so what? Surely that's not admissible evidence.'

'We're not in a court of law,' said Catchpole. 'Different rules pertain.'

Sol's attention was caught by a man in the audience. As their eyes met, the man half smiled and nodded gently. Sol puzzled for a few seconds, then pointed:

'The gardener!'

'That's right,' he answered, not with a country burr, but with the polished voice of a professional actor. He wore, not rustic garb, but a navy blazer and cravat. And he seemed much younger now, out of his disguise.

'You were very convincing,' said Sol.

'Thank you. My speciality.'

'I can see from the general reaction that you had most people fooled.'

'Here in the country an old yokel is considered a good source of information. Most people will give a lot of credence to his testimony.'

'Which is why a lot of people spent a lot of time pursuing red herrings.'

'Indeed.'

'And the fact that you were maundering on about "madhouses" didn't seem to suggest to most people that you yourself might indeed be talking nonsense.'

'It was a clue,' agreed the pretend gardener.

It had by now grown darker still, both in the room and outside. So much so that sensors had triggered the floodlights at the front of the hotel, even though it was mid-afternoon in the middle of summer. Above the trees at the edge of the grounds great banks of clouds had gathered, black as soot at their centre but tinged with light at the edges.

Then lightning and thunder: deep booms that seemed to

shake the very air and instil in the gathering a sense of awed respect. The rain began to fall, and the manageress hurried across the room to close the windows.

'That's just what we need!' someone remarked. 'A good storm to clear the air. It's been awfully close today. Awfully.'

Sol waited for the assembly's attention to return to the investigation. Then he stood up.

'I don't know if it's the consensus view that I'm the murderer in this case. But I have to say, I am not. A certain fax relating to the weekend's events was due to be sent to me at the hotel. I never received it, though I suspect it arrived and fell into the wrong hands. I suspect, indeed, that it may have been passed on to others. Or even sold.' He let his gaze dwell on Eustace, who was leaning against a doorpost listening to the proceedings.

'And if we're honest, is this not how crime is solved in the real world? By subterfuge and cheating! By bribery, bullying and blackmail! And by the most obvious thing: simply asking those who inhabit the same nether world as the criminal, and who can probably be banged up for their own crimes, "*Who did it?*"

'The notion of a super-intellectual sleuth, who builds up a picture of the truth from seemingly inconsequential clues is, of course, a Victorian fantasy. It doesn't quite work like that, as Swift well knew. His Lilliputians, like the modern detective, saw with great exactness. But they discovered that facts, observations, details could piece together in many ways, and they had nothing in their small minds that could look beyond the details. Their speculations took them no nearer the truth because they were little people with little minds.

'Likewise the Victorians, who liked to believe their towering scientific rationalism was the goal that evolution had been striving for. And we have inherited that prejudice. We

234

worship at the shrine of scientism, and we worship the image of detectives who use science and the intellect to dispel mystery. Sometimes, of course, they do. Just as often, though, they do not. And why? Because life is like that. To some extent we can order the world for our own convenience, but there will always remain mystery and disorder. Life is not all reason, and there is nothing reasonable about murder! So why should our reason be able to get to the root of it?

'To return to the fax, it was of course a red herring, although it seems some of you swallowed it. No, I didn't kill Shad. He was the victim, certainly. Very much a victim. I was going to say Shad killed himself, but in a broader sense many others killed Shad – his uncaring parents, all those who rejected him, ridiculed him, or shut him out from their friendship. Choy and Clowsie, and the other bullies in the Upper Remove. Even Old Cacknacker.'

Catchpole turned to Bowker, who had joined the gathering, and asked:

'What on earth is he blethering about now?'

Bowker shrugged.

'Pushed down and down and *down* by Life,' continued Sol, 'Shad just could not find the strength to resist. Why was he born to be crushed? Why was he dealt this cruel hand by Life? Who knows? That's a real mystery, isn't it?

'So we should perhaps say that rather than kill himself, Shad was the agent of his own final destruction.' Sol took a small, stoppered bottle from his pocket. He handed it to the sleuth nearest him and asked for it to be passed on to Catchpole and his group.

'I found this in the victim's room. The label says it's full of carbon, hydrogen, nitrogen and oxygen – as most things are. It's also labelled according to the recommended systematic nomenclature. Perhaps one of you gentlemen could tell us the common name.'

Catchpole took the bottle, held it at arm's length, squinted, and pronounced:

'Brucine.'

His young colleagues nodded their agreement and one of them added:

'Sometimes used to denature alcohol.'

'Related to strychnine,' continued Catchpole. 'Just as lethal; somewhat quicker-acting.'

'Not instantaneous, though,' added Sol. 'There was enough time after he had taken it to return the bottle to his suitcase, walk down to the lobby, return his key and then find somewhere secret to die. And, you know, I don't think we'll ever find out where. I don't believe we'll ever see him again at an event like this. Or anywhere.'

At the back of the room Rosie stood polishing – over-polishing – a wine glass. When Sol had begun to talk she grew concerned and pretended to be busy so she could stay in the room and listen.

But now Sol was eclipsed by an immense clap of thunder which rattled the windows and startled the guests. It was as if a field gun had been discharged on the lawn outside.

'Right overhead,' remarked one. 'Hardly a second between the flash and the bang.'

'I'll say!' agreed another. 'No-one's outside, are they? Not a safe place to be, a wet lawn. Saw a chap frazzled once. Golf course. Most spectacular.'

There was another crash of thunder and the lights flickered thrice in quick succession.

'Cor blimey!' exclaimed someone. 'What they trying to do? Flush out the epileptics?'

'We get a lot of electric storms at this time of the year,' said the manageress, smiling. 'There's no need to be worried.

The hotel meets all the safety standards. We've lightning conductors, you know.' And she pointed upwards to indicate where they could be found.

The rain now fell in sheets rippled by the wind. It drummed on the roofs and the bonnets of cars. It clattered on the tiles, then gushed through drainpipes, down to underground conduits and towards the main sewer. The water soon filled the gutters, sending stuttering cascades to the ground below. Pools appeared on the lawn, their bright surfaces furiously agitated by the harsh incessant downpour. Water covered the asphalt car park and then disappeared through gratings and was carried to the storm drain – where Shad's remains lay . . .

At first the water simply flowed around and over him, but as the pressure built his stiff-limbed body was shunted along. At one point it stuck and dammed the flow, so that water backed up along the drain and bubbled up through some of the gratings. But as the rain continued, the flood once more picked up Shad's body and with gathering speed carried him away . . .

'So,' said a voice from the floor, 'you've no idea where this Shad fellow is now? It's usual, you know, for the victim to join the proceedings at this stage.'

'As I said, Shad is no longer with us. I suspect that, as we speak, he's travelling inexorably towards the sea.'

The company was silent.

The Turks glanced at each other, and at Catchpole, puzzled.

Someone coughed, and another voice said:

'You know, for a minute I thought you really meant he was—' and he broke off in a chuckle at the absurdity of the thought.

'Don't be silly!' It was the manageress. 'It's all just pretend, isn't it? Another mystery solved.'

Sol smiled. 'Of course it is. A fantasy Murder Mystery Weekend. And while I'm on my feet, let me propose a vote of thanks to Juppy for such a wonderfully thought-out and well-organized event.'

People said, 'Hear, hear,' and applauded.

Sol pointed to the manageress. 'And a hand too for our hostess for her splendid hospitality.'

Clearly taken aback, she nonetheless accepted the applause with a gracious smile.

Outside the rain fell now as only a gossamer drizzle. The thunder had slouched off towards the eastern horizon, grumbling and growling like a curmudgeonly old yokel as shafts of golden light broke up the leaden banks of cloud.

'And of course,' concluded Sol, 'our appreciation for the hard-working, charming and most obliging staff.'

More applause.

Rosie looked uncomfortable as attention focused on her. She curtsied awkwardly and hurried from the room.

22

The Murder Mystery Weekend had officially ended. People were leaving the hotel, saying farewells and promising to meet up at future events. The air felt fresh. The sun shone from a blue sky, warming the earth and warming the cars, so that steam rose from polished surfaces. It rose also from the square metal drain cover.

Sol was outside, observing the departures. He was not himself ready to leave. Two of the Young Turks emerged from the hotel and loaded their luggage into a vehicle. One of them, Challoner, seeing Sol, raised his arm in greeting.

'Just want to say it was a really good show. Unusual but compelling. The fax was a nice touch. Yes, I'm afraid I swallowed it. Hook, line and sinker.'

'How's the hangover?' asked Sol.

The Young Turk grimaced. 'Never again. Still. Best be going. Long way. Maybe see you another time.'

Sol's response was non-committal. 'What was all that stuff about the stolen car, anyway? Just bluff, I take it?'

'It wasn't, actually. I can tap in to, er, certain police records, shall we say. Not that difficult, when you know how.'

'Sounds handy.'

'I do so from time to time, just out of curiosity, and, well, yes, there you are. Stolen car. I just threw it in to knock you off balance. Nothing to do with the Murder Mystery, really. Anyway, that's your business.'

Catchpole and Bowker appeared through the main door. They were heading for the city, for a show and supper.

'Ah! There you are,' said the former to Sol. 'Glad I caught you. Been a delightful weekend. Different. Kept us on our toes.' He turned to Bowker. 'Not often we don't crack it?'

Bowker nodded. He appeared a little sullen. Possibly the Execrable, of course, but Sol suspected he was not used to losing.

'Good team, though,' said Catchpole, referring to the Turks. 'Balanced. One of them's lucky, one trusts his instinct, another's painstaking, and the fourth can see patterns. Good combination.'

The men shook hands.

'Very nice meeting you,' said Catchpole.

'Pleasure's mine,' replied Sol.

'I was thinking. Could always use a bright chap like yourself on the paper. If you ever find yourself at a loose end, give me a ring.'

'Very civil of you, Catchpole. Might take you up on that.'

Sol made his way to Rosie's room. He knocked gently and walked in. She was asleep on the bed. She had removed her shoes, but still wore her working clothes. He sat down next to her, smiled and gently stroked her hair. She opened her eyes suddenly and stared at Sol.

'Blimey! What time is it?' She sat up and reached for the clock, and seemed relieved when she read its dial.

'That's all right. Got a bit o' time.'

'On duty again?'

'Yeh. Some tourists arriving, now you lot are out.'

'Poor old Rosie. Saturday's child are you? Works hard for a living.'

'Hard enough.'

'You work too hard, Rosie. I fear you're working your life

away. You'll be an old crone before you've had time to be a wife and mother.'

'Ent got much choice, have I?'

Sol removed his shoes and lay on the bed beside her. Rosie looked at him, perhaps wondering what he was up to. But he was moved by tenderness, not lust. He put his arm around her. They smiled at one another and she snuggled closer into his embrace.

'Perhaps you do have a choice.'

'What?'

'Well, I've been mulling a few things over. Try this. You had a dream about owning a hotel. Well, why not? Not here, but in the Med, say.'

'The where?'

'The Mediterranean. It's a sea, and a region. Cradle of Civilization.'

'Never 'eard of it.'

'Have to admit, I've never been there. Never been a great one for seas. But I don't know. I've a feeling I just might like it – if you were there too. Quite benign, as far as seas go, the Med. Not much in the way of tides, for a start. Anyway, I gather it's a lovely spot. Quite cheap to employ people too, in most places. You wouldn't have to do any work. You'd organize the staff and charm the guests. And you'd sit on the balcony with me, sipping Madeira and watching the sun go down. Sound nice?'

She shrugged. 'I suppose. But you ent got an 'otel in the Med, 'ave you?'

'Not yet. But they're there to be had. I do have a flat in the town which has gone up considerably in value since I purchased it. Reckon if I sold it I could pay off the mortgage and have a deposit on something modest. But this is all we'd be looking for. Something modest. And we could save, together. You can leave this place, come and live with me in the town. You can get a job. You're good at your work, you're worth more than they pay you here. And you wouldn't have to work such long hours. *And* you'd have me to come home to at night! What do you say, Rosie? Isn't this a wonderful scenario? You could leave with me tonight. Move into the flat. Just pack your bag, get in the car, and never see this place again.'

But Sol's enthusiasm didn't seem to fire Rosie. She sighed and looked away. 'You're forgetting two things,' she said.

'Two?'

'There's my old mum. I can't leave 'er, can I?'

'I wouldn't ask that of you. You can still visit her. It's not so far from the town, if we drive. Besides, you said yourself she's not . . . '

'Yeh, I know. I reckon another winter like the last one will kill 'er.'

'We all go through it, Rosie. We all lose our mum at some point. And what's the second thing I've forgotten?'

'Eustace.'

'Oh, Eustace! Yes, but,' Sol laughed, 'you're not really serious? You don't owe him *anything*, Rosie. Forget about Eustace. You've got one life. You can't waste it by shackling yourself to someone who – I was going to say someone you don't love, but it's more than that: tied to someone whose very being seems to irritate you. Someone you don't like. There are a lot more men out there. Better men than Useless.'

'Like you, I suppose.'

'Well, now that you mention it—'

'Least I knows where I am with Eustace. 'ardly knows you. All a bit rushed, 'ent it?'

'You can't always judge these things by the clock. I feel we've known each other for years. It's the intensity of interaction that makes a mockery of time. You know,

242

people can go through life, a long journey, side by side without . . . merging. Yet sometimes it can happen instantly. I don't know, I think this weekend we met on a different dimension, a place you can't go on your own. A place that two of us create together.'

'Don't always go jumpin' into bed with men. Don't want you thinkin' that.'

'You know, Rosie, I think I've been changed this weekend. They say these things don't happen with a fanfare of trumpets and drums, but gently and unobtrusively. Like a flower opening. And with Shad – he touched me. I think for the first time I felt another human's pain. As if his pain were mine. I sort of resonated with it. That's never happened before.'

'Yeh, and what about 'im? Gotta think about that. What about 'is luggage, for a start?'

'It's in the boot of my car, as we speak. Not sure what I'm going to do with it, but I'll think of something. Shouldn't be too difficult. It's sad, but I don't think he'll be missed. I don't think he's got any friends or family to wonder what's happened to him.'

'How did 'ee die, then? Was it like you said? Kill 'imself?'

'I don't know exactly. I did find the poison in his suitcase, but I don't know if he took any. I can guess why he carried it, but I have a notion that Rolling Roderick spoke some truth. "Out of the mouths of clowns and fools . . . ." Often people who speak the truth aren't believed.'

'He said it were two blokes done it.'

'Choy and Clowsie.'

'And who are they when they're at 'ome?'

'You needn't know, Rosie. They're real enough. Just take my advice and stay away from the old school grounds.'

'What school?'

'The ruins up the back. Cacknacker's School.'

'Can't think there were ever a school up there, let alone one with a daft name like that.'

'Whatever it was. Stay away, it has a bad feel to it.'

They drifted into silence for a time, alone with their own thoughts. It was Sol who broke it.

'Are you thinking about what I said?' he asked. 'About coming away with me.'

'Yeh. I'm thinkin'. Thinkin' it don't feel right. But also I don't want to end up just working away me life until . . . I dunno.'

Sol looked up to the top of the wardrobe, to where there was an old suitcase.

'Let's get your bag packed,' he said softly.

Rosie nodded. She took some clothes from a drawer, then seemed to hesitate.

'I'll 'ave to see 'im before I goes. Eustace. Say goodbye. Wouldn't be right otherwise . . .'

Sol nodded:

'Okay. I'll wait here. But don't be long.'

Rosie put her shoes on and left the room.

Sol looked around the cramped bedroom. He looked in the cupboard and drawers at the sum total of Rosie's possessions. There was a note-pad full of writing in a florid but childlike hand. He turned a page but then thought the better of reading it.

He listened for her quick steps in the hall, but heard nothing.

He moved the open suitcase to the floor, lay on the bed, looked at his watch and waited. Ten minutes later he looked at his watch once more. It began to irritate him that what should have taken two minutes was taking so long.

'I hope she's all right,' he said to himself. 'I hope that little prat's not done anything daft.'

244

Hearing her footsteps at last, he sat up on the bed.

'I tried,' she said as she entered. 'It's no bloody good, I tried to tell 'im.'

Sol could see she had been crying. 'What! What's happened?'

She sighed and sat on the bed next to Sol. 'I told 'im I was leaving. I told 'im I was goin', but 'ee wouldn't listen.'

'Well, you've told him. That's that. Let's go. You've said goodbye.'

'It's not as simple as that—'

'Yes, it is. Simple.'

'No, I want '*im* to say, "All right, it's over." *Ee*'s got to end it.'

'And has he not done that?'

'No. Sitting there bloody cryin' 'is 'ead off when I left. Says he'll kill himself if I leave him. Ee's been threatenin' as well.'

'Threatening what?'

'Weren't sayin' at first. I 'ad to give 'im a good shakin' to get it out of 'im. Says 'ee saw the body down the drain. Says 'ee knows 'ow it got there and 'tweren't no accident. Says 'ee'll go to the police if I leave 'im.'

'What's he going to tell them? We've done nothing. We've nothing to feel guilty about. It all unfolded under its own momentum. All we did was watch it. We were spectators, that's all.'

'Might make things a bit awkward, though. Ee might make up a story. And it might look a bit funny if I suddenly runs off.'

'I think he's bluffing. He might have certain suspicions.' Then Sol remembered something. 'I meant to ask you, did you place some blooms – hogweed – on the drain cover?'

'What would I do that for?'

Sol shook his head. 'I don't know. Just wondered.'

'Anyway, I've been thinking about the Med, or whatever it is. Don't know that I'd like it. Lollygaggin' in me bed 'til eight o'clock. Like you said, I got to work hard for a livin'. Saturday's child, and all.'

'That's not set in stone, Rosie. It's just a nursery rhyme, not some irrevocable universal law. You don't have to govern your life by it.'

She seemed irritated by his answer. 'No good saying that. I can't change the day I was born, can I?'

Sol smiled and nodded. 'No, Rosie. You can't do that. I think we have to accept that you're just a martyr. You have a self-denying side.'

'I dunno.'

'A little voice inside you says: you mustn't have anything you really want.'

Rosie remained silent, and rather sullen.

'We enter the world through piss and shit,' offered Sol, his tone consolatory. 'Know who said that? Tertullian. A Church father.'

'No. Can't be right. Wouldn't get no vicar talkin' like that.'

'Mind you, any midwife could have come up with the same observation.'

'Don't know what you're talkin' about 'alf the time.'

'Fifty per cent's not bad, actually.'

She smiled and clasped his hand. 'But I likes you, though. Bin good this weekend. Different.' She paused. 'We can still see each other. If you want.'

'Really?'

'Yeh. I quite likes comin' up to the town. I goes once a month, usually. But I could make it more often. If you want.'

'Oh, I *do* want, Rosie! But what about Eustace? Won't he get jealous?'

'What 'ee don't know won't 'urt. I'm 'ardly likely to tell 'im I going up town to get me oats, am I?'

'Ah. I'm glad we've got that part of it established.'

'Might as well make a day of it, if I'm coming up to town, eh?' she smiled.

'Indeed. Wouldn't have it any other way. I have to say, the more I think about it, the more I like this arrangement. It's all worked out nicely. So how about . . . next weekend? For a first conjugal visit?'

'No, can't come then.'

'Oh. Okay. The weekend after?'

'Yeh, all right.'

Sol wrote down his address and phone number. 'Here. Don't lose this.'

'Bloody 'ell! Look at the time. There'll be wonderin' where I am. I'll see you, then.' She kissed his cheek and hurried off.

'Goodbye, Rosie,' said Sol, although she didn't hear him. He looked up through the skylight. The day was drawing on. He hurried to collect his luggage from his room, wanting to be clear of country roads before dark.

23

Normally toward the end of his summer holiday Sol would have been counting down the days. But on this occasion he was not looking forward to returning to work. Indeed, and to his surprise, he was quite enjoying being idle.

Twice he had phoned the salon to arrange the return of Parlando's car, but each time received no answer. Nor was he in any hurry to take it back. He had enjoyed being in possession of it, and now thought he might even buy a car of his own; it would be handy when Rosie visited. Rosie! The Murder Mystery Weekend now seemed so long ago, despite the fragrant memories. Since his return Sol had thought frequently about his interlude with Rosie, and he was pleased she had not agreed to run away with him. To the Med? In the clear light of day it seemed a silly idea. He was not ready for a committed partnership. A looser, more occasional arrangement made much more sense – to a free spirit such as himself; didn't it?

In the afternoon Sol drove to the salon and was concerned to find it closed; locked; the blinds down. Even the sign had been removed. He looked up and down the alley. At the back entrance of one shop a van was being unloaded, while at another staff were putting empty boxes into a skip.

He asked the man unloading boxes if he knew what had happened to the hairdressing salon.

'Couldn't tell you,' was the reply. 'I'm new here.'

Sol walked over to the skip where the shop worker was depositing empty boxes and asked the same question. He looked to where Sol pointed, scratched his head, and smiled.

'I've been out in this alley so many times and this is the first time I've noticed the place. A hairdresser's you say?'

'It was there last week,' replied Sol.

'Why don't you go . . . ' and he recommended the hairdresser that Sol generally patronized.

'Thank you,' said Sol. 'I'll do as you suggest.'

Sol tried the door once more. It felt as if it was bolted from the inside, which implied there must be another exit. He walked twice around the block and along an interconnecting passageway, but found nothing. He stood on the pavement puzzling a while. He looked at the car. What the Turk had told him preyed on his mind. He locked the doors, dropped the keys through the letter-box of the abandoned shop, and headed for home.

As he walked through his front door, the telephone rang.

'It's the, er, telephone geezer. I've reason to believe you—'

'Erskine! That's extraordinary. I was about to ring you.'

''Ere, 'ow did you know it was me?'

'Oh . . . I don't know. Some sixth sense. Why are you pretending to be a telephone engineer?'

'This is just, like, normal procedures. When we've nicked someone we go through their phone numbers to see if the people are connected in any way. Ha! Geddit?'

'So you've arrested someone who was in possession of my telephone number?'

'Nah. I just dialled the wrong number, I reckon.'

'No matter, now that you're here . . . do you know what's happened to Parlando?'

'What, the 'airdresser nutter, you mean?'

'Yes.'

'Case closed, mate.'

'How do you mean?'

'Can't say any more on account of it's *sub judysea*.'

'He's been charged, then?'

Erskine hesitated before replying. 'Those are your words, squire, not mine.'

'I went to the salon, and it appeared abandoned.'

'Yeh, well, it was all a front, wannit.'

'A front? Never mind the short, back and sides, it was all a front.'

Sol wondered if he should mention the car, but he thought better of it and ended the call.

On the way home he had bought a newspaper. As he turned the pages a headline jumped out at him:

Just minging in the drain

In some alarm Sol began to read – but need not have worried.

Riddle of mystery pong solved, ran the sub-deck. A putrefying fish, about four feet long and torpedo shaped was the cause, much to the disappointment of neighbours and crime reporter Ron Bonsai, who had been hoping for a body. A prostitute, perhaps. The remains had been shovelled into a polythene bag and sent to the nearest fish research station for positive identification.

There was a quote from one man who said he knew all along it was a fish, as he had worked for many years on trawlers. He believed it would turn out to be a big pike, though he would not rule out barracuda. 'They're both long with a big mouth, he said, 'and these days people flush all sorts of things down the toilet.'

A policeman who attended the incident remarked that all dead things smelled the same to him. 'Putrefaction shows no favours,' he averred. 'The prince and the pauper decay in exactly the same manner.'

Dominating the letters page was a picture of a newborn baby, with red slime-smeared flesh, a gaping mouth like a deep-sea fish's, and eyes screwed up tight against the delivery-room lights, expressing with a lusty yell the outrage all babies feel on being thrust out into the world of fractured images. It was a reminder to Sol that his delightful time with Rosie could have unwanted consequences, for there had been no precautions. It unsettled him. Some couples bonked for years in an unsuccessful effort to conceive, yet some women could become pregnant standing next to a man at a bus stop. Sol hoped Rosie wasn't one of them.

Out of curiosity Sol read the letter that the picture was intended to illustrate:

> *Sir:* Allow me to reply to some of the criticisms made against me in your otherwise balanced story on surgical mortality statistics in the county's hospitals ('Butcher Beattie heads killer doc league'). In my defence I can only say that a baby fresh from the womb is very slippery and, contrary to popular belief, they do not bounce when they strike a hard surface. Moreover, I only dropped six – not seven as stated in your story – in the period covered by the statistics.

It was signed by one Roderick Beattie.

'Hmm,' mused Sol, reflecting on the name. 'That would certainly figure,' and he turned more pages.

In the business section there was a big piece on Chidzy Le Mer, the financier, under the headline:

Le Mer the merrier after water giant coup

It was a story of the acquisition of a water company on the continent by the said Chidzy. It was penned by the business editor, Flam Scorbax, and was full of arcane phrases such as 'parabolic clawback' and 'buyout Behemoth' that were no doubt intelligible to the eight or so people who would read beyond the first paragraph. There were two supplementary pieces headed, '*Eau la la! A French connection*,' which outlined the history of the company, and '*Zidane! You're blocking the vote*,' which detailed boardroom machinations and the sacrificial sacking of a director of that name. Apparently the financier had bought a mineral-water company in France, made some superficial improvements, cut costs through sackings, built up the share price by spreading rumours of an imminent take-over, and then made a killing. The 'panache' and 'robust style' of the financier seemed, in the writer's view, to adequately compensate for the fact that a small French town was likely to lose its principal livelihood. At least, that's how Sol interpreted what was an opaque and convoluted piece of writing, even by the standards of business journalism.

He turned back to the news pages. There was a story head-lined, '**Apocalypse not now!**', whose enigmatic terseness was partially expanded by a sub-deck which ran:

'*Space boffins in Armageddon blunder.*'

It was a follow-up to a story the previous day – a perennial favourite – in which scientists at a space centre had calcu-lated that an asteroid was on course for the earth and would make contact in the year 2022, obliterating all known life. But they had been precipitate in their prognostication, and on checking the calculations ascertained that a collision with the frozen methane wastes of nebulous Neptune was more likely. Sol had not read the original story, so his sense of relief was not as palpable as it might have been.

On the centre spread was a colourful feature headlined:

Full steam ahead for the Sprat and Winkle Line!

There was a big picture, printed across the double page, of a happy throng dressed as travellers from an innocent age, raising hats and champagne glasses towards the camera. A team of steam enthusiasts, explained the article, had resurrected the old Sprat and Winkle Line and were running excursions to the coast every weekend over the summer.

Sol was about to dismiss the venture with a jeer of derision, but to his surprise the piece engaged him and he read it, with some pleasure, to the end. He smiled:

'Rosie would love that, I know. I bet she's never been near the sea.'

He made up his mind to book a couple of seats on the excursion for her first visit. After all, they didn't want to spend *all* the time in bed bonking, and the sea air might do them good . . .

Sol could sit in a deckchair while Rosie splashed and frolicked in the sea, and then hold the towel around her while she peeled off her wet costume. He wouldn't have to go in the water himself – well, perhaps if Rosie insisted. And if the tide was slack. He had better take his trunks, just in case. They might even take a boat trip around the bay, but only if Rosie was positively enthusiastic about the idea, and if the sea wasn't choppy.

That was settled, then.

Sol took the double page, folded it, and stuffed it into an envelope, along with a note, which simply read:

'Fancy a bit of this?'

He was about to seal the envelope when he had an idea. He smiled as he hurried to write down the words that flooded into his head. Remembering her womanly concerns about her body he titled the ditty:

'*Light of my life* (or a considered reply to a lover on being asked, "Does my bum look big in this?")'

Hail your Featherness!
Light as the feyest of fairycakes
Full of air and fine flour whipped
So wonderfully light
(notwithstanding the sugar and butter)

If in boxing there were fleaweights
The title would be yours, hands down.

Diet and see?
Don't bother. Why torment?
Heightwatchers for me whose stunted frame
Won't support his naked appetites.
And happy with you, all sweetness and light,
A light to lighten the genitals.

After some consideration he omitted the last line, believing that to someone of Rosie's simple piety it might whiff of blasphemy (even if it was true).

Then Sol turned to the crossword.

'What have we here. Oh dear! "Doesn't cut with tradition." Has to be "front", doesn't it?'

He looked to the next clue:

'Islander makes mess of knocking off king's racehorse.'

'That's better,' said Sol, and filled in:

255

Cacknacker

He solved one or two more clues but then threw the paper down as images of the weekend just past filled his mind. He felt a pang of sadness at the thought of Shad, but it faded quickly enough. Instead, he looked ahead vividly to the weekend after next, when Rosie would be visiting.